Murder of a Sailor

JOSEPH RODERICK

PublishAmerica
Baltimore

First printing

At the specific preference of the author, PublishAmerica allowed this work to remain exactly as the author intended, verbatim, without editorial input.

Hardcover 978-1-61582-499-1
Softcover 1-4241-7184-9
PAperback 978-1-4512-6685-6
PUBLISHED BY PUBLISHAMERICA, LLLP
www.publishamerica.com
Baltimore

Printed in the United States of America

Joseph Roderick

To my sister Betty and in memory of Mom and Dad

Chapter I

Jack Crawford loved to reminisce about his early years as a sailor in the waters along the southeastern coast of Massachusetts. Jack is my neighbor and best friend, who lives on Westport Point diagonally across the road from me. "I really started sailing in 1946 just after the war," he would say, and although I knew the story by heart, I always enjoyed listening to him tell it. "Mom and Dad spent summers here on the Point even though we lived in Fall River only fifteen minutes away. I was fifteen years old at the time. Someone started giving sailing lessons and I talked Mom into letting me take them. The minute I started, I was in love with everything having to do with ships and sailing vessels and the water."

By nature Jack is not a storyteller. He is an exuberant man, filled with energy, but he tends to keep within himself. Tall and handsome and a wealthy widower, he is the object of affection for a great many women in the area who see him as the ideal match. I have said repeatedly that if Abercrombie and Fitch put out a catalog for older men, he would grace the cover. He is seventy-two years old and made his fortune in Manhattan, first as a textile broker, and then, as an investor in the stock market. His is a mathematical mind that deals in numbers and facts and figures. There are those people who lie hidden behind their numbers and their scientific minds and who use language only to communicate ideas as simply as possible for the rest of us. He is one of them. He is not prone to flights of fancy. I am afraid that that is more my inclination. He deals in proof and fact. One does not expect hyperbole from Jack Crawford and one does not get it.

"I admit that when I am on a sailboat or any kind of a ship for that matter, I feel one with everything around me. It is an indescribable sensation for me. I am utterly confident and completely absorbed in what I am doing and blind to everything else. So, I learned to sail right here in Westport Harbor. They said I was a natural and that my ancestors must have been the Vikings. At that time my grandmother and grandfather lived on the Vineyard, in West Tisbury, and I would spend a few weeks with them each summer. Of course, I spent every free minute down in the harbor looking for odd jobs on some of the yachts and sailboats coming in and out of the Vineyard. That was the best period of my life."

At that point he would fall into a reverie and sit very quietly for a few minutes as if he were visualizing the events of the past.

"In 1948, the summer of my junior year in high school, I signed on for a sail to Bar Harbor, Maine. It was a small craft, with only six for a crew, and it was hard work. The gentleman who hired the sailboat and his young son were along for the ride, but we worked hard. It was a great success and probably the finest single period of time I have ever spent doing anything. With that behind me, I hired out every summer until I graduated from college and found myself in the army for the tag end of the Korean War. There were some great adventures, a few close calls, but what I remember most was the sense of freedom and joy I got out on the water with the wind blowing against my face and through my hair. I have never felt anything like it in all my years. There is nothing that can compare with it."

"Except maybe a good steak with baked potatoes," I said jokingly.

"Well, maybe that comes close but even that doesn't quite give me the same feeling," he said laughing.

The subject of sailing came up because Jack received a call from an old friend who asked that he call on her at his convenience. She said it had something to do with his growing reputation as an amateur sleuth. She asked to see me as well because she claimed to have a mystery that might interest the two of us. Her husband, who had been dead for some twenty years, had been a sailor Jack had sailed with any number of times. Jack had a great deal of admiration for his skills aboard ship. Why she wanted to see us was a mystery and Jack admitted that he had not seen or heard from her in years.

The truth was that she was right. Together with Nelly McCarthy we had been successful in solving a number of crimes which startled everyone, considering that we were two old men in our seventies working with a young lawyer who was as inexperienced as we were in the criminal investigation field. She had not asked for Nelly, although if she knew about us, she had to have known about our partner. At any rate, Nelly had just had her first child and was not available.

I am the other half of the male team. My name is Noah Amos and I am a retired school teacher, having served thirty-eight years in the Fall River School Department as a teacher in a junior high school. I lived a solitary life for most of my adult years until I met Marge, the lovely lady with whom I share my house and bed. For the better part of forty years I was a lonely man after my wife of three years decided that she no longer wanted to be married to me. I came home from work one day to find an empty house and she was gone. I never saw her again although I did hear from her, asking for a divorce so that she could remarry. By then I had put her behind me and granted the divorce with no hesitation. I often wonder what she would be like now, the young pretty girl I married. If I walked down a busy New York street and bumped into her, would I know her? I can't even remember what she looked like; the color of hair, her eyes, her skin, those I can remember, but that is all. And yet, when I came home after school that day and found an empty house, I was devastated. She left nothing of herself behind. Not even a note of explanation.

What had I done? What had I done to make that woman walk out of my house without even a goodbye or an explanation? Never did I ask, why did she go back on her marriage vows? The fault was always with me. How many years did it take me to realize that I had nothing to do with her decision? That she had a devil in her brain urging her to another style of life. They had never explained any of this to me at the altar. It was their little secret.

The world turned upside down. Everything was divided in half. With only one salary, I still had to maintain a house and no one was nice enough to reduce my mortgage and taxes by half or my automobile insurance and house insurance. It was like an ambush coming from nowhere and I was completely unprepared for it. Life became slow motion. The dreamlike existence even surprised me. There was no ranting and raving, screaming, crying, anger or emotional outbursts. I pulled into myself and hid away and made the quiet, hardly evident adjustments to a new way of life. And, I was successful in burying myself in my work and taking great pleasure in teaching and the children with whom I worked.

Then four years ago I received word that a former student of mine had left me a fortune in money and property. I found myself, after years of living on a school teacher's salary, suddenly with more money than I could hope to spend in my lifetime. And with that, a beautiful restored house on Westport Point, something I had no right to expect in my wildest dreams. I found myself in the enviable position of having no restrictions on the amount of money I could spend. The odd thing was that I found that I had very few needs and my lifelong habits of penny pinching and cautious living did not leave me. I didn't run to Las Vegas to play the slots or indulge myself in the luxuries I assume the rich enjoyed. I was newly arrived in the realm of wealth, but Jack had been brought up with money and then made himself a multi-millionaire in his own right. I noticed, however, that he lived as frugally as I did on an every day basis.

We became fast friends. There were benefits to having money and we did some of the traveling that I had dreamed about all my life and could never afford. Europe had always been my favorite and the time I spent in the UK and Italy I would take to my grave.

Chapter II

"Wait until you meet Mrs. Macomber. She is quite a unique lady," he said. "I can't imagine why she wants to see us. You know she has to be in her nineties. When she called she sounded about the same as she did twenty years ago. I couldn't believe it was her."

"Do you have the address? I don't want to be driving all over Middletown looking for her house," I said.

"I have been there any number of times and I am sure I know the way, but just to be sure, Clarissa used Mapquest on the computer and supplied us with a map."

We drove through Adamsville and Tiverton where we picked up 24S. Before we knew it we were in Portsmouth, Rhode Island and then Middletown and Jack finally had to admit that the roads had changed so much in twenty years that he had difficulty finding the right road. Luckily, we had the map and followed it to the farm where Mrs. Macomber lived.

We turned off the road onto an entrace that seemed at least a half mile to the house that we could see in the distance. I had expected a farmhouse but instead came to a mansion by the sea. Alongside the road were fields of rhododendrons and azaleas enclosed in what looked like chicken-wire fencing that must have been ten feet high. To the right of the house we saw a large building that at one time must have been a carriage house or a barn from the looks of the two sets of large doors that opened out from it.

To the left and rear of the house I could see the water. It reminded me of the view from my own kitchen windows. We parked the car at the front entrance. Jack rang the doorbell, and it was opened by a young woman who invited us into a hallway.

"Mr. Crawford and Mr. Amos, am I correct?" she asked.

Jack said, "I am Jack Crawford and this is Noah Amos."

She was dressed in street clothes, and it was impossible to tell from her appearance or her manner what role she played in the household. She was a stunningly beautiful girl, one of those girls that people stare at involuntarily. She was tall and slim. Her blond hair was pulled tight to her head and tied in a pony tail. Her light hair and skin accentuated her beautiful green eyes. Even in jeans and a turtle neck she was what we would have called "statuesque" in my youth. God only knows what the young people of today would have called her; probably, "hot."

"Please follow me," she said. "Mrs. Macomber is expecting you."

We were taken into a room that was so dark it took me a few moments before my eyes adjusted to the light. Sitting very demurely in a wicker chair was a very slight, frail woman who I assumed was Mrs. Macomber. She sat with a blanket wrapped around her legs and she cradled a cup of tea in her hands. I couldn't be positive, but once my eyes became adjusted, I realized she was wearing a pair of overalls. Once we were introduced and I got close enough to see, I realized that I was right. She had on a pair of overalls with the straps over her frail shoulders and a high bib in front with straps attached by a pair of shiny brass buttons. My idea of wealth certainly didn't involve bib overalls for elderly women.

She pointed to seats for the two of us and in a clear, crisp voice she said, "Jack Crawford, how long has it been since I laid eyes on you? You are still a handsome devil. And this is Noah Amos. You two have made quite a name for yourselves without seeking publicity and managing somehow to stay in the background. I like that. Shows character."

She waited for an answer and I was struck by her verbal dexterity and her ability to speak without a quiver in her voice. Sitting so close to her, I could see that her eyes sparkled with a kind of pixie deviltry. A dull day suddenly turned into an exciting adventure for me, just being with this vital old lady.

Jack felt he was expected to answer and said, "It has to be twenty some odd years at least. The last time I saw you was at Jeff's funeral. When exactly was that Amy?"

"June 30, 1982 was the day we buried Jeff and I do remember that you were kind enough to come to the funeral. You have always been a good friend, Jack. But now let's get to business. Time is important to me as you can imagine. There are things I need done before I slip away from this wonderful life I have led."

"We're listening," Jack said.

"Well let me outline what I am interested in here. Let me say from the beginning that this is not going to be easy."

She sat for a moment and seemed to be deep in thought.

Then she said, "Give me a few moments. I can't waste talk. Let me think this through. Be patient with me. In the meantime, Jen," she called in a loud, clear voice.

Jen, the girl who had met us at the door came in and Mrs. Macomber said, "Could you please give these gentlemen something to drink?"

It seemed at least five minutes before she began again while we sat patiently waiting for her to decide to speak and for our tea to arrive. Then she seemed to be satisfied and began, "Jeff was murdered. He did not commit suicide. I want to know who did it and how it was done. I want closure. I have thought about this for twenty years now and I want to put it behind me. Do you understand me?"

"Yes," Jack said. "But Amy, you are asking the impossible. How in the world can two old codgers like Noah and me be expected to go back to an event that happened twenty years ago and come up with any sort of a solution?"

"That's not for me to say, Jack Crawford. The one thing I know is that I know you well enough to know that you'll figure out some way to get answers. You and your gentleman friend here. What I can do with my azaleas, I know you can do with this mystery."

"To begin with, how do you know that he was murdered, Amy? How do you know it was not a suicide?" Jack asked.

"I know and I knew right from the beginning. I know this sounds impossible but I want you to think about it. First off, you know he was killed or committed suicide on the day of a large party at which we had at least two hundred fifty guests including you and your wife. Could any of those guests have seen anything? You know him well enough Jack. You know he wouldn't contemplate suicide. You see, Mr. Amos, my husband was a womanizer. He was a charming, beautiful man even in his seventies. Women couldn't resist him and he couldn't keep away from them. So, that may have something to do with his death. Who knows?"

"So, we are going to have to spend some time with you, then, Amy. We are going to have to know everything you can give us to help us out. Can you take that? It may take hours," Jack said.

"I know and I haven't got forever. So let's get started tomorrow at ten o'clock. I can give you about an hour a day, that's all. I have work to do in my play pen and Jason and I have some work to finish together. Then, when I am finished my day's work, after dinner I work putting together my notes and I am exhausted and need my rest to refuel for the next day."

She began to think about getting up out of her chair then. She threw the blanket wrap off her legs and I could see that she was diminutive at best. She couldn't have been five feet tall when she struggled out of her chair. She held the sides of the chair with gnarled fingers. She saw me looking at her hands and she laughed and said, "Not a pretty sight, Mr. Amos. These hands are caused by New England arthritis. Years of working in the cold, damp ground have taken their toll on me."

"From the looks of it, Mrs. Macomber, you don't look too much the worse for wear for all of that. There aren't many people who live to be your age and there certainly aren't many who can do what you are doing."

"I'll have to tell you my secret of longevity one of these days. Right now I would appreciate it if you called me Amy. Remember gentleman, I expect to see you at ten tomorrow morning."

Jack laughed and said, "We haven't said we will take on this case Amy."

"You will," she said with an impish smile on her face.

Chapter III

We drove back to Westport Point without saying very much. Jack was in a contemplative mood and I could just imagine what was going through his mind.

Finally, he said, "You know, Noah, I always look to money first as the motivating influence behind any crime. I have seen more evil done for money than you can imagine. But, in this case it is hard to believe that money would play a role. Amy is rich beyond imagining, but she is not lavish with her money. In fact, you might call her tight-fisted, but when it came to Jeff, he never had to give money a second thought. Her checkbook was always open to him, but he never had a penny to call his own. I know that for a fact. So the motivation for killing him would never under any circumstance be financial gain because of his death."

Having said that, he kept driving and acting like he was concentrating on the road. I knew that was far from the truth. As for myself, I felt out of my milieu. I had said very little in Mrs. Macomber's presence and now I had very little to say as well. I had nothing I could sink my teeth into. This was the world of the super rich and everything that went with it. My family was working class and even though I had inherited a great deal of money, my whole upbringing was with me and would be until my death.

We drove the back roads to the Point and when we pulled into Jack's driveway he asked me to come into the house for a few minutes so that we could talk over a cup of coffee. I wasn't sure I could trust Jack's coffee, so I settled for a diet soda with ice cubes.

I hadn't been in the house since Clarissa had been living with Jack and it came as quite a surprise to see that everything was neat and clean. His study still had too many newspapers spread out on every available space and it was far too cluttered for my liking, but it now had a purposeful look that I had to credit Clarissa with. Once, when Jack had been hospitalized with a broken collar bone, I had come to the house to look for something and I had been amazed at the clutter. Even then, it had been clean with not a dirty dish in the sink, but it had a look of disorganization and chaos. Now it seemed the chaos was limited to his study.

We sat quietly on the back porch overlooking the water on the western side of the Point. My house was on the eastern side of the main road or on the opposite side of the road looking down on the Westport River.

Jack said, "What do you really think about this Noah?"

I sat quietly for a moment and then I said, "Frankly, I don't know what to think. How do we go back twenty years and come up with anything like reasonable answers? I wonder if we are not way over our heads here. This is a case for Hercule Poirot or Sherlock Holmes, but hardly for Crawford and Amos. But, I leave this decision to you because you are friends with Mrs. Macomber."

"Well, I thought about it as we drove back here, and I think we should give her a few days to tell us the whole story. If we see anything promising we can follow it up. Otherwise, we drop the whole affair and I extend my regrets. I was at the party you know, but it is all a haze. I always disliked parties and the drinking and the tomfoolery. My wife was practically a recluse and we could hardly wait to leave. I am going to try to recreate the whole affair as best I can and lay it out for you as I remember it. The one thing I do remember quite distinctly was that we left early. It was a tuxedo party and not my kind of thing. I felt uncomfortable in the outfit and could hardly wait to get it off. So the first chance we got, we left, but I'll try to hash over the particulars. Let me think every thing through as well as I can and then I'll tell you what I remember."

"Sounds good to me," I said. "Should be interesting at any rate."

The summer was coming and the weather was beginning to turn warm. The first of the crowds were beginning to show up at Horseneck Beach and Marge and I were limiting ourselves to morning walks before the crowds showed up and the traffic became a problem. The next morning early, before I was due to go to Middletown with Jack, Marge and I made for the beach just as the sun was rising. We parked the car in the Westport residents' parking lot and walked over the dunes to the western part of the beach. There was no one else on the beach and it was a particularly mild day. We were actually able to talk as we walked which was unusual. Normally, we were fighting the wind and holding each other's hands for stability. We walked easterly along the beach and it was breathtaking with the sun rising into a cloudless sky and reflecting off the incoming waves as they broke on the shore. We had never been warmer walking on the beach early in the season and we enjoyed every moment of it.

"So, what is this all about, Noah?" Marge asked.

I told her as much of the story as I knew. Marge had moved in with me about a year earlier. We liked each other from the day we met. Marge was a widow of five years. We enjoyed each other and she decided that she did not want to live alone. Neither did I after I met her, so we cohabited for a period of time on a trial basis and that had turned into a long term relationship.

I explained the little I knew about the case and Marge was befuddled.

"How in the world are you supposed to find out about a murder or suicide that took place twenty odd years ago? Is this woman crazy? Where would you even begin?" she asked.

"I suppose we'll begin by going over all the details she can give us. From there, who knows? If we don't get enough, Jack says we'll walk away. But you have to admit, it is interesting isn't it?" I said, and we both laughed that special laugh that we shared together.

We got back to the house in just enough time to meet Jack at my back door. I knew from the look on his face that he was looking for breakfast. We had been friends and neighbors long enough now that I could see that special look on his face that meant he was in the mood for food. I had enough time to whip together a three-egg omelet made with Portuguese chourico served with a large slab of Portuguese sweet bread with cheddar cheese that I know Jack has a soft spot for. Marge and I settled for our morning oatmeal with a glass of orange juice followed by a cup of coffee.

As was his habit, Jack was quiet while he ate his breakfast. He ate large amounts of food, but always slowly and with appreciation and very little conversation. When he finished his meal he poured himself a second cup of coffee and then said, "With enough documentation, Noah, this may be possible. We'll wait and see."

Chapter IV

Mrs. Macomber was waiting for us in her shaded sun porch. She was sitting in the same wicker chair with the stadium blanket wrapped around her legs. She had a cup of tea in her hands and for a moment I wondered whether it was the same one she had been holding yesterday.

"Right on time, gentlemen! I like that! Shall we begin? I don't like to waste time."

She said this with the same crisp voice that we had heard the day before. Whatever might be causing her ailments, it was not her vocal chords.

"First off," Jack said, "The party was held here, is that right?"

"Yes, you know that. You were here that day."

"But, Noah wasn't. Tell us everything you can remember about it," Jack said.

"Well, it was June 28, 1982. We were celebrating our 50th wedding anniversary. It was a big party. Daddy spared no expenses. I was worried that having so many people here might do real damage to my play pens and to the plantings going down to the water, so we hired security to guard them. Daddy set up tents outside with tables, a bandstand and a dance floor. Food was served buffet style with stations on the grounds, but not in the house. There were over two hundred guests and we had valet parking so the guests could drive to the front door and valets took their cars and parked them in the fields. So there was a great deal of activity, noise and movement. The party started at about noon and went on until close to midnight when Jeff's body was found in Daddy's study."

"Before we leave, can someone show us the study, please?" I asked.

"Of course. I was beginning to wonder if you had a voice, Mr. Amos. The study, incidentally was locked so that no one would enter it. I don't have any idea how Jeff got in there. He was sitting in Daddy's desk chair when they found him. He had been shot or shot himself with a small caliber revolver in the temple, the right temple. He was thrown back in the chair. I saw him and it was a terrible sight for me. It made me very upset. But, yes, you can go see the room before you leave today."

Jack asked, "Is there any chance that you might have a list of the people who attended the party that day?"

"Yes. Jen made copies of the list for you. I am trying as much as possible to eliminate the names of those people that I know for a fact, have died. I'll give you that before you leave. I've also updated addresses and telephone numbers on anyone that I have kept in contact with and who might have any information that might be valuable to you," she said with a bit of a twinkle in her eye.

"So, you were pretty sure we would take this on, then?" Jack asked.

"I know you well enough to know that you would. This is a puzzle that your mathematical instincts can't pass up, I think."

"I would like to know why you are so sure it was murder and not suicide," I said.

"It is a matter of character. Jeff loved life. He was seventy-four when he died. He was at the top of his game. He was planning a sail the week after the party. He was to leave from the marina at Portsmouth and had a crew ready to go. He loved sailing more than anything in this world. There is no way that he would have cancelled that sail. Jack knows that, as well as I do. Would you agree, Jack?"

"I would have to say, yes. Jeff was so single-minded about his sailing that I can't imagine any circumstance that would make him cancel or postpone a trip. You are absolutely right."

"How about his health?" I asked.

"Do you mean did he commit suicide because he had some fatal sickness like cancer that he had discovered? The answer is no. We had a thorough autopsy done and the doctor swore there were no signs of any problems. His heart was excellent and as far as he could determine he was in excellent health. There was no sign of cancer of any kind. I checked with his doctor and he said the same thing. Jeff was in tip-top shape for a man his age. At his semi-annual checkup he had blood work done and everything was just about perfect. Jeff was a perfect physical specimen, much like our friend Jack here."

Jen came into the room then with another cup of tea. She was courteous, but not subservient, so I suspected that she was not a paid servant. She asked if she could get us anything, and Jack asked for a glass of water. Mrs. Macomber was openly appreciative of the tea and again sat clutching it in both hands as if the cup were a hand warmer.

"Let me rest for a moment gentlemen," she said and then sat quietly holding her cup in both hands sipping from time to time. In the short time we had been with her I noticed that she was tiring. Her hands fascinated me. They were tiny and fragile and I could see blue veins running along the back of her hands and the tendons below the surface of her skin, taut and wiry.

We waited patiently for her to resume the conversation.

Finally she said, "Jeff loved life. I think Jack can vouch for that. He was a man who accepted every day as an adventure. He was not a man to take his own life. I know in my heart of hearts that he could not have done it."

Jack asked, "How was he for money? Did he gamble? Was he in debt? Had he made bad investments? Tell us about his money situation."

"He had none of his own. I was always free with money where Jeff was concerned, but he was on a tight leash. I realized very early in our marriage that he was a free spirit and the only hold I had on him was money. I knew he would never leave me because he wanted to be free of money worries. And as it turned out I was right. Was he in debt? Absolutely not. Was he a gambler? Not on your life. I took care of every expense he ever had. He lived high, but I had the money."

"So," Jack continued, "he had no money of his own? What I am trying to establish in my own mind is whether anyone would have had a financial stake in his death. What you are saying is that that is not the case."

"He had absolutely no money in his name. Back then my will left everything to him and to Jason, fifty-fifty. If anyone was to be killed for money, it would have been me. If I can say anything definitively, Jack, it is that money played no part in his death."

"Well, I will give up that line of thinking," Jack said. "If you are growing tired, why don't we go see the study while you finish your tea."

"I don't get tired Jack, I get anxious. I have a few things to do in my play pen and then I will have lunch and take my nap," she said this and threw the woolen throw off her legs and started to rise from her chair.

Jen appeared from nowhere and when Mrs. Macomber asked her to take us to the study, she smiled, turned and led the way. She had the copies of the guest list prepared and she gave us those in a large brown envelope.

The study was in the back of the house. Jen took a key off a shelf outside the door of the study, opened the door and let us in without saying a word.

It was a very impressive room. The first thing that caught my eye was that there seemed not an inch of wall space not covered with floor to ceiling book cases, stacked with books. I took a quick look and was surprised to see that they were not all in English. Many were in German and either Japanese or Chinese. Some were in what I assumed to be Russian and a number of other languages that I did not understand. These were not the typical leather bound classics that came in sets and were meant as much for ornament as to be read. They appeared to me at first glance to be scientific books and journals, although I couldn't decipher what kind of science they dealt with at a quick glance. The whole back wall of the room was in glass. There was a double glass door leading out to a terrace and on either side of the doors were windows that rose at least twelve feet to a casement that ran the length of the room. Above the French windows, were stained glass windows which gave the contents of the room a tinted appearance as the sun at eleven in the morning came slanting through the windows from the sun high in the eastern sky.

The room was divided into three areas. There was what I took to be a reading area with three leather chairs with side tables and floor lamps providing light for each chair. The leather was old and beautifully maintained so that it had the rich look that only old leather has. There were a number of books neatly stacked on one of the tables and a throw was folded neatly on the seat of one of the chairs. The area was wonderfully inviting and my first thought was that I would have liked Marge to see it. Further delineating the section was a beautiful Persian rug which marked the area in richness and taste.

Another section of the room was distinguished by a large, rectangular library table in what I suspected was solid walnut. It was a beauty and would be a grand addition to any room. This one was accompanied by cushioned captain's chairs and looked like a work area. Again the table was highly polished and I wondered if it was ever used. For some reason, I had the feeling that this room was used and was not merely a decorative setting for pieces of expensive furniture. Suspended from the ceiling and directly over the table was a large metal canopy containing a bank of lights which when lighted would shine directly down on the table. Jack found a switch and turned it on. The result was startling. The light was intense and made the table gleam. On the table were large, old-fashioned ledgers that showed a great deal of wear and tear.

In the third section of the room was a large desk with a computer, a scanner, and a printer. Next to the computer were several in and out trays containing sheaves of paper that were annotated with colored markings. The desk was placed so that it was facing a bank of French windows from which one could get a great look at the water below.

It was quite an impressive arrangement and showed great use of a large, oversized room. By dividing the room into three areas and with the walls covered in book cases there was a feeling of enclosure, but on the other hand the windows opening onto the distant waters below opened it up to the sun high in the eastern sky. Looking through the windows of the door and those making up the wall, we could see the water down below in the bay leading to Newport and the ocean beyond and it was truly a dazzling sight.

The book cases and the walls and doors were mahogany. They had a polished look and were obviously well-cared for. I was surprised because I hadn't seen a servant in the house, and I couldn't imagine Jen or Amy Macomber taking care of this much house by themselves.

We both had a number of questions that had to be answered.

I said, "Let's make note of anything we want to ask Mrs. Macomber tomorrow because we may not see her again today."

Jack agreed.

We listed a number of questions.

(1) Was this arrangement in place when Jeff Macomber was found dead?

(2) Was the room in use at the present time?

(3) Was the room her father's study and did anyone else use it on a regular basis?

(4) When Jeff Macomber was found, were the French doors leading to the terrace open or closed. If they were closed, were they locked from the inside?

(5) Were there any pictures of the room as it existed then?

(6) Were there any pictures of the body?

We spent considerable time checking the French doors to the outside. There was no outside lock. The doors as they now existed could only be closed from the inside. There were two slide bolts, one at the top of the doors and one in the middle above the handle which, when pressed down, allowed the door to open. For anyone to have entered the doors from the outside they would have had to have been open at the time of the suicide-murder. Jack even tried unsuccessfully to slip the door bolt with a credit card. We both felt confident that if the door was closed or locked, that anyone entering the room would have had to come in by the inner study door. If the desk had been in the same position as it was now, which might be unlikely, then the killer, if there was a killer, would have been seen by Jeff Macomber when entering through the French doors.

Jack left the room to find Jen or Mrs. Macomber so that he could leave the list of questions we had prepared for Mrs. Macomber. I began to feel more comfortable as I found myself thinking about something specific that I could dig my teeth into. It was entirely possible that someone might have come into the room unseen and unheard while Jeff Macomber sat looking out at the bay below him with his back to the door. That same person could have brought a pistol to Jeff's temple and pulled the trigger and then very quickly placed the pistol in Jeff's hand to make it appear like suicide. The size of the room though, made me feel that although it was possible, it was highly improbable. The room I was standing in was at least thirty feet wide and twenty-five feet from the inside entrance to the French doors. I next checked the book cases to see if there could be a sliding panel or a hidden entrance behind the book cases and although I couldn't give a definitive answer, the one thing that I did see was that the construction of the book cases seemed to me to be solid horizontal pieces of wood supported by uprights. I didn't see any openings or joints in the long stretches of board that would allow for a swinging section or anything of the kind. I checked each section slowly and carefully feeling for breaks in the long horizontal boards, and found none. It seemed to me an odd way to build book cases, but the upright sections seemed to be sturdy so that there was no sagging or lack of support at any point. I finished my search just as Jack came back and said that he had finally found Jen and given her the list.

We hadn't done much but I found myself feeling tired. I was tempted to sit in one of the large comfortable leather chairs and to take one of my famous naps. I have found that nothing is quite as rejuvenating as a short nap and the leather chairs were inviting.

Jack must have known what I was thinking because he said, "No way, my friend. I am absolutely starved and I need something to fuel my system and the sooner, the better. I say we head over the Mount Hope Bridge to Bristol and go to Tweet Balzano's for lunch. I need a big plate of pasta and meatballs and hot Italian sausage to fill the hole in my stomach. Are you game, Noah?"

I knew that Marge was busy for the day, and I knew that Jack was in dead earnest, so I decided to let my nap wait for later and found myself driving out of the Macomber farm and looking for the road to the Mount Hope Bridge.

Chapter V

Jack wanted his usual enormous lunch. Tweet Balzano's was the place to get it. The restaurant was famous for its more than plentiful portions and people like Jack with huge appetites made their way to Bristol specifically to eat their fill. I was more interested in getting the background on these people we were investigating, one dead for twenty years and one very much alive, with whom I had suddenly come into contact. Let it be known that I have tunnel vision. I admit that without reservation. Whether I am focusing upon chess, or the New York Times Sunday Crossword or Double-Acrostic or a case such as this one, I have the capacity to think about nothing else for days on end. I don't know whether this is a gift or a curse, but it is something that has been with me since I was a child and I am now in my early seventies. This case was becoming the subject of my obsessive and singular method of thinking in a very short period of time.

A man had been dead for twenty years. Suddenly he had come back to life in our consciousness. There was so much to learn. What kind of a person was he? Where should I begin? A hedonist, from what we had heard already. I hadn't even seen a picture of him.

Jack, as was his habit, ate his meal slowly and without much conversation. I had an antipasto that could have been suitable for a dinner party of four, but I too ate slowly and enjoyed the different flavors. Jack had a large dish of pasta with Italian sausage and meatballs, a glass of red wine and a double portion of Italian bread. When he had finished eating his dessert, I asked him to tell me what he knew about the marriage of Amy and Jeff Macomber.

"Well," he began, "As you would suspect after visiting what was Mr. Goetzel's summer house, Amy was a rich, young lady. Her father was a research chemist who, working independently had discovered the key to producing fungicides for use on plants. His fungicides were non-toxic and 98% effective, so when he began marketing them, he made a fortune. In no time at all he had a factory in Maryland producing the product and developing new and related products. With the increase in farm production and new methods of farming, his production barely kept up with demand. He had two children, both girls. Amy, of course, you know, and he also had a younger daughter, Susannah."

He stopped then as if to catch his breath. Then he said, "Noah this is a long story. Are you sure you want to hear it all?"

"Yes."

"Okay. Amy was a serious girl while Susannah was very flighty and sort of a good time girl. She just couldn't settle down to anything. Amy was a good student and ended up going to Radcliffe which at that time was the female version of Harvard. In her senior year she met Jeff who was a law student at Harvard Law. She fell head over heels in love to hear her tell it. He was the golden boy. He was handsome; tall, blond, clean cut. I remember his long wavy hair and beautiful white teeth. It was a whirlwind romance and they married almost immediately. She couldn't believe her luck in getting such a handsome man. She told me more than once that he looked like a Greek God as far as she was concerned."

"How did he feel about her?" I asked.

"That's a tough one for me to answer. I just don't know. I know he was always attentive to her and loving in her presence. I also know that when he was sailing or docking in various ports when I sailed with him, he always had a woman. He was never faithful to his wife."

"Did she know?"

"I don't know. I doubt very much if she didn't. But their real story begins on their honeymoon. He was a great sailor. He got together a crew and they sailed across the Pacific to Japan from California. At the age of twenty-two, perhaps because she was in love and saw everything in a special light or because she was truly affected by their beauty, she fell in love with azaleas."

"What do you mean azaleas?"

"You know, the shrubs that flower in the spring. She saw them in bloom in different ports in Japan and fell in love with them. From that time on she devoted her life to breeding them, to crossing them, and to trying to develop her own special varieties. I'm sure she'd be willing to tell you all about her work."

Jack stopped to think for a few minutes. It was his habit when he was telling a story to stop and pull his thoughts together from time to time as if he were reviewing what he had said. Now he just sat looking at the empty plates in front of him and toying with a teaspoon which sat next to his plate.

"Jeff Macomber was a complicated man. You know he never practiced law. He used to laugh and say that he wouldn't even know where to stand in a court room. He was from money himself, but, of course, not the kind of money Amy brought to the table. At any rate, she led her life raising and breeding her "pets" as she called them, and he spent his time sailing."

I felt I knew a little about them now although Jeff Macomber remained a mystery. I couldn't quite get a picture of the man in my mind. I knew that would come sooner or later. The bigger question for me was what kind of a person would dedicate her life to raising and breeding azaleas? That struck me as much more of a curious question than the problem of trying to get a fix on Jeff Macomber. But, it would all come in time. I knew that, and I made up my mind to be patient and let it happen rather than trying to come to too many conclusions too quickly.

We drove back to the Point and were at home in less than thirty minutes. Marge wasn't back from her business when we arrived, so I sat down in my favorite chair and decided to listen to a Nielsen symphony. I didn't want quiet and tranquility. I felt I needed music to stir my soul and Nielsen always did that for me.

I wanted to think. That ruled out taking a nap. I sat for an hour or so listening to the music and trying to puzzle through what I knew about the case. I really found that I didn't have sufficient information. It was like doing a picture puzzle with too many pieces missing.

Marge came back to the house to wake me from a deep nap. I was in the habit of taking naps but in this case I had fallen deep into sleep. It hadn't been my intention but I suppose it was a carryover from the soft leather chairs in the study in the Macomber house that morning that had been so tempting to me. I woke refreshed and Marge and I began to attempt to decipher the guest list that Jen had copied for Jack and me. Jack had his copy and I could have bet that he was sitting down right at that moment doing the exact same thing as I was, that is, trying to make some sense out of the list.

The brown envelope that Jen gave me contained a copy of the original guest list. Amy had crossed out the names of those people she knew to be deceased. Marge counted 210 names that were originally on the list. Of those at least three quarters were married couples. That meant we had approximately 150 who had come together as man and wife. The remainder of the people were listed singly. Since it was a fiftieth wedding anniversary we felt justified in assuming that most of the couples were older if they were friends of the celebrants. On a separate sheet were the names of those people who Amy knew had passed away. Someone had taken a yellow highlighter and marked the names on the original guest list as well. Where only one of the couples had died, the highlighter went half way through the name to indicate that only one of the couple had passed away.

On a separate sheaf of paper were the names and telephone numbers as well as the addresses of at least fifteen people with whom Amy had kept in contact. That was the most useful information to us. So, at least we had a place to start. At a glance we could see that most of the names on the sheet with phone numbers were women.

Marge said, "It should be an easy matter to begin contacting the people on the list, but what good will that do, do you think?"

"I have no idea, but it is a beginning."

There was another list in the envelope as well, and this was a list of the names of the servants who were present that day. Most of these, according to a note on the bottom of the page, were fulltime employees who lived in the area of Middletown at the time. Unfortunately, there was neither a telephone number nor an address next to any of the names. Tracing the hired help was not going to be an easy job, but if the help was mainly local, I supposed it could be done.

"Well, Marge, unless I am wrong, I think we have our work cut out for us."

Jack was not long in showing up with his copy of the list. He had started in right away from the time he got home, and he had done so without a nap intervening.

"It's quite a puzzle, Noah," he said brandishing the envelope in front of him as he came through my kitchen entrance. "This is going to be difficult to tackle. I can't figure where to start. Not much of it makes sense to me right now. There are a lot of people listed, but do we talk to them on the telephone or try to meet them personally? I, for one, don't feel like flying all over the country."

"I haven't had a minute to really think about it. Most of the people on the list must be elderly women, so maybe it would be best if Amy were to contact them first. Then Marge could follow up. That way we wouldn't be scaring women half to death."

Marge said, "Are you going to show this to Nelly?"

Not only did we want to show Nelly the contents of the envelope but we also wanted to go over the case with her from the beginning. Nelly had worked with us on every one of our cases and she was a crucial part of our success. At the moment she was at home with her newborn baby. She had had a little girl and she and her husband Patrick, the District Attorney of Bristol County were delighted with their little girl and with their new life. Her mother, Peggy, our dear friend, was living with them for a short period of time to help out with the household chores and with the baby, but mostly, I suspected, to be near her daughter and her new grandchild.

We called first before going across the road to Patrick and Nelly's house. The house had belonged to the Jackson girls but when they decided to leave the area, Jack and I had bought it for the McCarthys as a wedding gift. It had been in a rundown condition but the young couple was slowly making improvements to it and it was becoming a lovely home for the three of them. Nelly said that the baby was napping and that we were welcome to come over, especially if Marge came along as company for Peggy.

We spent about an hour explaining what we knew to Nelly. She couldn't believe that we thought that we had a chance at explaining an event that took place twenty years before.

When we had finished, she said, "Only you two gentlemen could find yourself in the middle of something like this. You are nothing short of a panic. I don't know how you do it."

As she said it, both Jack and I had to admit that if it was at all possible, Nelly looked more beautiful now than she had ever looked. She was a classic beauty to begin with, but now she had a glow that she had never had before. One always sensed in Nelly a certain vulnerability and the feeling that she had been hurt terribly and that she carried that pain with her. She had in fact been married to a cocaine addict and had been awarded an annulment. She had suffered. Now she was blooming with love for her husband, Patrick, and her new baby girl and it showed in her appearance and in her body language.

Her mother, Peggy, who was always with a smile on her face, was now the vision of happiness. She was filled with love for her daughter and the wonderful grandchild she just could not get enough of.

"So, where do you go from here?" Nelly asked.

"We continue to meet with Amy Macomber for starters and then I think we chase down some of the people who were there that day and try to get some information from them," I said. "If nothing shows, then we have nothing to work with and we have done no harm. The real question is whether Amy Macomber is right in asserting that it was against her husband's character to commit suicide? She feels definitely that he would never have taken his own life. I have to assume that she is right."

"I agree with Noah. I have never seen anyone so sure of anything. The woman is convinced that Jeff Macomber was murdered. If he was, I think we should take a shot at finding out if she is right. The only thing I don't understand is why, with all of her resources, she should turn to two old buzzards like us. She could hire anyone she chose to and get a real professional investigation done. Why us?"

Nelly laughed and said, "For two old buzzards you have done pretty well. Maybe more importantly, you have done it with no fanfare."

Chapter VI

We met the next morning with Amy Macomber in what had become our normal setting. There we were sitting in the darkness in a sun room with the blinds drawn and not a light on in the room. She was wrapped in her stadium blanket and for all of her apparent frail appearance, had the usual sparkle in her eyes.

I had some questions and I started right in with them.

"I notice that the books in the study are all of a scientific nature," I began. "Some of them are very old. Who do they belong to?"

"This young man is very observant," Amy said. "They are half Daddy's and half ours. Daddy used that room as a working study and so do we. We meet every night to work out details of our progress. As you can see, we have the computer set up which is mostly Jen's area, then there is the large table where we map out our crosses and the sitting area where I tend to stay and read the journals to try to keep up to date."

"What exactly are you doing?" I asked.

"Well, I continue to cross azaleas to try to develop very hardy, wind tolerant varieties for the northeast. I have introduced several varieties which have become quite successful commercially. Jason is attempting to develop multicolored varieties of dwarf rhododendrons using Yaks as a basis for parentage. Yak is short for yakushimanum. Jason can explain his work to you when he gets a little time. This is a very busy season for him right now."

"So you meet every night in the study and work? I notice it is spotless. Everything is shining clean. It is hard to believe that a working space could be so neat and clean."

Amy laughed. It was the first time I had heard her laugh. She had a high shrill laugh that didn't seem to fit her age or her shrunken body. It was the laugh of a child.

"That's because I insist on it being clean. I have one cleaning girl who comes in three days a week just to clean that room. Jason says that I have a cleanliness fetish about my study. That's because when I first started work in my "play pens" I would track dirt into the house. I taught myself to stop in the greenhouse and to change my shoes there before I come in. After working in soil and dampness all day, I want a clean atmosphere to finish off the day after I have my shower and an evening meal. This is it. We may not have cocktails after dinner, but we do work, and it is refreshing to come into a spotless room at the end of the day."

"You mentioned that your father used that room as a working study. Exactly what does that mean? Was it set up in the way it is now?" I asked.

"You are persistent, but I suppose that is why you are successful at this business. The room is exactly as it was when Daddy used it. The only real difference would be the quality of the lighting over the table, the reading lamps and, of course, the computer. When he summered here, he used the room mornings when the sun first rose and then in the evening when the sun had set. Like us, Daddy was a record keeper and he liked to have everything in order. No one was allowed in the study when he was working. You'll find some of his records intact. They are in the large black binders, much like Jason and I use today."

Jack interrupted by saying, "We have both gone over the list of guests. We need you to make contact with those that are close to you, so that we can follow up with phone calls. We will probably visit any that we feel will give us valuable information, but it would help if you talked to people first, particularly women who might distrust a call out of the blue."

"That isn't easy for me. I hate to talk on the phone, but if it has to be, I'll do it. I know what you mean by alarming some of the ladies. At this point in time, those who are still alive are well along in years."

I couldn't pass up the questions I had on my mind.

"Could you tell us why you became so enamored of azaleas?" I asked.

"Oh that is a complicated question. Let me think for a moment."

Amy Macomber sat very still and she was almost serene in her stillness. She seemed at peace with herself. At her age she should have been feeble and weak, perhaps suffering from dementia, but there was none of that here. She may have been feeble physically, but even then there was an inner vitality that showed through her old body.

Finally she said, "First of all, I was struck with their sheer beauty. There was not only the beauty of the flowers, but I loved the way the Japanese gardeners grew them in lovely graceful shapes and in wonderful clean backgrounds. To me, they shone like precious jewels in perfect settings. That sounds mushy I know, but it was really love at first sight."

She stopped for a moment and seemed to reflect back to a period some seventy years before when she was a newly married honeymooner.

"Then when I began talking to the gardeners using a translator, I learned that they bred their own varieties from seed. I couldn't believe that. They actually made crosses and grew plants. They introduced something completely new into the world. That excited me beyond imagination. My husband thought I was crazy. It was all I could think about. I spent my honeymoon learning how to make crosses and how to grow azaleas from seed. To make a long story short, the whole process appealed to me."

She stopped again and sat for quite some time in silence. I did not want to break the spell so I signaled Jack to wait for her thoughts. She rocked back and forth very gently and slowly and her eyes took on a far away look. She had her own special thoughts and she was happy.

Then she said, "This is complicated. Daddy became rich by discovering fungicides. He spent years all by himself in his laboratory working on formulae that would allow him to defeat the deadly funguses that were killing off plants. It was his life's work. Why did he choose that life or that work? Who knows? But it required his special skills. He was methodical, clear headed, unrelenting, and, finally, successful. He kept the most detailed notes of everything he did to the point where 99.99% of the people on this earth would go mad in frustration. He was trained to be a chemist when chemists didn't have half the tools they have today. Is all this clear to you?"

Jack and I both nodded.

"Then think about it. I do the same thing with my azaleas and Jason does exactly the same with his rhododendrons. For seventy years now my laboratory has been the greenhouses and my play pens. I come here every night to make meticulous notes of crosses, successes and failures. In all those years, nothing has stopped me. Do you know why? The answer is simple. I am my Daddy. We are one and the same. And, Jason, who is my sister's son, is my Daddy too. Somehow the genes skipped a generation in my sister but were waiting to reemerge again in fertile soil. Jason is that fertile soil. So, that is a very long answer to a very simple question. Does it all make sense to you, Mr. Amos?"

"Yes, it does, and thank you for the effort," I said.

"You see, this is all about genetics, isn't it? Whether we are talking azaleas or rhododendrons or people, it is all about the same thing. Daddy, Jason and I are all from the same mold and we breed true just as Jason's dwarf rhododendrons breed true. All I know is that my life's work has made my life worth living. The azaleas I have produced have made all the work and effort worthwhile."

At this point Jack did break in with his questions. "Let's take a few minutes to prioritize this list. First off, we are looking for information of any kind that will relate to your husband's death. Are there any names here that will be more helpful than others?"

"I can't see in this light. Let's go into the study for a minute and then I am going to go outside and get some work done. This is the busy season, believe it or not."

We went into the study and she moved under the canopy and put the lights on. The brightness shocked her for a moment but her eyes became accustomed to the bright light and she adjusted quickly. She took a highlighter out of the bib pocket of her overalls, made a few marks on the sheet of names, gave the sheet to Jack and said, "Those should be contacted first. I'll call tonight and tell them to expect a call from one of you. Who will be calling?"

I said, "Marge will. She is my companion and she will make the calls so as not to frighten anyone."

"That's a new phrase for me, companion. Does that mean you are living together?"

"Yes, it does," I said and left it at that. I didn't feel I needed to explain my relationship to Marge and I certainly didn't need to justify it.

Chapter VII

Jack dug back in his memory trying as much as possible to remember the details of the party that he felt might be useful to us. That night he sat down to tell us what he recalled. Nelly and Patrick had come to the house and we were all sitting around the kitchen while Jack began his story. Nelly needed a break from the baby. Peggy was probably hoping the baby would wake up so that she could have her all to herself.

"It was a big do," Jack began. He was tall and slim and as he talked his hands seemed to have a will of their own. It was like watching a conductor leading an orchestra. From time to time he would stop talking and then his hands would disappear into his pockets before coming out again as he continued his soliloquy.

"My wife was down for the summer and was working on some sketches for a book. I was in Manhattan working. I drove down the day before the party and we got all decked out for the big day. They had feared rain, but it was a beautiful sunshiny day with only a few clouds in the sky. I remember that because the breezes off the water kept everything nice and cool. We drove up to the front door and a valet picked up our car giving us a slip tag so that he could retrieve the car for us later. I asked him not to bury us because I didn't think we would be staying late."

He explained to Marge and Nelly and Patrick that the drive leading to the front door seemed endless. The house had been built on the site of a farm and the land was flat from the road to the house and then sloped down to the bay below. You could almost imagine a field of potatoes or sweet corn on either side of the road. Instead there were large fenced in areas lining the drive.

"We entered the house and were ushered into the dining room and through it to the terrace that ran the whole width of the back of the house. I can't remember whether the study doors were closed or open. Jeff and Amy met us on the terrace. He had had a few drinks. Since it was only mid-afternoon I was a little surprised. If nothing else, Jeff always put on a good appearance. His speech was a little slurred and he looked the worse for wear. He was tall and slim. He was dressed in a black tuxedo with a lacy white shirt and he looked like something out of a formal magazine advertisement. His naturally blond hair had a touch of gray that made him look distinguished and his tan was perfectly set off by the whiteness of the shirt and tie. Dressed as he was, he exuded muscular strength and vitality. I can still recall how strong the man was. I was always in good shape but I was never a match for him even when I was in my prime. Amy, of course, would much rather have been in her bib overalls, as we see her now, than all dressed up in clothes she never wore and in which she had to be terribly uncomfortable. I remember her in a long blue gown that was too loose in the shoulders and around her hips. Either it was a bad fit or she had put it on hurriedly without attempting to fit it to her body. Amy had never been a beauty and she made no pretense, at the age of seventy she was going to play a role she had avoided all her life."

This was a long speech for Jack and he seemed quite surprised at himself for having made it.

He laughed and said, "I haven't strung so many words together in years. I think I am catching something from Noah."

We sat quietly waiting for him to continue. Finally, he began again by saying, "Mr. Goetzel also stood on the terrace. For a man of his age he looked like a million dollars. He had to be in his nineties, but dressed in a tuxedo you would never have guessed it. He was not a handsome man. He was small and too heavy, but he had the same intensity about him then that Amy has now. He seemed distracted by the time I reached him, but he concentrated on me long enough to thank me for my advice on investments he was making for his grandson, Jason. Amy's sister, Susannah, stood next to him. Even in her late sixties she was a beauty. She was a commanding figure even though she wasn't much taller than Amy. But there was a quality about her that made you stop and look and finally, admire her."

According to Jack, there was a reception line to meet the celebrating couple and Amy's father and sister.

Marge asked, "How about Mr. Macomber's family? Were they there?"

Jack thought for a moment and then said, "I never even thought about that. No, I don't think any of his family was there. I certainly didn't meet any of them. We'll have to ask Amy about that."

Jack was silent again as he tried to recollect that day.

"At the far end of the terrace beyond the study, a dance band played. If I remember correctly it was the old Glen Miller band under Tex Benecke. They were playing all the old favorites and the crowd was old enough to appreciate the old swing tunes. Those who were dancing were having a great time. The band was playing facing the terrace outside the study where a temporary dance floor had been set up. Now I do remember, the doors to the study were definitely closed and the drapes had been pulled."

"It comes back to me slowly. Then on the lawn below the terrace there were a number of food stations.. There was one with little Italian things and there was a Mexican stand, I ate at those two. Then there was a fish table where there were raw oysters and little necks. There was sort of a barbecue pit where they had Texas style barbecue. All little fancy stuff served on little plates that were hardly a mouth full. I think people were doing more drinking than eating. I know I kept poking away at the food and when my wife and I left I was still hungry."

I asked, "Did anything of any importance happen while you were there?"

"Not that I can remember. It was the usual dull big party. There was too little food, the music was too loud and too intrusive, the speeches and toasts were too corny for words. Amy was so obviously miserable that she made everybody uncomfortable. All in all I know I could personally have done without the whole day. The only people who enjoyed themselves were those who drank too much too quickly. As for the rest of the visitors I think they were much like I was, definitely wanting to get out of there and get home or to their hotel rooms."

"Where was Mr. Macomber while all this was going on?" Nelly asked.

"Well, when we first saw him he was on the terrace behind the dining room, meeting everybody as they came in. From time to time as the afternoon went on I saw him walking across the lawn or talking to someone alone. Amy pretty much did the rounds and then disappeared for an hour or so while Susannah held court seated in a wicker chair under an umbrella. She was beautiful in what my wife described as a lavender chiffon Grecian style gown. She had silvery gray hair pulled back in a chignon. She was truly lovely. She didn't have a wrinkle on her face and Susan said that she had had so many face lifts that wrinkles would be afraid to show themselves. At that time I think she was living in a villa in Tuscany and she affected a slight accent that made her all the more alluring. To be honest with you, I liked Amy far more than Susannah and so did my wife. But that afternoon the men were all paying her court. She was the queen sitting in that wicker chair half in the sun and half in the shadows sipping lemonade with 'just a splash of vodka, dear, just the slightest splash.'"

"If a shot had been fired, do you think you would have heard it?" I asked.

"I doubt it. The orchestra played most of the time although when they took a break the silence was deafening. Remember almost every inch of the grounds was taken up by people wandering around and talking. There was clinking of glassware and the usual noise when people are being served. It was party time and the more people drank, the louder voices became. When that shot went off in the study, I doubt that anyone outside could have heard it. I don't know about inside though," Jack said and the way he said it sounded like he had had enough talk for a while.

"So, as far as you were concerned, when you left the party that day, there was no reason to think that anything was wrong. Would you agree to that?" Nelly asked.

Jack nodded and sat thoughtfully in the chair that he had been sitting in before he started pacing the floor. We all sat quietly thinking about what he had said. If nothing else, I thought I could now visualize the setting at the house and the party on the day that the death had occurred. With the information Jack gave me I was able to recreate what I remembered of the front of the house. The front doors opened into a wide hallway that looked directly at a marble staircase that led to the upper floor of the house. To the right was a sitting room that led directly to the dining room behind it and to the left a formal parlor complete with chandeliers and fireplace. Somewhere out of sight was the kitchen which

I hadn't quite placed in my mind's eye. Beyond the staircase was the study which occupied a central location in the house. In a separate building to the right of the main house was the barn which had long since been used as a garage for the family's automobiles and as a storage place for the tools and vehicles related to the business of growing rhododendrons and azaleas.

I tried to imagine myself that day looking over the whole vista from a perch atop the terrace. There would be the sloping green lawn, the terrace itself sitting in a dominant position above the rise, the small pine trees leading down the slope and the winding walks which ended in a wide walk at the bottom of the slope a hundred feet or so from the water's edge. Then of course, there were the yachts and sailing vessels anchored in the bay below in a sheltered lea near the wharf that was part of the property and in which several of the guests must have arrived.

All in all it was quite an impressive background for a party. Most importantly, as far as Amy was concerned, her "play pens" were not harmed in any way. She called them play pens because they were fenced in areas where she set out her young plants after they had been started in the greenhouses. They were fenced in because when she had first started laying out her azaleas, the young plants had been devastated by the deer which ranged freely in Middletown and Portsmouth before the housing developments came in to drive all the wild animals out. She never forgot her terrible disappointment when she discovered the damage the deer and other animals had done to her first couple of year's work and would never take the chance again.

She grew the crosses and seedlings in the greenhouses until the danger of frost was past and they were large enough to set out in rows in the fields. They were put out and labeled very carefully with metal markers that were set in the ground in front of each plant. The markers had the crosses listed on them and each cross was given a number which was recorded separately. The work was meticulous and there were times when it demanded every ounce of discipline that Amy had, but, she did it every year for sixty years without losing her faith.

In addition to Amy's work with azaleas, Jason joined her with his rhododendrons when he graduated from Harvard. Harvard had been a tradition in the family only broken by his mother Susannah, who had flunked out of Radcliffe after her freshman year. Jason's interest in hybridization was a direct outgrowth of his time spent with his Aunt Amy when he was a teenager and the time he had spent working in the fields with her.

Chapter VIII

We decided that it was time that we met Jason, so Jack called Amy and asked that he be present at our meeting the next morning. Jack remembered him only briefly from the funeral of Jeff Macomber he had attended, but even then he didn't have much of a picture of him in his mind. We hadn't seen him since we had been visiting the farm so it came as a surprise when Jen ushered us into the study to find him sitting there waiting for us.

He stood when we entered and only then did we realize how tall he was. He seemed to unwind as he rose to shake our hands. I would have to guess that he was at least six feet four inches tall. He was slim but muscular and when he shook my hand I could feel his strength coursing through his fingers.

Jack was taken aback at first sight of him. Amy saw his surprise and said, "Yes, Jack it is what you think. No more need be said now unless we forget to get down to business."

Jason was a handsome man. There was no question about that. He had a shock of rough cut, wild blond hair above a handsome face with a few distinctive wrinkles that added to his beauty rather than detracted from it. His gleaming white teeth set off his deeply tanned face to perfection. There was a confidence about him that, like his strength, showed through without any effort on his part. Like, Jack, he had not a bit of fat on him and his clothes fit him to a tee. He wore a pair of jeans that looked like they had seen considerable service, a thin, long sleeved cotton shirt that was tucked in at the waist and a light vest that zipped up the front. That together with heavy leather boots made up his work attire. He appeared to be in his mid-forties, but his youthful looks made it hard to tell.

Amy began by saying, "I thought you would like to meet Jason before he starts working outside. If you have any questions for him, please ask them so that he can get to work. He is rather anxious to get started today since he has quite a bit ahead of him."

Jack began by asking, "Were you here the day of the party?"

"I was. But, I pretty much kept out of the way. A group of us went upstairs to the other library and spent all of our time in there. It was really a party for adults, so except for the food, the younger people kept out of sight."

Jack said, "I don't even remember seeing any young people getting food."

"No, we had one of the maids bring us the food upstairs on trays. We had more than enough without coming down. She got rather tired of it, but with a little prodding, she made the trek back and forth any number of times. It was sort of fun for us, but the poor girl must have been exhausted by the end of the day. She kept bringing us food from one serving center or another all day, I think."

I said, "So, you saw nothing that would give us a hint as to what happened to Mr. Macomber, is that right?"

"That's right."

He spoke in a matter of fact way that suggested that he was totally uninterested in what we were trying to discover for his Aunt Amy.

"I'm rather surprised that you and your friends didn't mix at least a little with the older guests," I said.

"Actually, someone had gotten a bottle of vodka and one of the kids was making an ass out of himself, so we kept him close so he wouldn't be discovered. It was embarrassing and rather foolish, but there you have it."

Jack then said, "If you have anything that you think could help, can we depend on you to come forward?"

"I will, Mr. Crawford, but, I can't think of a thing that would be of any use. So, if there is nothing else, I'd like to get my day's work started. Nice to meet both of you."

He left us then and as soon as he left the room, Jack turned to Amy and said, "Tell us now, please."

She smiled and said, "There isn't much doubt is there? He is the very likeness of Jeff. He may be taller and more serious, but he is Jeff all over. He is definitely Jeff's son. Before my sister died I visited her in Italy and she made the big confession that she and Jeff had been carrying on for years. That is really why I wanted you to meet Jason. Now you know, Jack. I don't know if it will shed any light on the problem, but there it is."

She had made her point. Now that she had gotten it off her chest she seemed to relax as the tenseness went from her body. I could see the change in her face and in her posture. She didn't slump or become diminished in any way but rather became whole as if she had gotten rid of a weight and was now free of it.

"We might as well get this out of the way now. I knew about Jeff and all his affairs. They were endless. It was his fatal flaw. Women, including myself, loved him for all the wrong reasons. He was a golden god, a Greek statue. Look at Jason. Do you see why he is so attractive to women? They love him too. He attracts them just as Jeff did. Jen is his daughter, incidentally."

She stopped again to reflect on what she wanted to say. There was no confession here but more like a statement of the facts as she saw them. There was no sense in which she was sad or apologetic; she was merely stating the case as it was.

"The odd thing was that Jeff was a brilliant man who wasted his life on sailing and on women. That's why I could never divorce him even though I knew what he was doing. You see, I stole his promise. I lured him with money. Never knowingly and with intent, but I did nonetheless. That's why his family wanted nothing to do with him. He showed great promise and then threw it all away because I gave him the means to do it. As brilliant as he was, he was weak and gave into his impulses rather than join the battle to make his life worth something. Without my money he would have gone on to make an outstanding career for himself in the law."

Jack said, "Was his family here the day of the party?"

"No, by then his mother and father were both dead and had they been alive they would not have come. They never forgave me for letting him lead a wasted life. You know he graduated fourth in his class at Harvard Law School which was a great achievement. He was offered jobs in the most prestigious law firms in the country and he turned them all down for sailing."

Jack said, "We all make choices Amy. Jeff chose a way of life and who knows why. Your money may have made it easy for him, but he made the choices, not you."

"Thank you, Jack, but at this point it is neither here nor there. As you well know once we make the choices there is no going back. Well, when Susannah was dying she called me to Italy to her bedside so that she could confess that she had long been in love with Jeff and that they had had an affair that had lasted well over forty years. She had never married because of her deep love for Jeff. Even I was shocked at that. It was quite obvious that Jason was their son, but I had had no idea that they had been together so long. My first thought was that it had been a terrible waste. I had long since given up any love that I had for Jeff. I can't even remember now when I realized that I didn't love him and never had. I would gladly have given him to her. We had nothing in common, Jeff and I. She was in the same financial condition as I was, so he would have lost nothing by going to her and staying with her permanently. There was no real reason why he should have stayed with me if he could have gone to Susannah."

It was quite a surprise to me to hear her talk as she did. However, she was in her nineties and had seen quite a bit of life. She needed none of the justification that most of us have to have to make our lives have meaning. There was no looking back with regret. She didn't have time for that. What she was doing was putting the facts on the table. She was looking back at a time some twenty years before when her husband of fifty years had been killed or committed suicide. She wanted to know the truth. She had had a loveless marriage, and in some twisted turn of events she had learned that her only sister had loved her husband for most of her adult life.

"I have had enough of this for today. Now you know as much about my personal life as anybody ever did. What more is there to say?" she said and seemed to withdraw into herself. I had to admire her. She was what Peggy would have called "spunky." Everything about her was strong and without equivocation; there was no fence-sitting with this lady.

"We had a couple of questions," I said. "Was the help mainly local? Were the people who worked here as servants or caterers from the local area?"

"Yes. Evangelica who will come in today to clean the study is the daughter of our oldest cleaning woman. Her aunts and uncles as well have worked for us for years. Her mother is Deolinda. She is still alive and doing quite well, I understand. Maybe you can talk to her today. She may be here now. In fact she should be."

"Did you make any calls for us?" Jack asked.

"Yes, Jen has the names and numbers of three people who will be expecting calls from you," she said with a dismissive tone that we knew meant that the interview was over for that morning. I felt it had been a very revealing morning.

"Is there any chance we might visit you at work to see how things are done in the gardens?" I asked.

"Not today. I have too much to do. Maybe I can arrange to have Jason take you around so he can show you the whole process. I don't think it will help you to solve our case, but it may be helpful to you, who knows?"

She threw off her stadium blanket then and pulled and pushed her way out of the wicker chair and walked rather unsteadily for the door to the outside and to her beloved work.

Jack and I went to the study in the hope that we would meet Evangelica and perhaps get some information that might be useful. It seemed we were constantly grasping for straws here. Except that the case was growing more and more interesting for me, it didn't seem that we were learning anything substantive about what happened to Jeff Macomber. The facts about Jeff's love life didn't seem to add up to very much. Although listening to Amy tell us about it, shocked me a bit.

When we entered the room, we saw the lady immediately. She surprised me by her appearance. She looked like she must have been in her fifties. Somehow I had expected someone younger. She was a Portuguese woman through and through. She was a short and heavy woman and had a no nonsense attitude about her work. We had to ask her to stop bustling around so that we could talk to her. I had the impression that she would have preferred to be anywhere at that moment other than having to face us and answer our questions. We finally asked her to sit in one of the large brown leather chairs so that we could sit across from her and keep her still.

I began by saying that I too was Portuguese and should she want to express herself in Portuguese rather than English at any point I would be more than capable of understanding and translating for Jack. She seemed to relax a bit then and Jack began the questioning.

"Now, Evangelica how long have you been working here?" Jack asked.

"Oh, I been here for many a year sir. Look out the back window down over the garden. Go ahead," she said pointing at the glass doors. "Go ahead, I told you."

We didn't know what to make of it but we both rose from the leather chairs and walked to the windows.

Then she said, "See the garden just off the terrace to the right, the one with the big stones and the plants growing over them? Do you see them?" she asked while she remained seated in her chair.

"I do," I said.

"Okay. Those are Missy's first azaleas she made herself. Those go back to when I was a little girl. My daddy brought those rocks in and Missy set them up. They look real good don't they?"

Jack said, "They do."

"You should see them in flower. See the one in the far corner? You know what that is called? It is Evangelica. That was planted on the day of my First Communion. So, how long have I worked here? I can take you through every garden going down the hill to the water. And then Mr. Jason started bringing in his special rhododendrons too. They are here too. Does that answer your question?"

From where I stood I could see at least five of what Evangelica called "gardens." They were Japanese styled gardens with raked stones surrounding large boulders with azaleas and rhododendrons planted strategically for the greatest effect. Even from where we stood at quite some distance, they were quite lovely. They were placed on the slope sweeping down to the water's edge almost giving the sweeping lawn a terraced look.

I asked, "Are all of the plantings Mrs. Macomber's and her nephew's?"

"Yes, they are. Too bad you can't see them in bloom, they are really beautiful."

"So," Jack said, "You were working here when Mr. Macomber was found dead, is that right?"

"Of course. I wasn't working in the study then. The day of the party I was taking care of the kids upstairs. Mr. Jason was there too."

"Did you see anything out of the ordinary?" he asked.

"No, I was too busy taking food up to the kids and the group upstairs. Quite a few of them were drinking quite a bit and they were getting cute with me. Mr. Jason stopped them. He took charge of them and he kept them under control. He was a man by then and he was with one of his girl friends."

"Where were they?" I asked.

"They were in the upstairs study right over the room where they found Mr. Jeff."

"Could they have heard a gunshot?" I asked.

"I don't know. There was a television on. It was noisy."

"How many were there?'

"There was Mr. Jason and his lady friend. Then there was the guy who was drinking. I don't know his name. There were a couple of young girls maybe in their early twenties and two more boys about the same age. I don't know any of their names. I know they ate a lot of food. I had to keep going in and out all afternoon. The windows were open and you could hear the band music coming from the terrace. Jason and his friend danced quite a bit. I could tell he was very restless. He wanted to get out of the fancy clothes and get to work outside."

"Do you like Jason?"

"Oh he is very nice, but he is a workaholic. I had a terrible crush on him when he came to live here. He is the handsomest man in the world, and, he is a real gentleman."

"Was Mr. Macomber as nice?" I asked.

"Depends. When he wasn't drinking he was a real gentleman. When he had a few drinks in him, he was very nasty. When he started drinking we all kept away from him. Especially the men. He was very strong and he liked to fight. For such a good looking man you wouldn't believe it, but my father used to say he was a 'barroom brawler.'"

Jack said, "Come to think of it, she's right. I remember him looking for a fight on shore any number of times. He really was good with his hands. He was fast and powerful, Rocky Marciano with a pretty face."

I asked, "Did you know that Jason is his son?"

She laughed at that. "We are not blind you know. You would have to be blind and stupid not to see that Jason is his son. But, Jason is not like the father at all. For one thing you will find out that he never drinks anything stronger than beer with food. I'm wasting a lot of time. I better get to work."

"No, don't worry about that right now," I said, "Mrs. Macomber wants you to talk to us. It's all right. I have a few more questions for you. Did your mother work here too?"

"Yes, my mother and father worked and my two brothers still help Mr. Jason with the hot house, the play pens and the gardens. The family has been very good to us and we have worked for them and no one else for many years except for my father who worked for the family and other people too doing special stone work. He died twenty-five years ago."

"Do you think we will be able to interview your mother?" Jack asked.

"I think so but you will have to come out to the house. She won't come here. She doesn't like to leave the house too much now."

Jack said, "Okay, we come here almost every day. Leave a note with Mrs. Macomber to let us know when we can visit. Is there anything else you think we should know before we let you go?"

At that point I think she had just about come to the end of her line. She looked nervous and edgy and when Jack asked her if there was anything else she could add, she saw that as an opportunity to escape. She rose from the deep cushions of the chair, smoothed down her skirt and began looking for her cleaning things. Our interview was over, but I felt we had learned quite a bit. We thanked her and left her to her work and I decided to take a walk outside the house to get a closer look at the gardens on the slope going down to the water.

The first was the garden at the end of the terrace that Evangelica had told us about. It was a small Japanese garden with three azaleas planted around and over the rocks. They were low growing plants, two of which wove through the stones like rock garden plants while a third mounded up in a perfect semi-globe nestled in between two large boulders. In front of each was the name of the azalea and the cross which had produced it and the date it had been introduced etched into a metal marker stuck in the ground. One of the plants was named "Evangelica", another was named "Sam Goetzel" and a third was named "Eleanor."

Jack had disappeared. I had no idea where he had gone, so I continued my little walk by myself. The gardens were loosely connected visually by paths of flat, bluish stone that looked like they had been laid on the raked sand on which they were set. The second garden was some thirty feet away from the first and held two azaleas named, dated and with the crosses noted on metal markers as in the first garden. There were six gardens in all and the very lowest contained what I assumed were rhododendrons that resulted from Jason's work, one of which bore the name "Aunt Amy" and another the name "Jen". I did make note of the fact that none of the azaleas bore the name "Jeff." I gave myself a mental reminder that I would ask Amy Macomber about that when the opportunity arose.

I wondered if Mrs. Macomber had any introductions other than those in the gardens. Had she spent roughly seventy years of her life to produce so few azaleas or was the number I had seen typical of what a hybridizer would produce in a lifetime working alone? I had no idea but I did think it worth looking into, not in terms of the case, but merely to satisfy my own curiosity.

I had lost track of Jack and it wasn't until I found Jen that she told me that he was in the basement kitchen. She showed me the way and we found Jack sitting at a rough work table sipping the remains of a cup of coffee and eating a sandwich that the cook had rustled up for him using leftover roast beef and some pita bread. He apologized for the fact that he had been "starved" and needed to find something to eat. I waited until he finished and then we left for home.

The question of how many azaleas Mrs. Macomber had introduced into the plant world stuck with me for the rest of the day. It wasn't that I questioned the value of what she had done, but that I admired the fact that she had stuck to her task all those years. In some respects it was no different than what I had done with my life. I had spent 38 years teaching and it wasn't as if I could look back at that many great accomplishments. Many of my kids had done well, but many had gone on with their lives and I had never heard from them again. Amy Macomber had plants in gardens all around the plant world and had a great deal to show for it in comparison. Unlike Jack, who had spent his life making money, Amy Macomber had no need to devote herself to typical pursuits. She could have become a socialite or a bon vivant as her sister had done. But she had fallen in love with azaleas. Her husband was in love with the sea and they both had the means to follow their pursuits.

So, what was the difference in what Jack and I had done and what the young couple has chosen to do. We each went our own way. I went to the classroom not so much by choice as by chance. Jack chose to make money. The couple made their choice as well. But each of us brought skills to what we had chosen to do and that ensured our successes.

I had difficulty relating to each of their choices. I could understand Jack's desire to make money because for years I had been living with just enough to get by. Every Friday when I sat down to pay the bills, there were always a few that had to be delayed or set aside for a week. When I inherited the money from my former student I never had to face that problem again, but I could understand need and the desire to amass a fortune. I had been on a sailing ship only once in my life and that had been the previous summer when Jack, Marge, Clarissa and I had taken a cruise from Miami to the Bahamas. We had had a full crew aboard to manage the sailing vessel and although Jack had been in charge, he knew his limitations at age 72. It had taken some adjusting by Marge and me, but it had been pleasant and we had not met any adverse conditions. Would I have devoted my life to sailing? I could see no chance that that would happen. Even Jack, who had a great love for the sea and of sailing, felt that he had better fish to fry than spending his life sailing.

I had never grown anything in my life. The fact that Jason and his aunt devoted their lives to growing things and creating new plants from seed or from crosses was completely foreign to me. If someone said that they loved to cook, I could understand that. If one person liked to decorate his or her home, I could relate to that. Marge laughed when I told her how I felt about growing things.

"I'm sure as a descendant of Azoreans, you have horticulture in your blood. I'm sure there were more farmers in your ancestry than fishermen," she said.

"I'm sure you are right. You know my father kept a little garden and I never so much as cut the grass. It was his special hobby and he was jealous of it. He kept the chores to himself because he enjoyed the activity out of doors. Then when I bought my house, it was on a postage stamp of property wedged in between two other houses. I added a deck to the back and that was it for the back yard. The front was landscaped with a few feet of grass in front of overgrown foundation plantings and that was it. So aside from four feet of grass going across a fifty foot lot, I can't say that I grew anything."

"But, it's there. But just think maybe it isn't horticulture that is the key to Amy's and Jason's fascination. Maybe it is method. Wasn't her father a scientist? And isn't what they are doing science in a real sense of the word? So we may have a case here of not so much the hobby or obsession as such but the process that we call science in action. Just as you and Jack must call on some special cast of mind that comes from deep within you to solve these mysteries of yours, so maybe Mrs. Macomber and Jason have something that drives them to discovery in this particular way."

"It could be," I said and I suddenly felt like a walk on the beach. It was the wrong season and certainly the wrong time of day to even consider a walk on the beach. It was the height of the season and the beach was sure to be packed with swimmers and sunbathers. Marge caught my mood and we decided to dare it.

We drove the five minutes to the beach and parked in the Westport Town Resident's Parking Lot. We were lucky enough to find a parking space and then trekked over the dunes to the beach. Horseneck Beach is located on the very western end of the Buzzards Bay Watershed and is a strip of beach fronting the Atlantic Ocean to its south. About two hundred feet at its deepest, it is bordered on its northern edge by sand dunes which are typical of the beaches along the coast leading to Cape Cod. We entered the beach close to its westernmost part and so we walked with our backs to the sun in the later afternoon to the eastern end of the horse's neck. It was beautiful. As we had suspected there was not an available inch of sand left for those people hoping to throw down a blanket and stretch out in the sand and get some afternoon sun.

Marge looked very becoming in a floral blue, long skirt with a white top with long sleeves. She wore sandals and as we walked along the edge of the water I could see the water swishing between her toes. I wore only a pair of shorts and sandals hoping that the sun would give me a lift. The breeze coming off the water made the hot sun tolerable and the cold water washing over our feet was refreshing.

Mothers and fathers had their hands full chasing back and forth after their little ones while the older children were watched intently by the life guards. Horseneck Beach was notorious for its undertow which managed to kill at least one swimmer each year. The swimmer tended to move out too far into the water and at times the undertow was so strong it was capable of dragging even excellent, strong swimmers under and pulling them out to sea.

We wove our way down the beach and since the beach was a local attraction, I had any number of young people walk up to me and reintroduce themselves. Thirty-eight years of teaching means that a great many students come under a teacher's purview and it was no surprise to me that out of the thousand or more people on the beach that afternoon, any number of my former students were present.

Marge was a little surprised that it took us so long to walk a mile and a half, but it was a pleasure for me to meet old students, some of whom had families of their own to worry about. They were all grown up now and those with beards and mustaches looked a great deal older than they had as students and were almost unidentifiable until I heard their voices or looked at their eyes. Most of them I did recognize after they introduced themselves and we joked about the changes in their appearances.

We often walked the beach early in the day and had the beach pretty much to ourselves. This was a different experience, but still gave me a chance to clean the cobwebs out of my bemused brain. The walk back down the beach was into the sun and even with my tinted glasses I had to shield my eyes from the descending sun. By then the sun had heated my skin and I was pleased to feel the ocean breeze cooling me down. It took another fifteen minutes to get back to the dunes and to the parking lot. I had left the windows open a hair so that we would not be baking when we got back but even then the seats were red hot when we entered the car. Marge had thought to bring some towels and she placed them on the seats and we managed to avoid getting our bottoms and backs scorched. It was then that I thought that the answer to the problems we faced were more likely to come from inside the house than outside. Why my mind should have been on the case at that moment was beyond me, but I thought of the information Evangelica had given us that morning and realized that her mother would hold a great deal of information in store for us.

We drove the very short distance back to Drift Road which was the first exit on the highway over the bridge fording the Westport River in twenty minutes because we were facing bumper to bumper traffic as the crowds began deserting the beach and making their way back to Fall River and New Bedford via Route 88. It was slow but we knew we had only a short distance to go so we were patient while many of the young people were irritated and road rage was in the making.

When Marge had said that there was something in our backgrounds that molded our ways of thinking that allowed Jack and me to be successful detectives, I had dismissed it as so much twaddle. Now I realized that she was right. What my ancestors had given me was patience, forbearance and persistence. My father had often said to me, "Noah always remember that you are Portuguese through and through. You may not be the smartest or the wisest, but we have learned over the years to put our shoulders to the wheel and never give up." Suddenly, on that hot summer afternoon in a traffic jam, waiting for cars to get over the bridge in single file and onto the two lane highway to Drift Road, I knew that my father was right and Marge had once again proven to be right. Jack had his gifts and I had mine and patience certainly wasn't one of his.

The first thing I did when I got back to the house was to call Jack. I wanted to have him call Amy so that we could set up a meeting with Evangelica's mother as soon as possible. I had suddenly become convinced that the only way we were going to succeed was from the inside out.

Chapter IX

We set out for Middletown the next morning. Marge had begun calling the people on Amy's guest list and had several appointments set up for us during the following few days, but in the meantime I wanted to keep busy. We were to visit Mrs. Arruda that morning. She lived not too far from the Goetzel mansion and we found the house with no difficulty.

Jack immediately noted, "This is quite a house for a maid. She must have been paid very well indeed to end up with this."

The house was located in an upscale development on a large lot of land. It was a two story colonial house located high on a rise and overlooking the bay in the distance. We pulled into the wide driveway and parked and took a moment or two to admire the beds of roses along the side of the house. The garden, from what we could see, was a showplace of annuals and perennials and it seemed to be very well kept. The lawn was perfectly manicured and the walks leading around the side of the house and through the side gardens that we could see were meticulously set in Portsmouth stone. All I could think of was that my father would have loved what he saw.

Mrs. Arruda was waiting for us. My first impression of her was that she must have been a handsome woman. She was taller than her daughter and quite slim for a woman in her seventies. Although her hair was gray and did not look like it had been touched up, it still hung naturally and didn't look like the beauty parlor hair that so many older women have. The wrinkles around her eyes and on her forehead and around the mouth didn't hide the beauty that had once been there. She wore tinted eye glasses, but her brown eyes showed through the lenses.

We were escorted into a formal parlor that could have been my mother's. The minute I saw the inside of the house I knew that this was

Mrs. Arruda's house. No interior decorator had been allowed to bring his or her "fancy" ideas here. I had seen this a hundred times. This was not where the family lived. I could have bet my last dollar that there was a large finished basement below the living quarters. There would be a recreation room and more importantly a kitchen with all the facilities in the basement. The family ate in the basement, entertained themselves in the basement and for all intents and purposes, lived in the basement. The bedrooms on the second floor were used for sleeping. A bathroom was used by the women. If the children were young enough they might be allowed to study in their bedrooms. Otherwise all activity was in the basement. The bathroom on the first floor was never used except by guests. The children were trained from the earliest to use and to preserve the house in its prescribed manner. The women of the house all worked, with rare exceptions, so there wasn't time for cleaning rooms once they were arranged. The show rooms were cleaned once a week and kept in pristine condition the rest of the time.

We were sitting in one of the showrooms. This was the parlor in which the chairs and sofa were probably covered with plastic all week and taken off on Sunday and any time there were guests expected. I could imagine the frantic energy employed when we were announced as visitors. Jack thought the idea was ludicrous, but I had seen it many times among my mother's friends. Furniture for the parlor and dining room was a once in a lifetime buy and was not about to be ruined by misuse or faded by sun light.

We sat in the parlor and waited for Mrs. Arruda to bring out tea and Portuguese tea biscuits called bisquettes. These were doughnut shaped biscuits with just a touch of lemon. I loved these as a boy and I enjoyed eating a few of them now. I hesitated to dip them into my tea, but that is how I remember eating them when I was young. I finally worked up the courage to do just that and Mrs. Arruda began laughing and said in Portuguese, "You go back to your boyhood in your mother's kitchen, I like that."

There were no airs about this lady. She exuded confidence which was rare in the Portuguese ladies I had known. They ruled their roosts with an iron hand but felt very insecure once they left their domain or were confronted with people outside of their usual circles. Not Mrs. Arruda, however. She struck me as a very interesting character. She saw me take notice and she laughed a coquettish little laugh that took me by surprise.

Jack began with, "Mrs. Arruda can you tell us how long you worked in the house?"

"Please, my name is Deolinda, please call me that. I am old enough without being Mrs. Arruda all the time," she said this with a smile and just as Mrs. Macomber had talked to Jack during our sessions, it was apparent that Deolinda Arruda was going to direct all her talking to me. I represented the comfort zone and just as Jack had felt right at home with Amy Macomber, so too did I feel in my own milieu talking to Mrs. Arruda.

"I started when I was in my thirties when the kids were big enough to be home alone. My husband worked for them when they were building the house. He was a stone man. When the Mrs. said she needed someone to help in the house, Manuel told me and I went for the job. That was around 1960 and I stayed until two years ago when it got too much for me. Now Evangelica and two of the boys work for them. The boys work in the gardens and the greenhouse for Mrs. Macomber."

"What do you remember about the day Mr. Macomber died?" Jack asked.

She seemed a little taken back by the question. She looked at Jack for a moment as if she wanted him to repeat the question so that she could have time to think. Then she quickly changed positions in the chair she was sitting in, crossed her legs at the ankles and reached forward to place her tea cup and saucer on a napkin she had on the coffee table in front of her.

"I can't remember much. I was very busy making sure everyone was taken care of. It was a big party, and I had to supervise the caterers and the new waiters and waitresses to make sure everything was done right and that no one was stealing liquor and stuff. At a big party the outside help can steal you blind. You have to be very careful. Silverware and bowls and glassware can disappear. So, yes I was too busy to pay attention to what Mr. Jeff was doing."

She seemed to recover very quickly, but I wondered why she had reacted so openly to a simple question.

"Did you believe that Mr. Macomber committed suicide?" I asked giving her what I thought was an easy question before getting back to the more interesting questions.

"Who knows? I couldn't believe that he would take his own life. He was a man who loved life. He loved what he did with his sailing ships. He loved women. Women loved him. But, I could never figure him out. I never trust a man who doesn't eat and that man didn't eat you know. For so strong a man I couldn't figure him out. He ate like a bird. Peck a little bit here, a little bit there; give him a steak and potato and he would eat half the steak and leave most of the potato. What kind of a man eats like that? He was so strong too. When they built the Goetzel house they put in a cast iron bathtub and the Mrs. wanted it out of the house. She gave it to me for my house. I saw that man pick up the bathtub all by himself and carry it to the hall just to show the men he could do it. It took two men to lift it when he set it down. Tenha muito forca."

She said the latter in Portuguese for my benefit and it meant "He had great strength."

"So, you don't think he would have committed suicide."

"I don't think so. But, I'm telling you I couldn't figure the man out. He was a puzzle. Whenever I walked into the room, I could feel him looking at me. I know I don't look it now, but I was a good looking woman. He looked at me and I knew he wanted me, but he never said a naughty word to me and he never touched me or my daughter," she said.

"Did it bother you that he looked at you that way?" Jack asked.

"No, it didn't. He made me feel like a woman. He was a man who made women feel good about themselves. They loved him for it. You have to understand that he could have any woman he wanted and he had plenty of them from what I heard. They were always after him. So, why would he commit suicide? He had all the money he needed. He had women chasing him even when he was in his seventies. He was getting ready to take another cruise. So then he takes a gun and kills himself. I don't think so."

"Were there any tensions in the house because of his womanizing?" I asked.

"At first, maybe, yes. But Miss Amy gave up years ago. By the time I was working for them I don't think there was anything between them. They slept in different rooms and even though they never had fights or anything, you could see that whatever they had once was over. Mr. Goetzel had a tough time dealing with Mr. Jeff. He didn't like him at all.

Miss Amy was his special girl, you know, and he hated to see how Mr. Jeff treated her and how he fooled around."

"Did they ever argue that you knew of?" Jack asked.

"Oh yes. All the time. When Mr. Goetzel came here we were always waiting for the explosion. Then Mr. Jeff would get out and go somewhere. They didn't stay in the house together too much and since Miss Amy didn't care, Mr. Jeff would go sailing or go to Europe or something. Miss Amy liked having her father here, so Jeff would leave the house."

"I don't understand then, why they would have a big 50th Anniversary wedding party," I said. "If they didn't have a real marriage and they didn't love each other, why do it?"

"That is the question we all asked. Mr. Goetzel was the one who wanted it and there was no changing his mind. The money was like nothing you ever saw. It was enough to keep a family around here for a whole year. There was no marriage for at least twenty years and they were going to celebrate. Celebrate what? The Mrs. was dead then, so she couldn't try to change her husband's mind. She wouldn't have allowed it, if you ask me. But she was crazy as a loon anyway."

"Why do you say she was crazy?" I asked.

"Maybe not crazy. Maybe what is the word? Eccentric. She was eccentric," she said laughing.

"How?" I asked.

"Well when she wanted to build a fireplace, the one in the parlor, she hired my husband to make it. So every day he goes to the house and the lady is waiting for him. She is dressed in what they call it, riding clothes with big boots. They take a walk in the fields looking for stone. She finds two or three stones she likes. My Manuel takes her back to the house and then comes out with a wagon to pick up the stones. He takes them back, mixes mortar and then sets them in the fireplace. She comes before they are dry and set. If she likes them they stay. If she don't, out they go. Sometimes, a whole day's pay for nothing. I wonder what's going on. Manuel is no looker but he is strong as a bull. I figure she is using him for sex. Nope. She wants the perfect fireplace and it takes him more than a year to make it. Every Friday he gets paid cash so he don't care.

He's doing other jobs after he leaves there. He could have built twenty stone walls for what he built that fireplace."

We laughed at the idea. I had a vision of this woman getting dressed each morning and getting her morning constitutional by searching for the stone in the fields that would be perfect in size and shape for her fireplace. And I could imagine, Deolinda's husband at the local Portuguese club dramatizing the affair for the unbelieving workmen who met in their club every night for a few beers or a glass of wine after a hard day's work as laborers. To them Mrs. Goetzel was a dream, the kind of contract they had yearned for all of their lives. The most important part was that Manuel Arruda had work every day and got paid cash every Friday. That's the part that amazed them. Mrs. Arruda laughed all the time she was telling us the story and when she finished there were tears in her eyes.

"So how long ago did Mrs. Goetzel die?" I asked.

"Oh she died two years before my husband. Manuel died in 1975 and she died in 1973. She died of pneumonia the poor thing. She wasn't sick long. She was home with a bad cold and then she got worse after a few weeks even though the doctor was with her every day. You can't trust those guys. All they want is money. She went into the hospital in Boston and the poor thing never came out alive. It shows you no matter how much money you have, when God wants you, that's it."

"And, your husband, what happened to him?" I asked.

"The doctors never got him. He fell off a roof and died right then. He was fixing a slate roof at the church and the roof let go and he fell and died right there. The poor man never knew what happened to him."

"What kind of a man was Mr. Goetzel?" Jack asked.

"That is the hardest question of all," she said and then took our teacups and disappeared for ten minutes or so leaving us sitting quietly wondering what she was doing. She came back in due time with more tea and another plate of biscuits. While we had been talking Jack had not stopped eating for a moment and had devoured every biscuit.

She placed the biscuits on a napkin on the coffee table and then placed the tray holding the tea things on the table. She struck me as a handsome woman even now. She must have been seventy, but she certainly didn't look it. She was a good looking woman and I sensed that she knew it. She was not a modest, shrinking violet.

"Mr. Goetzel," she began, "was a very smart man and a hard worker. He never rested. He was up very early and then started working in his room when he was here. I had to come in to give him coffee and breakfast sometimes before the sun came up. He worked until about eleven o'clock and then took a nap. He slept for an hour and then came down for his lunch in his room. He had a big bowl of oatmeal with raisins and walnuts and a glass of orange juice. Sometimes he had a cup of tea. Then he would go back to work and nobody could go in his room except Miss Amy. By the time I started working here, Miss Amy was working on her plants and she spent a lot of time like her father working in her books and writing things down."

"Did you like him?"

I could have sworn that she blushed. She was taken aback by the question and I knew I had hit on something.

She recovered her composure and said, "He was a very nice man and he was good to me. When he died he left my family money to take care of us."

She waved her arm as if to include what we saw around us as her heritage from Mr. Goetzel.

"When did he die?" I asked

"About six months after Mr. Jeff. Miss Amy took it hard. We all missed him."

She sat quietly, then, sipping her tea and she seemed to be far off for a moment.

"He was a special man. Even when he was an old man he was special. In the morning I loved to see him at his desk. Sometimes, before the sun even came up, I would bring him his coffee. He would be bending over his journals in the light from the desk working and writing."

"What journals?" I asked.

"He wrote in them every morning. He told me all the time that when he was dead they would have all his secrets. They were black books."

"Where are they?"

"They should still be in his room. He always put them away on the shelf when he finished. They are still there."

Jack got interested now and said, "Can you show us where they are?"

"Of course. Drive me there now and I will show you," she said.

She rose from her chair and walked to the entrance. She looked back at us as if to ask what we were going to do. She was a woman who was used to ruling her roost and she obviously included us as well when she decided to move.

In no time at all we were back at the Goetzel house. She told us she would meet us in the study. First she went to see Mrs. Macomber. We both knew she was asking permission of the lady of the house to show us the journals. We didn't want to interfere so we went to the study and waited for her to appear. She was gone no more than ten minutes. She entered the study and without hesitation went to a shelf next to the windows and reached up as high as she could to bring down a black leather binder.

She handed it to me and said, "There are a lot more of these on the shelf. Can you see them?"

We both nodded and thanked her for her troubles.

"Do I get a ride back home, or do I walk?" she asked with a smile on her face. Again I was taken with her beauty and I sensed that she knew it and was on stage. She didn't prance or wiggle, but there was no need for that. She was a seventy year old woman who somehow exuded sexual attraction even at her advanced age. I was buying none of it and she knew that too. Jack per usual was completely indifferent to women and their sexual advances. Since the question had been addressed to me, I offered to give her the ride. I needed to ask her something else that had occurred to me.

I took her to the car and opened the door for her. When we had both put on our seat belts I said, "Deolinda, you are a very beautiful woman."

"Thank you. I know. I thought that you have no interest in me. Are you married?"

"No. I am not. But I have a woman who is very dear to me. We live together and I love her." I said.

"I know that. I can tell. When you get to be as old as I am, things don't have to be said. I knew that. But now, why are you telling me I am a beautiful woman?"

"Because I think, unless I am wrong, that there was something special between you and Mr. Goetzel. The way your eyes shine when you talk about him and the look that comes over your face, means something. Am I wrong?"

She fiddled with her seat belt and didn't say a word as we drove the three or four miles to her house. I waited for her answer. I didn't persist and I had the feeling she was thinking it through. She didn't move her body at all, but her hands were busy smoothing and adjusting the seat belt until she finally said, "Yes, he was special and I loved him. After his wife died he was a very lonely man, and he was a man who needed a woman. I am a woman who needs a man. Manuel was dead, his wife was gone. One day when I went into his room in the morning he came to me from behind the desk and I knew what he wanted. We made love then, and we never stopped until he died. He was wonderful. And he always treated me like a lady, never like a puta. He was an old man who made love like a young man and I have no shame in what we did together. I don't want every one talking about it because I don't want to hurt his memory. You know how people will talk. So I tell you this because you knew it already. You are a wise man who sees things that don't need to be said."

"I understand. I will say nothing about this, but I think it is important."

"You have to promise me."

"I will."

"Well, we were together right after my husband died. I knew he wanted me before that but he was a gentleman and respected my time to put my husband to rest. This house he gave me the money to build when he died. But he never bought me. I gave myself to him because I wanted to. It had nothing to do with money. It was love for him and I do not want it spoiled with talk."

"I understand and you can trust me. But does Mrs. Macomber know this?"

"Probably. There is not much that Miss Amy does not know. She is a very smart lady, but she is a good lady too, so she would never say anything to me."

We were at her house by then and I thanked her and dropped her off. She refused to have me take her to the door, but as soon as I pulled up in her driveway, she opened the door and without saying another word, was gone into the house. I drove back to the Goetzel house and found Jack still reviewing the journals he was taking down from the shelf.

I had never seen anything quite like them. They were made of black, soft leather and they were the size of large ledgers. The pages they contained were sewn into place as if they were a bound book. Each was roughly two feet wide by two feet high. Mr. Goetzel must have spread the journal on the desk and then leaned over to write. It would have been difficult to reach the top of the page from a position sitting back in a desk chair.

We opened one and we could see that each page contained at least ten handwritten separate notations. The first one we saw at the top of the page had a day of the week and then a note following it.

"MONDAY, JAN 18

ELEANOR FARES BADLY. SHE IS A SICK LADY AND SHOWS VERY LITTLE SIGNS OF COMING OUT OF THIS. WHAT HAS CAUSED THIS TERRIBLE BOUT WITH HER LUNGS IS A PUZZLE TO THE DOCTORS. SHE HAS BEEN TAKEN TO MASSACHUSETTS GENERAL FOR TREAT-MENT, BUT EACH DAY SHE SHOWS MORE AND MORE DECLINE. AMY AND I VISIT HER EVERY DAY. AMY FEELS SHE WILL RECOVER UNDER ADEQUATE CARE, BUT I HAVE NO SUCH ILLUSIONS. SHE SHOWS GREAT COURAGE AND MY ADMIRATION GROWS FOR HER. IT HAS BEEN MORE THAN A MONTH NOW SINCE SHE TOOK SICK AND SHE HAS NOT COMPLAINED ONCE TO ME."

The writing was cramped and written with the blackest of ink. The quickest glance gave me the impression of care and attention. The large white sheets upon which the diaries or journals were kept were unlined, but there was none of the sloping that one would anticipate in writing on such large material. It was as if Mr. Goetzel had written with a ruler for a guide. As a school teacher I had always felt that handwriting was at least an opening toward understanding a student. I wondered what Mr. Goetzel was telling us about himself in these journals unintentionally. Jack had begun sampling some of the pages by the time I returned and he was not overly impressed.

"There isn't much here. I haven't read much, but most of this is very personal. It is as if he reviews each day in a very personal way. He talks about a tooth getting loose, what he did or didn't do with his favorite pen, or the price of a stock he bought and then sold. He has little reminiscences that are purely personal. But, I know you Noah, I'm sure you will spend hours with these."

"I suppose I will," I said. "Let's show them to Mrs. Macomber and get her permission to read them."

We found her in her 'playpens' directing some of her workmen in what they should or shouldn't do. I enjoyed watching her set out the work for the day. She drove a golf cart that maneuvered the rows between her azaleas with no difficulty. I had to smile. Here was this old lady sitting in a golf cart riding between long rows of plantings. She explained to us that this play pen contained the yearlings which she had set out that season. They had been grown in the hot houses over the winter and had been set out in the fields in May. In the seat next to her was a large bucket containing colored stakes which she gave to her foreman as he walked along next to the cart. At the top of each row she gave him a blue stake which he drove into the ground. As Amy explained to us, a blue stake meant that that particular row had to be watered. As she went along she gave her foremen the different stakes indicating what had to be done. Weeding was marked by a yellow stake which Amy explained meant "weed with caution."

"Azaleas are shallow rooted so the weeding has to be done so as not to damage the tender little roots just below the surface. If that happens, they quickly dry out and we lose a potential winner. Every plant here is precious. When they finally bloom we will probably discard 90% of them on the first run through, but in the meantime, we have to be patient and make sure that each plant is treated as a precious commodity."

Our day had been an interesting one. We had begun by learning a great deal from Deolinda and she had led us to the journals. Now we were watching a professional at work delegating work to her field hands. I have always admired professionalism whether in my own profession of teaching or in others. Here I could see a woman who knew exactly what she was doing. The foreman looked vaguely familiar and then I realized that he bore a resemblance to Deolinda and Evangelica and I knew he was another member of the Arruda family working for the Goetzels. I could sense the faith these two people had in each other. I am sure he would have known what to do with each plant and row without Amy Macomber pointing out every step to him, but I am also sure that it was part of a method they had developed together and that worked very well for them. There was no question about who was in charge but at the same time I had a feeling that she had absolute trust in her foreman and knew that what she gave him to do would be done as she requested. Not much was said between them because there was probably little need for words.

When she had finished giving her work orders for the day and Mr. Arruda went his way, we asked Amy Macomber if we could talk to her about our discovery. She was obviously shocked to hear of their existence.

"I had no idea. How could I live in the same house all those years and not know that my dad kept a journal? I can't believe it," she said and there was no doubt that she meant it.

"Mrs. Arruda claims that he worked on it every morning. It was almost the first thing he did when he went to the study to start his day. She claims that she would bring him his coffee first thing in the morning and that's when she saw him making his entries. She saw his ledgers and realized what they were long after he had died."

"I never went to the study early, so I guess I never saw him working. Isn't it strange how close one can be to people and still not know very simple things about them? Now I am faced with a decision. Will I read them myself? Do I want to? This is a turn of events that I have to think about. God, who would expect something like this? Supposing I were to find out things about my dad that I didn't want to know? Wouldn't that be upsetting? I read a story once in which a woman going through her deceased father's effects, finds out that her father had a collection of pornographic materials. The discovery is terrible for her to deal with. I don't want to find out something that I don't want to know. You read them first and then you can tell me whether I should read them or not."

Jack laughed in his eccentric way which was a half guffaw and a giggle and said, "Now, where does that leave us in terms of having access to the diaries or journals, whatever you choose to call them?"

"I see no problem if you feel they will be productive for you. But, I think that I would be a great deal more comfortable if they were not to leave the study. I would hate to see something happen to them. Is that acceptable to you gentlemen?"

"I don't see why not," I said. "I think keeping them here would be wise." I did get Mrs. Macomber to agree to have Marge read them along with me. I thought she might bring an intelligent woman's insight to the journals and that might prove to be valuable.

At that moment though, I was tired. My seventy-two year old body had had enough and my mind was running blank. There comes a time when we are forced to listen to our minds and bodies, and I had reached that time. I needed a good old-fashioned nap and I could hardly wait to get home.

Shortly after taking a shower I sat in my favorite chair, put Mozart on the stereo and listened to a few bars before slipping off into a nice quiet sleep. I probably slept for less than an hour but I awoke refreshed in body and spirit.

I explained what we had learned that day to Marge and she was elated to hear that we would be reading the journals together. She was eager to get involved and I looked forward to working with her on this case.

The idea of the journal bothered me. I explained my feelings to Marge. How many times had I started one only to end up putting it aside because I had nothing really of importance or significance to enter? What kind of a man kept a journal every day? Was he taking the trouble and time because he was thinking of posterity? Was he merely keeping tabs on his life? Did he think that what happened to him daily was so important that he had to get it on paper? We would know the answer to these questions and more, I felt, when we sat down and read the journals. Marge agreed.

She said, "But, how do we know that after we spend hours and hours reading the journals, we will come up with any of the answers you are looking for?"

"That is the problem we face in doing this kind of work. It is grinding slow work and you just plow ahead and hope for the best," was all I could say in answer to her.

Jack and Clarissa had planned to come to dinner that night. Clarissa was home for a few days. Clarissa was a young lady in her thirties who was attending Brown University as a special student. She was living a dream. She had been raised in the Bahamas and had been well educated by her teachers and mother. We had visited her home in the Bahamas the previous summer when Jack had relived his youthful days on a sailboat. It was my first experience on a sailboat and both Marge and I enjoyed ourselves. We weren't expected to do any work since Jack had hired a crew. The raison d'etre for the trip was to allow Clarissa to revisit her mother and the islands on which she had been raised. It was a peaceful trip. Marge and I as two novice sailors did not encounter stormy seas. Marge in particular had had fears about sailing but it turned out that she did better than I did. On the one day in which we experienced choppy water for a short time, I hadn't felt very well and had to retire to a bunk below.

Jack, of course, was delighted with the trip. He was once again at the helm of a sailing ship. Like Jeff Macomber, it had been his first love as a boy. The crew and captain of the vessel showed some trepidation the first time Jack took the sails in his own hands, but it took very little time for them to realize that they had an experienced sailor in their midst. He returned to his old form very quickly. From that moment on, the crew had no doubts of his ability. He may have been old, but his skill had not left him.

We spent two happy weeks going to and from the islands and on the island itself where Clarissa was reunited with her mother and her family. When we returned in late August, Clarissa had very little time to prepare for her academic career at Brown and was thrown right into the fray. Jack, I suspect, had planned it that way. Clarissa naturally felt a little humble knowing that she would be competing against some of the brightest young people in the country. The less time she had to be nervous and to worry, the better off she would be.

The year had been a good one for her. She had spent the first semester commuting from the Point to Providence and then, as much as Jack knew he would miss her, he had made the sacrifice and found her an apartment with a few other students. The drive in and out of Providence wasn't easy during rush hour and Jack felt she needed an intellectual environment which she would get by living on campus. So she made the move and we all missed having her with us every day. It was an adventure for her, and since she was older and wiser than the younger students, she was determined to get the most out of it. For her it was more than a dream come true; it was a chance for her to realize her potential, something she never thought would happen to her after her experiences working as a clerk in the United States in entry level positions and for minimum wage. Fortunately, she had the work habits in place that served her well doing what she liked best, reading and studying literature under the tutelage of knowledgeable and appreciative professors.

For dinner I put together a baked scrod with a Ritz cracker topping and Marge made some sliced baked potato rounds that came out of the oven very crisp and tasty. They were made on an oiled baking sheet and for such a simple dish were very good. Along with a freshly baked French bread that I made from frozen dough and a salad for the three of us, excluding Jack, we had an excellent meal and yet a simple one. Jack loved the scrod and did more than justice to it. I had had the good sense to get enough for six people knowing that Jack would eat twice as much as we ate. The fish was new to Clarissa who had eaten fish as the main protein in her diet for most of her life, but she enjoyed the taste and texture of the scrod which she found quite different from the fish in the Caribbean.

Even as I was enjoying my meal, I kept thinking about the journals. It did seem odd to me that Amy Macomber would not know that her father had kept a journal. Not only did he keep one, but he approached it like a woman saying her morning prayers or a priest reading his breviary. It was not an on again off again affair with him. She claimed to be close to him. Yet she did not know something as simple as his habit of waking every morning and working at his desk.

Jack finished his main dish and said, "Think back to when you were living at home. Did you know everything your Mom and Dad did, much less what they were thinking? Is there anything that you could discover about them now that would surprise you?"

"I admit that my father was quite a mystery to me in many ways. But a revelation about my mother would be a surprise," I said. "She lived a very simple life at home, so I can't imagine too many surprises in her life."

Marge laughed and said, "When I was in my forties, I remember my mother making a revelation to me that really shocked me. My father died of a heart attack when he was in his mid-sixties. We buried him and about a month later we were sorting out his things, when my mother suddenly began sobbing uncontrollably and burst into tears. I tried to soothe her by saying that I knew she would miss my father and that life would go on and saying all of the normal tripe we tend to say in those situations."

She was very serious so we all sat still knowing that she was about to reveal something that she felt deeply.

"She then told me that she had had a terribly unhappy marriage," Marge continued, "and that she would not miss him at all. She claimed that she had stayed with him only for me, to protect me. My father, she said, had had one affair after another and that she was well rid of him. I was stunned. I was used to seeing my father flirt with women, but I thought he was just amusing them with his banter. He could be a charming man and I thought it was part of his persona. At first, I was angry at her because I thought she was making it up, that she was actually lying to me."

Clarissa said, "When my father left us, I felt the same way. I blamed my mother, poor thing."

"Isn't it amazing?" Marge said, touching Clarissa on the arm, "We blame the person who is innocent because the real villain isn't there. I got over it pretty quickly, but for the life of me, I still can't understand how my father could have been doing what he was doing without me having even the slightest idea. Remember, I was in my forties when I was told. I was not an innocent, unknowing child. But, I was truly unaware of it."

She looked at all of us for a moment and then said, "So a thing like keeping a journal might very well escape Mrs. Macomber's notice."

"I suppose you are right," Jack said, "I do know Amy was shocked that she had no idea."

We spent the rest of the night going over what we knew, even though it was very little.

Jack finally said, "Things don't add up here, but they never do, do they? Why would Jeff commit suicide remains the big question that we have to come up with an answer to."

We left it at that and decided to call it a night. Clarissa and Marge cleaned up and put things away. I was too tired to help and I begged off and prepared myself for a good night's sleep.

Chapter X

The following morning, Marge, Jack and I drove to Fall River before going to Middletown because Jack had to stop at Dunkin Donuts on Quequechan St. to get his breakfast fix of a medium coffee with cream and two sugars, a large coffee roll, a scone and a coconut jelly stick. Marge laughed so hard that tears came down her face when she saw Jack lay out his treasure in the back seat and begin devouring his breakfast in absolute silence.

"If I ate that breakfast Jack I would put on five pounds. There are more carbohydrates and sugar there than I eat in a week. I can't believe it."

Jack took time out from his morning snack to say, "It's all in the genes."

Talk about genes made me want to learn more about the genetics of what Amy and Jason were doing in their crosses. I knew something about genetics in general, but I knew very little about the specifics of how one goes about crossing azaleas or rhododendrons. I determined that I would sit down with Jason as soon as I could without being an annoyance. I realized that it had nothing to do with the case, but my curiosity was peaked and I felt that I needed to know the details of their work if I were to understand it.

We met with Amy Macomber first as was becoming our routine. We introduced her to Marge and they seemed to take to each other almost immediately. Whether we were due to meet her or not, we realized that Amy Macomber made it a practice to sit in her room every day at ten o'clock in the morning after she had finished washing and dressing for the day and after she had eaten her breakfast. It was her time for preparing her thoughts for the day and setting her schedule. As it turned out, we found that she had followed the same routine for years. Routine was as important to her as it had been to her father.

She would rise at eight, bathe and dress and then have a light breakfast which never varied from day to day. She ate alone in the kitchen to make it easy on the cook who was very accommodating but was getting along in years. After breakfast she would sit in the darkened sunroom to prepare her thoughts for the day. I couldn't help but think of the women in my neighborhood, who would go to early mass every day in the darkened church. The two widely separate habits most likely served the very same purpose. Then, it was to the greenhouses or fields depending on the time of year to work for several hours. Then, she would return to the house for a very light lunch and a bath and a nap. The nap grew longer as she aged and felt the hardships of work become greater and greater. In the evening she ate a very light dinner and then went to the study to record all of the work that needed documenting. The schedule meant that she and her father had rarely met early in the day since their separate schedules, which they both adhered to religiously, did not allow them to come together until their late lunch in the afternoon.

As it turned out, Jason was free to talk to me for an hour or so. He had made time in his busy schedule to talk with me. Marge sat down at the table in the study and began reading the journals. Jason was in one of the greenhouses when I caught up with him. He had given a crew instructions to hose it down, clean all the surfaces, allow it to dry, and then spray. He left them at it and we walked out into one of the older fields to inspect the plants and to make notes on some of the crosses. He made entries in his notebook which contained the numbers of each plant that was still growing in that field. He spent considerable time at each plant inspecting its growth and the condition of its foliage. In this field, which was the oldest field, many of the plants had been removed. Those that remained were the best of the crosses he had made in that particular year.

"We are going to give these plants one last look before the final thinning. As of now I have three that I am rather excited about," he said bending over one of the plants.

He was a tall man somewhere in the range of six foot four or so, but when standing upright he did not stoop or bend. My fourth grade teacher would have been delighted with his posture. He held his handsome head high. He had a full muscular chest and hard sinewy arms. There was nothing soft about him. He had the look of a man who had done hard labor.

"What I am looking for is a Yak with colors other than pink and rose and white. Those are very beautiful but I am breeding for a color variation that opens new doors in this particular line of dwarfs. Yaks are dwarfs and their dwarfness breeds true so no matter what we cross with them, they seem to maintain their small size. Their natural color seems to be pink or rose which gradually turns to white as the flower matures. I am trying to keep the dwarfness and hardiness but develop colors in the yellow and gold ranges as well as deep reds and purples. I've developed some good reds but I still haven't broken the other color barriers with what I consider to be quality plants."

"You say your Yaks breed true as dwarfs. Is there any special reason for wanting dwarfs?" I asked.

"Modern properties, city gardens and the like, call for small, manageable plants. Think of the small homes that need foundation plantings. Seven and eight foot rhododendrons worked beautifully on big estates, but something else is needed in the cities. My dwarfs are beautiful in bloom, have handsome foliage, and remain small in size and are extremely hardy. I am looking for hardiness of 20 degrees below zero. Those are qualities that are hard to beat in today's market. It gives me quite a thrill to be driving down a side street in a crowded city and suddenly see one of my crosses in bloom in a little city garden."

"What got you started doing this?" I asked.

"Definitely Aunt Amy. She got me interested in cross-breeding when I was a teen. I enjoyed being with her and then I started working with her pollinating the azaleas. The process fascinated me and made me feel useful. We would collect the pollen and then pollinate the pistils of the mother plants. Next, we would cover the recipients with little silver cones so they didn't get contaminated by other pollen. We recorded every pollination meticulously and waited for the pollen to take and the seed to grow. Finally, there was the whole process of recording, labeling and growing."

"It sounds like an arduous procedure," I said.

"Actually it is quite simple, but one has to be very careful in doing everything just so. We have to be sure that we record every cross that is made, the donor and recipient, that is, including as much as we know about the parentage of both plants for future crossing so that if the cross is successful we know exactly where we stand."

"Is that why you work in the study at night?"

"Yes. What we do is to go through all of the crosses we have made among other things, check those that are unsuccessful and compare those to crosses we have made in the past to try as much as possible to eliminate fruitless effort. Then we take the fruitful crosses we have made and document the parentage for future attempts. We are not looking to duplicate the crosses but want to take advantage of good parentage to produce other plants. This involves a great deal of detail work. I check the parentage of both donors to determine what characteristics of each emerged in the offspring. Plotting can be long and arduous."

"I begin to understand this a bit more. How long does it take for you to determine if you have made a successful cross?"

I think if I had been talking about any other subject, I would have had a difficult time keeping his attention, but this was a topic he loved and I also suspected that he had little opportunity to discuss it. I had found over the years that in teaching I had been forced to simplify quite often and this helped me to clarify things in my own mind. It could have been that he was doing the very same thing for me. He was a quiet, reserved man by nature and he seemed reluctant to get involved with people and I wondered if his father, Jeff, was similarly disposed.

"A successful cross has a number of characteristics including color and bloom. I am looking for a color breakthrough. The bloom has to be of sufficient size and substance to hold its own. Then there is the quality of the foliage which, since the plant is out of bloom most of the year, should be attractive in itself. Then we look for ease of reproduction and duplication since these are produced largely for universal distribution. Then there is the matter of hardiness which is very important for distribution again. And then there is the matter of growth habit and resistance to disease. So all in all, and since I am under no pressure to rush things on the market to make a living, it takes anywhere from six to ten years before I am ready to introduce a new plant. If the plant does not meet all the requirements along with early bloom production, I discard it."

"I would never have thought that it was that long a process. However, it must be very satisfying when you reach the final decision."

"The moment of bloom is the exciting time. We have pollinated, collected the seed, sown it, and watched it germinate. Then we pot up the little plants, raise them in the hothouses, and finally set them out to harden off. The last step is to grow them in the playpens until they bloom."

"What are the playpens, incidentally?" I asked.

"Oh they are just enclosures that protect the young plants from the deer. The deer feast on the tender young leaves. Unless we close in the growing areas, we can suffer great losses during the winter months. We found that the deer will not attempt to break into the growing areas if the fences are high. Height seems to deter them. The fences could easily be knocked over without much difficulty, but their height tends to keep the deer from approaching them. We string light chicken wire over the upright posts to allow the sun to get in."

"How much of this is luck and how much science?" I asked.

"Jen is trying to make it more of a science, but I would say about fifty-fifty. I have been working on tracking crosses on the computer and trying to predict results. I find this almost impossible because of the infinite variables involved. Even the computer can't deal with it and the unknowns confuse the situation even more. The one characteristic of the Yaks that seems to breed true is their dwarfism. So using that as a starting point we can almost assume that any successful cross will be a dwarf. There are exceptions but for the most part dwarfism will hold true."

"You must really get a great deal of satisfaction out of it to work so hard at it and stay with it so long," I said. "Did you study genetics in college?"

"Oh, no. I began as an English major at Harvard. I really enjoyed literature and I still do. I took my junior year abroad in Paris. I spent a year learning the French language, studying French lit and living the life of a student in the student quarter. It was great fun. I loved the French women and the whole atmosphere. My mother was living in Tuscany so I spent holidays in Italy. I became an art aficionado. It was a wonderful life."

"Really. Jack and I visited Florence a couple of years ago and we enjoyed it tremendously."

"Well, you can imagine a twenty-one year old boy in the Sorbonne in Paris. There I was spending hours on end in the Louvre and the art galleries in every side street. Eating great French food, sitting for hours sipping coffee at the sidewalk cafes, the great conversations and discussions; it was quite a life style."

"So, what caused you to leave it?"

"Aunt Amy. For all of the fun I was supposed to be having, I felt completely unfulfilled. I saw Aunt Amy having a wonderful time doing her work. I had taken an interest in what she was doing during my teenage years, and when I finished school and went to live in Tuscany for a couple of years, I realized that I need something substantial in my life, some purpose. Then one day, a woman I was having an affair with attempted suicide, and I realized that I couldn't continue my womanizing and doing nothing of any significance with my life. I didn't love that girl and I realized that I was just using her for my own personal pleasure."

He said this with the same lack of passion and intonation in which Amy spoke. There was nothing emotional or self-pitying about his manner. His face had not a bit of smile or smirk or any sign of feeling; he was serious and spoke directly to the point without embellishment or emotion in almost a monotone.

"You may not believe this, but it is very difficult being rich and needing something serious to do. Things come too easily and there is no need to make a living. What was I going to do with my life? I tried writing, but I found I had nothing of any importance to say. I found I had no special talent. I could have gone into my grandfather's business, but I had no interest in making money and the creative part of the business, working in the chemical production business was way over my head. It required special training and education and there was no way that I was willing to embark on that. Then by chance, Aunt Amy visited my mother in Tuscany on her way to Germany where she planned to attend an azalea and rhododendron show. She invited me to come along to keep her company."

He was smiling then for the first time since we started what I knew was a long dissertation for him. He was still standing very erect but now he was walking toward one of the playpens very pensively, distracted by thoughts of what he was saying.

"It was quite interesting. There were some dwarf rhododendrons on display that had been developed in Germany and a few Yaks from the US. I wasn't impressed with the German introductions but I really liked the Yaks. They had great flower size and their foliage showed an inudentum which I thought was quite unique and made the plants eye-catching. I had no idea where to begin work on them, but I started doing some research and got caught up in the process. Of course, I used Aunt Amy's knowledge with azaleas as a basis and that was a great time saver. The whole project served my purposes very well. It gave me something to work at that would require my attention over a long period of time and it satisfied my need for method. I suppose that was the discovery about myself that was the most revealing to me."

"In what way?" I asked.

He became quite thoughtful then. He stood very quietly and his hands came to rest by his sides.

"The discovery was that my mind runs in a systematic, methodical way. Up until then I had worked in my own fashion without realizing how much I relied on method, order and repetition. The more disciplined I am, the more I enjoy the work. Crossing rhododendrons requires everything I enjoy. For me, the outcome is miraculous. When I was a boy I often went to the kitchen in the villa in Tuscany to watch our cook work. I was amazed that she should mix flour and water and yeast and put the result in the oven and make a loaf of bread. The transition from raw ingredients to a finished product that was edible fascinated me. In a sense I am doing the same thing; taking those little bits of pollen and turning them into a beautiful blooming plant. You can't imagine the excitement when we see a final product that is an entirely new introduction. I've had a number of successes but I haven't had the color breakthrough I am working toward. But, I have faith I will. I have been narrowing my ranges of crosses more and more and I know I will have what I am after soon."

"I hope so for your sake. It must take a great deal of patience and endurance to keep up what you are doing."

"Not really. The odd thing is that it is completely satisfying. Every small step is important. That is what I have in common with Aunt Amy and grandfather. All three of us were cut from the same mold and I suspect that Jen will follow in our footsteps."

"What is she doing?" I asked.

"She is at Brown right now majoring in mathematics. She is also working with some geneticists at URI on gene splicing. She has already begun working on some crosses of her own and we will have to wait to see where those take her. She is taking a far more scientific approach than we are. We'll have to see if she gets faster results than we do."

"Sounds like she is following in your footsteps. Would you like that?"

"The old cliché is that I really don't care as long as she is happy in whatever she chooses to do. But, of course, having her do the same kind of work would be very satisfying because she would be sharing so much with Aunt Amy and me. What is interesting is that we are using divergent methods and procedures to get to the same end. Who knows? You know, Mr. Amos, I have done more talking to you than anyone with the exception of Jen and Aunt Amy for as long as I can remember. You do have a skill Mr. Amos, but I had better get to work and get some things done before the morning slips away."

I thanked him for all the information and even though I hadn't done much of the talking, I found myself wanting to sit quietly for a while to get my own thoughts together.

Marge took to reading the journals with relish. She had collected all of the journals and put them in chronological order and begun reading them methodically. She purchased a loose-leaf notebook for the express purpose of having a place to keep notes as she read.

She seated herself at the large table with the overhead hanging lights shining down on her work so that she had more than enough light. As she sat in her captain's chair leaning forward with a large, black leather book laid out open and flat in front of her, she was the picture of an academic searching through arcane material for a special research project. She looked lovely when she was concentrating. Her gray hair was cut close so that it framed her lovely face. Her face was comparatively wrinkle-free, although as one would expect of a woman in her sixties, she had her share of them especially around the eyes and above the lips. Through a reasonable diet, she managed to keep her weight under control and she had very little of the extra fat which has become the hallmark of Americans.

I hadn't really looked at the journals in any detail so I was eager to sit next to Marge and to hear what she gleaned from her quick reading of some of the pages of the first one we opened.

"Well, from what I can see," she said, "Mr. Goetzel was largely noting what he had done the day before or commenting on something that he had read or had happened. It wasn't as if he was making acute and brilliant observations or giving the world his brilliant thinking. This one is probably typical of what I have seen so far.

TUESDAY

WET AGAIN. THE RAIN DOESN'T STOP. AMY IS WORRIED THAT TOO MUCH RAIN WILL HURT HER SEEDLINGS. JASON IS BEGINNING TO GET FRANTIC. IT SEEMS TO ME THAT TOO MUCH IS LEFT TO CHANCE IN THEIR LINE OF WORK. THE LABORATORY, UNDER CONTROLLED CONDITIONS, IS MUCH MORE TO MY LIKING.

AMY AND JASON ARE LIKE TWO PEAS IN A POD. THEY ENJOY EACH OTHER TO NO END. IT IS A PLEASURE FOR ME TO WATCH THEM WHEN WE RETIRE TO THE STUDY AT NIGHT.

"If anything comes through it is that he is a nice, simple man, spending his remaining days in the peace and quiet of his home," Marge said.

"Well, let's see if there is a pattern of thought that emerges here," I said, and we sat so that we could read the same entry together. Sitting so close to Marge made me think of how fortunate I was to have found her after over forty years of living alone. I could smell just a hint of her perfume and in the short time we had been living together I realized that something as simple as the scent of a woman's perfume is what I missed all those years. These last months made me realize how much time had been lost, never to be reclaimed. I made up my mind to make the most of the time I had left.

On the same page there was another entry that I found quite interesting. It appeared about five days later than the first.

SUNDAY

WE GOT INTO A DISCUSSION YESTERDAY THAT I FOUND INTERESTING. JASON WAS SAYING THAT WHEN HE WAS STUDYING ART IN EUROPE, PARIS AND FLORENCE

MOSTLY, THAT EACH OF THE ARTISTS HAD A STYLE PECULIAR TO THEM; THE GREATER THE ARTIST. THE GREATER AND MORE UNIQUE THE STYLE, HE SAID. HE CALLED IT THEIR VOICE. HE SAID THAT WHEN YOU WALKED INTO A ROOM YOU COULD SEE A REMBRANDT OR A FRA ANGELICO IMMEDIATELY AMONG A HUNDRED PAINTINGS. HE CLAIMED THAT, EVEN AMONG THE WRITERS HE HAD STUDIED, AFTER READING TEN PAGES OF DICKENS OR FAULKNER THEY WERE IMMEDIATELY RECONIZABLE. THE SAME COULD BE SAID FOR MUSIC. WHEN I ASKED HIM ABOUT HIS VOICE OR TRADEMARK, HE SAID "ENDURANCE AND DOGGEDNESS." AMY LAUGHED AND SO DID I, BUT LONG AFTER THEY HAD LEFT ME FOR THE NIGHT, I REALIZED THAT HE WAS RIGHT. I HAD SUCCEEDED BECAUSE I HAD PERSISTED WHEN OTHER PEOPLE HAD GIVEN UP.

"So, Jason studied in Europe?" Marge asked.

"Yes, he tells me he was a lit major in college and that his mother lived in Tuscany. She lived outside of Florence. Then he spent a year in Paris at the Sorbonne. You have to be a little jealous of him," I said.

"To say the least," Marge said.

Jack spent the hour with Amy Macomber talking about money, which along with food, was his favorite subject. We drove back to the Point at the end of the morning and he told us a bit of what he had learned.

"It seems that when Jeff died he was in Amy's will for fifty percent of her income and what she would inherit from her father at his death. The rest was to go to Jason. At her death Jeff would have complete control of his share of the money. Jason who would inherit all of his mother's money and money left to him by his grandfather and his Aunt Amy, would, of course, be a millionaire. Then, it seems that as far as Amy knows, Jen is the sole beneficiary of her father's estate should anything happen to him. That is assuming that Jason doesn't marry. All in all, we are dealing here with some very wealthy people. According to Amy, Jason supports Jen's mother quite handsomely, but that is hardly anything of significance to him in terms of his income.

"We both agreed that there would seem to be no motive on Jason's part to hurt Jeff in any way since he would eventually inherit more money than he would ever hope to need from his mother alone. As it turned out, that was indeed the fact. When she died she left everything to Jason."

"It would seem that their life styles are not lavish. At least that is what is apparent here in the way they live.

"No, not in the least. Jason sold his mother's villa in Tuscany but still maintains an apartment in Florence and in Paris. He visits each place about once or twice a year. Jen has them at her disposal as well. Other than that, they spend money sparingly. Surprisingly, Amy is very careful with money. She never passes up the opportunity to tell you about her rules for spending money," Jack said laughing.

Marge couldn't resist asking, "What are the rules?"

"Well, first, never spend money that you don't have. Secondly, never buy anything you really don't need. Thirdly, and most importantly, since you can buy whatever you want whenever you decide to, give yourself at least a few days before you buy whatever it is you have decided to buy," Jack said laughing. "This from a woman who has an endless supply of money."

"Doesn't make much sense if you ask me. What is the sense of having money if you don't use it?" Marge asked.

"I'll leave that subject for you and Amy to discuss," Jack said.

Chapter XI

The weather suddenly turned hot. As we drove through the city we could see the tenement dwellers sitting on their stoops to escape the heat that made second and third floor flats unbearable. The number of cell phones in use was remarkable. Ten years before we would have seen "boom boxes" on every porch and stoop, but now the blaring music interfered with the private conversations on cell phones, so they had pretty much disappeared from view. Cell phones weren't cheap and I wondered how so many relatively poor people were managing to pay for them and at what sacrifice. I remember when I was teaching that the most catastrophic event that could befall a teenager was the loss of his or her telephone at home. It was the worst disaster in a teenager's life to have a parent or parents who could not pay the telephone bill. The telephone was the link the young people had to each other and without it they were isolated and deprived of the companionship that was so important to them. Nothing brought depression and tears faster than a dead telephone line.

We made our way through the city and to Billy's Café, so that Jack could get his chourico and chip sandwich. Clarissa was staying in Providence until late and wouldn't be home until long past dinner, so Jack was doing his version of take out. Billy's was justly famous for its chourico sandwiches which were made up of half inch rounds of Portuguese chourico which were fried in wine and their own fat in heavy cast iron skillets. The chourico is made of chunks of pork which are seasoned with hot pepper, forced into sausage casings and then smoked. Billy's takes the cooked chourico and places it on long Vienna breads which are sliced lengthwise. The sandwich is served as is or is topped by

French fries. It is a big favorite with blue collar workers who want a tasty and large sandwich for lunch. Marge and I begged off on a sandwich. My cholesterol count rose at just the thought of all the grease, animal fat and pork involved in the sandwich.

When we arrived at the Point, Marge changed into shorts and a light top and I put on a pair of shorts. She made a pitcher of sugarless lemonade and we made our way to the lawn at the back of the house and our Adirondack chairs where we could sit in the mixed shade and sun on the east side of the house away from the gradually lowering sun in the southwesterly sky. It was mid-afternoon and we both felt that we needed an hour or so of inactivity to make up for a strenuous morning's work.

We felt we had a few things to talk about, but we were no sooner seated and relaxed than Jack came across the road from his house carrying his sandwiches and a bottle of beer. He was excited.

"Believe it or not, I just checked my call waiting and we have a call from a Mr. Maurice Desrosiers saying that he must see the two of us immediately, Noah, about a major emergency. I tried to return his call, but his line was busy each time I called. This detective business is getting out of hand. I think I am better off going back to work."

"What could he possibly want with us?" I asked.

We finally sat back in the semi-shade as the sun was covered from time to time by large cumulous clouds drifting slowly across the sky. A light breeze came off the Westport River below us that was just cool enough to cause Marge to go back into the house for a light sweater to throw over her shoulders. Jack was speechless as he ate his lunch and sipped his beer. I knew him well enough to know that he was deep in thought. Marge was in a talkative mood.

"The Goetzel house is quite a place. The study would seem to be the nicest room in the house. The dining room is not very noteworthy, and the parlor aside from the fireplace which dominates the room is not very exciting or even comfortable looking. I suspect that poor woman had very little to say about the décor of the house or even the layout," Marge said.

"Actually it seems from what Deolinda Arruda told us, that each and every morning Mrs. Goetzel and Mr.Arruda who was a stone mason went walking through the fields looking for stone to build the fireplace. Many times she would pick out only one stone in a day and he would bring the stone back and work that day to set it in its place," I said.

"That follows. The fireplace is beautiful and is definitely a standout. So he gave her a bone while he designed the rest of the house, I bet."

Jack laughed as he wiped his hands and mouth after finishing his sandwich. "You women are all alike. Here you are building a case against Goetzel with the slimmest of information. Any man who would allow his wife to hire a workman to put in one or two stones a day into a fireplace must have been pretty lenient, if you ask me."

"Either that or he gave her a small piece of the action so that he could control the rest of the building."

Jack laughed and said, "May I use your phone, Noah. I want to call this guy back again."

I nodded and Jack went into the house to make his call. Marge sat silently next to me, looking out at the water down below and I suspect, continuing to build her case against Mr. Goetzel. It was a pleasant place to sit as we savored the cool breeze and watched the sailboats bobbing in the waves from the power boats plowing through the water. Marge and I had reached that point in our relationship at which we didn't feel required to keep a steady conversation going on between us. We had become comfortable with interludes of silence.

Jack returned with a quizzical look on his face and uncharacteristically his brow was wrinkled. He was normally free of any signs of anxiety so I knew something was wrong.

"Well, we have a case of a stolen safe which cannot be reported to the police. We were recommended to this gentleman by our friend the investor in Providence who handled the affairs of the LaFrance sisters. Remember Mr. Deschenes?"

"Yes, I do. He was a nice gentleman," I said.

"Well, I don't know how much of a favor he has done us here, that's for sure. At any rate, I told the man I talked to on the phone that I would be willing to see him tonight. Can you make it Noah?"

I looked at Marge and she nodded, so I said, "Marge and I have nothing planned, so I have no problem seeing him if you want me to."

"Okay, then I'll call him back and we'll meet him at his office," Jack said, and went back into the house to make his call."

Marge smiled and said, "I think you two should open a detective agency. For a fee, I'll try to come up with an appropriate name. We can run a banner across the road from Jack's house to this one, although you don't have much traffic here to see it. Give me time, I'll come up with a good name."

"This detective is more inclined to sleep more than anything else at this point. I think I'll go in for a nap."

Between phone calls, Jack was able to find out a little about Mr. Desrosiers. He was a reasonably successful defense attorney in Fall River who had managed to pick up some notoriety as a drinking man who would go on long toots from time to time. I hoped this was not one of those times. We parked on North Main St. next to the Fall River Public Library. We found the office which was on the third floor of a substantial building which I remember as housing one of the major banks in the city before the older local banks were gobbled up by the big Boston banks. I remember opening an account as a young boy during World War II when I began making a few dollars a week with a paper route. The deposits I made in my new bank account gave me the excuse I needed to visit the library at the same time. I would tell my mother that I wanted to make a deposit so she didn't object to me taking the long walk to Main Street if I was going to the bank.

We found the elevator to the third floor and we emerged into a suite of offices the moment we stepped off the elevator. It was after working hours, so there was no receptionist to meet us and we had to mosey around looking for the right office. We finally became accustomed to the dimness in the unlighted room, and Jack thought he saw a light coming out from under a door at the end of a hall to our right.

Mr. Desrosiers must have heard us coming so he came to the door of his office to meet us. The moment he came to us I got a strong whiff of whiskey. He had been drinking, and he made his way to greet us with some difficulty.

"Glad you could make it gentlemen," he said, reaching out to shake our hands.

He was a big man with gray, close cropped hair, who looked like he had seen better days. He wore no suit jacket and his shirt was sticking out of his pants. His tie was unknotted and hung loose from his shirt collar.

Not only had Mr. Desrosiers been drinking, but he had an attitude that I did not particularly like. I would learn in time that he became particularly nasty after he became inebriated. If he wasn't drunk when we met him, he was getting close to it. He was on his best behavior although I could sense the edge, I knew that he was trying to stay under control. He needed us, and he was playing the subservient role as best as he could.

His office was as sloppy as he was. There were piles of typed pages stacked on every surface that was available. Some had fallen to the floor. His suit jacket was thrown on one precarious looking chair that had been used as a temporary bookshelf. It was hardly an office to encourage faith in an attorney's thoroughness.

He pointed to two chairs in front of his desk, and he stumbled to his own chair behind it and slumped into it unceremoniously. He busied himself for a moment, I suspect, putting his bottle and glass of whiskey away in his desk drawer before he began to tell us his story. At that point I was tempted to get up and walk out of the office and leave the whole affair behind me.

"Where to begin?" he started.

Jack said rather snappishly, "From the beginning." I knew then that Jack was as unhappy about the prospect of listening to this man as I was.

"Well, I was a lifelong bachelor. Then at the age of 72, I made the mistake of getting married. What can I say? It was the stupidest thing I have ever done in my life, and I can't say I have led a perfect life by any means. It wasn't a May-December marriage. She was 68 and had been married twice before. Both of her husbands had died. She has one son from the first marriage who is in his forties."

He stopped then to mop his brow and I thought that he might just reach down into the drawer where I suspect he had put his bottle of whiskey and take a quick drink to give himself the courage to go on. He had the look of a man who was coming apart.

"She swept me off my feet. One look, gentlemen, is enough to tell you that I am not a handsome man and have never been. I have lived with the problems of alcohol abuse all of my life. I have gone through long stretches of sobriety. Then the curse returns to haunt me. Obviously, you can see that I am drinking again."

He stopped then and I felt a bit of pity for him. His admission was not an easy one for him to make. That didn't take away my reservations about becoming involved in his problems. I knew that I had a full schedule working on the Jeff Macomber death, and I wasn't too sure that I wanted to take on even more.

"Everything was lovey-dovey at the beginning and then slowly she began demanding more and more from me. I have been close with money all my life. I say close, but some people might even say miserly. I don't know. Money has always meant a great deal to me. I worked hard for it, and I was not a person to spend it foolishly. She began spending money at an alarming rate and demanding more and more. I had planned to retire shortly after we married but I had second thoughts about that. I never lived with anyone for any length of time and I found her rather nerve-wracking to be with all the time. I thought I should keep working to allow me some space. My problem was that the more space I took, the more money she spent. Then it reached the point that I cut off some of her charge cards and things went from bad to worse. Things have been deteriorating badly for weeks and months."

Jack had been sitting very quietly, but now he sat up and began paying attention. I could tell that Jack was not a happy man dealing with this rather dissolute rogue. I knew he would think of him as a rogue even though he hadn't said anything or given me a sign of any kind.

"So, then what happened?" Jack asked.

"My safe was stolen from my house and carried off. It was a large floor safe. I'm pretty sure she arranged to have it stolen. I would bet that she and her son are responsible for the whole thing. I can't prove it, but I would put money on it," he said. "I hate to admit it, but I have already put my money on it."

"How long have you been married?" I asked.

"Three years as of the end of June. We are in our fourth glorious year," he said with a voice dripping in self-pity and sarcasm. "I'm sure she'll be talking divorce now with a large settlement."

Jack said, "Now comes the big question. How much was in the safe?"

"Close to a million in cash. I can't go to the police with this, the IRS would be on my doorstep tomorrow. I have enough enemies in the Police Department to have fifty reports made to the IRS. If I hadn't been drinking

I would have seen this coming, but I have been on the booze for six months now. I suppose it is too late to do anything, so I am asking for your help after the barn door has been closed I suppose."

"I'm not sure that is the case," Jack said. "But I won't make any promises."

"Do you think there is a shot here of getting my money back?" he asked.

"I don't know," Jack said, "But, let's get a few things straight at the beginning here so we understand each other. I think this whole affair stinks. Your greed in stowing money away to avoid taxes really irritates me. Then I am offended by the sloppy way in which you did it. Why didn't you open a Swiss bank account, for instance? That would have been safe and worry free. Instead, I would guess, you wanted the money nearby so that you could count it and gloat over it."

Jack sat still looking at the attorney a moment. I suspected that he wanted to see if the message was getting across. I thought it was. Mr. Desrosiers was not so drunk that he didn't understand what was being said. He looked like he wanted to burst out in an angry tirade, but thought better of it under the circumstances.

Jack continued, "So, I can do some things here, I am sure, but you have to give me some help. I want to know everything there is to know about your wife and her son. When I say everything I mean just that. If it means you have to hire a detective agency to get every bit of information you can. I want to know who your wife was married to, every affair she ever had, what kind of money she had when she married you, what her husbands died of, who her doctor is. I mean everything. The same thing goes for her son. This is no holds barred now; it is dirty pool all the rest of the way. Can you handle that?"

"Of course I can. I have a man that I have used for years to dig up the kind of information you want. No problem there. He is very good at it."

"Secondly, you are pretty sure she will sue for divorce, right?"

"That is coming very shortly I think."

"Then, I want you to drag out the divorce proceedings as long as you can. Make it seem like we are talking years here. Can you manage that?"

"I can do that easily."

"I'm sure she'll have a good divorce lawyer ready to go. I want him to understand from day one that this is going to be a long drawn out affair and that there will be no quick settlements."

"That can be managed."

"Then I want to meet with both of them, along with my financial aide Clarissa and with Noah. You have to understand from the outset that this is going to cost you plenty of money. You are not getting off scot-free here. As of now you are running a total loss. My job is to try to get back as much as I possibly can, but there is no way that you will come out of this clean."

"How much are we talking?" the attorney asked.

"As of right now, you have lost every penny in the safe and probably half of what you own. As an attorney, does that sound reasonable to you?"

Attorney Desrosiers sat still for a few minutes. I thought for a moment that he would be reaching down to his draw to take out his bottle of whatever he had been drinking, but he just sat and stared over our heads. Then he said, "You're right. I was pretty stupid, but I'd like to save what I can now. In a case like this one you are probably even talking more."

"So our job is to use every bit of leverage we can to come up with a settlement that costs you as little as possible. Let's work on that. But we know that we are not working against an amateur here and that means we are playing with very little room to maneuver in."

"So, I'll get my guy working on background checks right away. Do you want to drop into the house to meet them informally?" he asked.

"No. I want them to understand from the very beginning that we are representing you in the money arena. Any meeting with them is to be presented as a formal business meeting without you present. This is not going to be pleasant. Unfortunately Noah and I have a major project on our hands and we haven't got endless hours to spend on this."

With that, Jack rose from his chair and seemed to unwind to his full height. Unlike Mr. Desrosiers who was sloppy and disoriented, every one of Jack's movements was purposeful and directed. He reached out his hand and said, "Think this over. We can try to do whatever we can to straighten out some of this mess, but you may feel more comfortable with one of your lawyer friends who deals in this kind of thing full time. Make a decision overnight and then call us one way or the other."

The attorney didn't rise. I hadn't said a word during the whole meeting because I had nothing of value to say. It was Jack's field and I left it to him. But, I had my own thoughts on the subject and I voiced some of them when we were in the car driving out of the city.

"He is a despicable character. I frankly don't know why we should even bother with him," I said.

"Agreed. But, imagine what she must be like. I hate to see her get away with what she has pulled off. She has taken this drunken, miserly character for all he is worth. And, I'm sure she did it with malice aforethought. Think about that. He is a despicable character, but what must she be like. Do you think for one moment that she fell desperately in love and then became embittered as the marriage went sour? I'm sure Marge has seen this any number of times or something similar to it. Also I think here, we are dealing with the top of the line. I'm sure right now she is planning her getaway. She is getting far too old to keep doing this, so I am sure she is going to cash in all her chips on this one play and then disappear into the lap of luxury. He probably deserves it, but I hate to see her get away with it."

I had to agree with him as I normally did. Jack had the ability to get to the core of things without much subtlety maybe, but he saw the essence of what he was dealing with in a very direct way. We were not going to be working for Mr. Desrosiers as much as against his grasping wife.

When I told the whole story to Marge over dinner that night, she was not the least bit surprised. She claimed to have seen the same thing in many forms and dealing in large and small sums of money.

"Both men and women can be such fools when they are lonely and searching for love. I have a girl friend who was so lonely after her husband died that she became almost desperate. She shifted all her need of companionship and affection to her son who was an absolute fool. Whether he did it purposely or through stupidity, I don't know, but he ended up costing her her home and everything she had ever saved. She was penniless and homeless at the age of sixty-five. Fortunately a few of us had enough to help her out, but she could have been in terrible straits," Marge said this and I almost felt that she was about to break into tears as the memory of her friend's plight came back to her.

I couldn't help but think how lucky we had been to find each other. We both were independently well to do. There was no concern about money between us. She had all that she would ever need and I could never spend the money I had been left.

"I have seen this kind of thing before too. You would expect that the woman would be beautiful or at least handsome, but oddly enough looks have nothing to do with it. Quite often, it is true, you find an older man marrying a young girl who is very attractive sexually, but in a surprising number of cases, you find two older people with no particular physical attraction for each other. It has mostly to do with fulfilling a need. Remember when I first stayed overnight here? I said that I was tired of sleeping alone. I was tired of being cold. Well, that was true, but I was also tired of not having anyone to depend on. I needed you, and, hopefully you needed me too. But supposing you wanted to take advantage of me. I like to think I'm pretty cautious and alert, but I could have fallen for some trickery, I'm sure."

"You haven't escaped my clutches yet," I said laughing.

Chapter XII

Jack and I had a full plate. Here we were two retired men who should have been sitting on our back porches drinking lemonade or something stronger getting ready to interview our client who had sent us back twenty years to determine if her husband's death was murder or suicide. There was no question that our minds were actively engaged. I missed my walks on the beach with Marge and my very wonderful restoring and reinvigorating naps in the afternoons, but I learned long ago that there are tradeoffs in everything we choose to do. As a teacher who took the power of the intellect seriously, I have always been concerned about losing my intellect and the power to think. Alzheimer's is the sickness I dread more than any other. I suppose I have no control over it, but I feel that by keeping my mind active, I forestall its advent. We were keeping our minds active. There was no question about that.

I had no idea where Jack intended to go with the case of the stolen safe. I felt that there was nothing that could be done there, but I also knew that Jack would never take on a hopeless task. I couldn't imagine myself playing a role in that investigation so I made up my mind to concentrate on the Jeff Macomber death.

We met with Amy Macomber again the following morning and I decided that there were questions that had to be asked even if they might prove to be embarrassing. We met once again in the dark room which was most certainly meant to be a sun room but which had been converted to what was more like a mausoleum. Once again, Amy was wrapped in her football blanket, and for some reason, she looked particularly vulnerable and small to me. I almost decided to postpone my line of questioning, but I knew she was a great deal stronger than she looked.

I began, "I have some personal questions that I think need answering. If you prefer not to answer please tell me."

"Go right ahead."

"First of all, you say that you knew that your husband was having affairs with different women. That must have given you a great deal of pain. Can you tell us about how you felt about his transgressions?"

"Well, at first. they were very painful. I wanted to be a good wife to him and to satisfy him sexually just as any woman would. But as time went by I realized, not only that I did not appeal to him, but that he actually only slept with me out of pity for me."

"How did you know that?"

Amy looked at me as if she couldn't believe that I could ask such a question and then said, "I just knew. The first time I felt it, I remember I got out of bed and dressed and took a short walk down to the water's edge. I can lead you to the very spot today. I sat on the grass and cried and cried all night long. When I went back to our room at daybreak, he was fast asleep. I was so exhausted I got back into bed. and when I finally got up and met him at breakfast, I realized that he hadn't even known that I was gone. I knew that night that I was in a loveless marriage. I never let myself be fooled again," she said.

There was no remorse in her voice. She spoke as she had before, very matter-of- factly. She was a strong woman and had put all feelings for her former husband aside many years before.

"Then there followed a whole series of women. I have no idea whether he was in love with them or merely used them. It made no difference to me because I slowly came to the realization that I didn't really love him."

"Did he know that?" I asked.

"That is the difficult question. Jeff was very bright, you know, but he was also blinded by his egotism. People loved him because he was beautiful. His looks took him a long way. He never had to work as hard as other people to get what he wanted. He once told me that he was every teachers "teachers' pet" from the day he entered school. He assumed automatically that people loved him. Of course, that women especially, did. So, did he know that I stopped loving him? I don't think so. Then, about six years into our marriage I fell and broke a hip. I used that as an excuse to sleep in separate beds."

"Do you think that led to his pursuit of women?"

"Not on your life. He could have been having sex with me every night and still have been looking for women. Jack sailed with him and he knows what he was like."

"How did your father feel about him?" I asked.

"Dad felt he was beneath contempt. He thought he had wasted his talents, and Daddy could never tolerate that in anyone. He tried to get Jeff interested in the business any number of times, but Jeff would have none of it. As time went on it was as if Jeff didn't exist for him. That drove Jeff to distraction. Every time Daddy came to the house, Jeff would leave and stay away as long as Daddy was here."

"Did they ever have words?"

"Daddy wasn't the kind of person who got angry or argued with people. He thought there was no point. At work he would dismiss them physically by having them fired; in private life, he dismissed them psychologically. He told me over and over again that there was no point in wasting his valuable time and energy on people he disagreed with. So, he did exactly that to Jeff and Jeff couldn't stand it."

"That put Jeff in an awkward position as far as money was concerned," Jack said. "If your father pulled out he was in a difficult fix."

"Not at all. I had my own money because of my partnership in the corporation. We were in a fix to use your term, only if the corporation failed for any reason. Other than that, Jeff was safe as long as I supplied him with money. I did that, as you know."

"How did you feel toward your sister?"

"I loved her very much. She was everything I wasn't, and I think she felt the same about me. She was lovely and exciting. I was drab and dull. She was our mother and I was our father. When we were children she would spend hours playing dress up in mother's clothes pretending to be all the characters she read about in her books. I would sit and watch her and laugh at all the things she did. I could never join her though, because I would feel so foolish."

"Did you know that she was having an affair with your husband?"

"I guessed at one point. Then, of course, when Jason was born, there was no question about it. Jack can certainly see the resemblance between Jeff and Jason. On her deathbed my poor sister confessed to me that she and Jeff had had a long-term relationship as if the world couldn't see that Jason was Jeff's son. Did I know how long they were together? No, I had no idea. I didn't care."

"How did Jason feel about this? If everyone knew, he certainly did. What kind of a relationship did he have with his father?" I asked.

Again, I got no overt reaction to my question. Amy Macomber sat as quietly as she had before and answered my question without hesitating or showing any embarrassment whatsoever.

"I think you have to ask Jason that question. If you are asking whether they had a normal father and son relationship, I would have to say that they didn't. There was no playing ball together, or going fishing, and never did Jeff teach Jason how to sail. Jason was always respectful, but I would have to say that they were never close. I think Jason was closer to me than he was to either his father or mother. From the very beginning we seemed to understand each other. But again, I think you have to ask Jason how he feels."

Jack broke in with a question of his own, "It seems to me Amy, that your father would have had some problems with Jeff when it came to money. The Sam Goetzel I knew did not like to give money away. I wouldn't call him tight-fisted, but he was close to it. How did he accept the idea of Jeff living off your money?"

"You know the answer to that. He did not like it one bit. It was always a bone of contention between us. He wanted me to divorce him years ago, but I had my own reasons for staying married. One I have already explained to you. I felt guilty about the fact that I had let him take a route in life that was not productive and I couldn't very well punish him for something I had encouraged or at least allowed to happen. Then as time went on, and Jason was born and began to grow into a man, I became more and more attached to him and I realized that Jeff had given me a gift. I couldn't leave him then."

Things were becoming clearer to me, but I still had to ask, "Why, then did your father insist on having the 50th Anniversary party? It seems foolish considering the fact that he had no love for Jeff and wanted you to end the marriage."

"If you are suggesting in any way that Daddy planned to kill Jeff and used the party as a means to that end, I think you are definitely wrong. It was not in Daddy's nature to do such a thing. Jack has already suggested that he was hard and ruthless; that I'll grant you, but he was not a cold-blooded killer."

With that, Amy seemed to have had enough. For the first time since we had met her, she looked tired. The lines in her face, even in the semi-darkness in which we sat, suggested that she had had enough of the questioning and, instead of going to work this morning, would rather have gone to bed and taken a good, long nap. She slowly removed the blanket from her legs and gripped the sides of her chair for support as she lifted herself out of her chair. She did it with difficulty and both Jack and I leaned forward to offer our support. She shook her head. We stepped back and let her struggle to an upright position. We respected her pride.

I returned to the study and found Marge talking to Evangelica who had come to clean the study and been quite surprised to find Marge reading Mr. Goetzel's journals. From the looks of it, Marge had been talking to her for some time when I entered and was just finishing up. I didn't feel I was interrupting anything.

Marge said, "I'm glad we had a chance to talk. Next time you come to clean, you won't be so surprised to see me here."

She bowed slightly and left Marge and me alone.

"I'm afraid I shirked my duty a bit. I really didn't get to the journals to speak of, but I think I learned a few things," Marge said.

"For instance."

"I think that lady had a terrible crush on Jeff Macomber."

"What makes you think that?" I asked.

"I don't know. I can't put my finger on it, but when he becomes the center of conversation, she takes on a particularly sympathetic demeanor. She claims he was always a gentleman to her, but I wouldn't be too sure of that."

"Well, it bears looking into."

Chapter XIII

It was Jack's opinion, which he was willing to document in a hundred different stories, that money was the cause of most of the world's evils. He gave religious fanaticism a distant second.

"Look at what our favorite attorney is going through right now. That woman hooked onto him for money and money alone. The poor fool thought that he had found true love. I hate to tell you how many times I have seen the same kind of thing. I worked with a genius once who could make money grow. He had an instinct for knowing where money was to be had. He could do no wrong except when it came to people. He had a blind spot for women. He married a woman I called the "spider woman." She wove a web around him that had him so entrapped he couldn't move. Here was a man who could go to a race track or a gambling casino and actually come out a winner on a regular basis. At the same time a woman could enmesh him in lies and chicanery that would make you laugh. At one time or another, the "spider woman" was sleeping with every one in our office, and this poor fool with a million dollar mind could never see it."

"Not you, of course," I said seriously.

"Absolutely, not me. I couldn't stand the woman. When I looked at her all I saw was evil. She knew it and couldn't pass up the opportunity to make passes at me at every office party or celebration. She was so obvious that I became the subject of jokes in the office."

"The instances of that kind of thing are endless. But with Jeff Macomber it would seem that none of this applies. He was in no need of money as far as we can determine. I recall a very good friend of his who sailed with us. I am hoping he is still alive. I remember he lived in Key

West. I am having difficulty remembering his name. I keep forgetting to ask Amy. If he is still living he would be in a good position to fill us in on Jeff's financial situation as he saw it. He lived high off the hog and was married at least three times when I knew him some forty years ago. He was in a very different position than Jeff was in."

Marge asked, "Do you think Jeff married Amy for her money? Was that his real reason for marrying her? Do you think he really loved her?"

Jack thought for a moment before answering. Then he said, "I can't answer that. On our trips together I saw a man who attacked life savagely. Everything he did was in the extreme. He was a strange man. Once, for instance, we were cruising the Caribbean and on board with us was a beautiful, French woman who would do justice to the front cover of the best of the fashion magazines. She had everything; beauty, style, class and intelligence and she was passionately in love with Jeff. So, on the whole trip he romanced her and made love to her to the point where it was definitely embarrassing to the rest of us. They were literally all over each other. Then one day we reached a port and she felt mildly ill so she decided to stay on board. I went on shore with Jeff and a few members of the crew. We ended up at a little bar where we decided to sit in the shade to cool down. I can remember the terrible heat and how good it felt just to be seated in the shade and under a cooling fan. Our waitress came to the table and she was so beautiful she took my breath away. She had a chocolate brown skin and the most beautiful face imaginable. Before we knew it, Jeff was in hot pursuit. If her husband hadn't appeared from outside the cafe, Jeff would certainly have made more than advances toward her. Now, here he was with a woman on the boat that was tied to the dock, a woman that any one of us would have given a month's pay to be with for one night, and he was making a move on a complete stranger. On the other hand, I have been with him when he had women chasing him around and he couldn't get away from them. Now, the question is, would he have acted in that way if Amy were on board? My answer is that he would not."

"It sounds to me like he would have done just that," Marge said a little indignantly.

"That's the difficult thing about this. It was like he lived two lives. He was one person on board and a completely different person when he set foot on shore. I think he lost all of his inhibitions on the water. It was the milieu in which he was an unconditional success without expending his energy in tension and anxiety. He was a bright man but he was always unsure of himself in an environment like Harvard where he was one of many bright people. When he stepped aboard that vessel, he knew then that no one was his equal. I am sure that Sam Goetzel intimidated him on land, but had he set foot in Jeff's domain, Sam would have been shocked at the change in his son-in-law. I could imagine him sailing a Yankee Clipper in the China Seas or even as a captain of a whaling ship out of New Bedford. But, sitting in a stuffy law office in Boston or New York would hardly have suited him. He was the wrong man for the twentieth century. He was meant for the 18th or 19th centuries."

However, Marge said in a disapproving tone, "He was married in the 20th century."

Jack didn't say anything for a few minutes. His hands were still in his lap which was unusual for him when he was talking. Then he said, "Understand, Marge. I don't approve of what Jeff did. I certainly wouldn't live the lifestyle myself. But, I have tried to explain some aspects of Jeff's behavior as I saw it. You asked me if I thought he really loved Amy, and I have to say that I don't know the answer to that question. On the surface it would seem he did not, but who knows what was below the surface?"

Chapter XIV

Marge found an interesting entry in the journal the next morning:

SATURDAY;
I RETURNED LAST NIGHT. AMY AND HER HUSBAND AND
SUSANNAH WERE IN THE STUDY WHEN I CAME IN. AMY HAS
JUST INTRODUCED A NEW AZALEA WHICH SHE CLAIMS IS A
LOW GROWER, ALMOST A CREEPING VARIETY, WHICH SHE
FEELS WILL BE A BREAKTHROUGH IN THIS COUNTRY
BECAUSE IT IS SO HARDY. SHE WAS TRYING TO NAME IT AND
THE THREE OF THEM WERE IN THE PROCESS OF TOYING WITH
DIFFERENT NAMES. JEFF WAS PLAYING WITH ANAGRAMS
AND I HAVE TO GIVE HIM CREDIT HE IS VERY CLEVER WITH
WORDS; WHAT A WASTE THOUGH . BUT I HAVE BEEN OVER
ALL OF THIS BEFORE WITH AMY AND IT IS A WASTE OF TIME.
THE SAME CAN BE SAID FOR SUSANNAH. SHE HAS DEVOTED
MOST OF HER ENERGY TO HER APPEARANCE AND IS JUST
BEGINNING TO SHOW THE ILL EFFECTS OF ALL OF THE WORK
SHE HAS HAD DONE ON HER FACE. ANOTHER WASTE,
ALTHOUGH SHE HAS NEVER SHOWN ANY PARTICULAR
TALENT. SHE IS HER MOTHER ALL OVER. STILL I MISS THE
OLD LADY. SHE HAD HER MOMENTS. THE HOUSE SEEMS
COLD WITHOUT HER. I'LL BE GETTING MAWKISH IF I KEEP
WRITING AND TALKING ABOUT HER.

AMY IS MY GIRL. THERE SHE WAS LAST NIGHT LETTING
JEFF STEAL THE SPOTLIGHT WITH HIS CLEVERNESS WHILE

SUSANNAH DRAPED HERSELF IN A SHAWL ON THE LEATHER COUCH IN A POOR IMITATION OF ELIZABETH TAYLOR PLAYING CLEOPATRA. AMY HAS DEVELOPED A NEW PLANT THAT WILL PROBABLY GET WORLDWIDE RECOGNITION AMONG AZALEA ENTHUSIASTS AND THERE SHE SAT AS HUMBLE AND UNASSUMING AS EVER. NEITHER OF THE OTHER TWO HAVE ANYTHING TO SHOW FOR YEARS OF BEING ON THIS EARTH.

EXCEPT JASON. I LIKE THAT BOY. HE SPENDS MORE AND MORE TIME WITH AMY AND HE LOVES TO WORK. I PRETEND TO BE ANGRY WIH HIM FOR TRACKING DIRT INTO THE STUDY, BUT HE IS WORTH A THOUSAND JEFFS. I HAVE BEEN SPENDING SOME TIME SUPPOSEDLY TEACHING HIM CHESS. AT THIRTEEN HE IS FAR BETTER THAN I EVER WAS OR COULD HOPE TO BE. I GIVE HIM CHESS PUZZLES THAT I CLIP FROM THE HERALD TRIBUNE AND HE SOLVES THEM IN SECONDS. HE IS VERY INTENSE AND I DON'T UNDERSTAND WHERE IT COMES FROM. MAYBE I WILL NEVER KNOW BUT HE REMINDS ME SO MUCH OF ME WHEN I WAS HIS AGE. ADMITTEDLY HE IS A BETTER STUDENT THAN I WAS, BUT HE IS VERY MUCH LIKE ME. I WOULD LOVE TO HAVE HIM TRAIN TO TAKE OVER THE COMPANY, BUT IT MAY NOT BE TO HIS LIKING. THE FUN IS OUT OF IT ANYWAY; ALL IT DOES IS MAKE MONEY NOW. IT DOESN'T TAKE THE KIND OF TALENT THIS BOY HAS TO RUN AN ONGOING ENTERPRISE. THE FUN WAS IN PUTTING IT TOGETHER.

I CAN FEEL MYSELF GROWING OLDER NOW. I HAVE TO START THINKING ABOUT WHAT I LEAVE BEHIND BESIDES MONEY.

Marge said, "You have to admit that our Mr. Goetzel was an interesting man. I doubt if his employees saw that side of him. By the way, this is the first mention I have seen of his son-in-law in the journals thus far. Jack worked with him on some financial planning, you said. What did he think of him?"

"Jack hasn't said much except for the fact that he was close when it came to money. We'll have to get him to talk about his relationship with him."

"We'll also have to get Jason to talk about his grandfather," Marge said. "I'd love to know how he felt about Mr. Goetzel."

"The big question that I would like answered is how Jason felt about being a bastard son in a house where he lived with his father and his father's wife knowing that he was not her son but the son of her sister. That was certainly a stressful situation especially when he was so close to his aunt. Under normal conditions that would have made for an explosive situation, to say the least."

Marge looked at me with an odd expression on her face and asked, "Do you think there could be a connection between Mr. Macomber's death and the fact that he fathered Jason?"

"I don't know, but I wouldn't rule it out. Doesn't it strike you as strange that the boy could remain in the same house as his father without being acknowledged by him?"

"How do you know that he was not acknowledged or recognized by the father?" Marge asked in return.

"I suppose I don't," I answered, "I just assumed that was the case. I think we need another session with Mrs. Arruda to shed light on some of this. She was close to the family as an observer without being directly involved emotionally."

Marge seemed to be enjoying digging around in this case which I found a bit frustrating. Like so many women of her generation she had chosen marriage for a career. Unlike Clarissa and Jen who would most certainly be looking for careers outside of marriage, or Susan who had become a successful doctor or Nelly who chose to be a lawyer, Marge had become what we in our generation called a "housewife". Her career had been to be a mate to her husband and to tend to his needs at home.

The next day we arranged to meet with Deolinda Arruda again, but this time I did so with Marge rather than Jack. Jack was chasing down the information he had received from Attorney Desrosiers concerning his stepson.

Mrs. Arruda met us in her home. Again we sat in the parlor in exactly the same seats in which Jack and I had sat on our previous visit. I sensed that Mrs. Arruda had made an effort to look even nicer than she had on the previous visit knowing that Marge would be present. There was no question that she was a handsome woman. Even at her age, her figure was lush and appealing and she exuded sexuality. In comparison, Marge was appealing in a different way. She was thoughtful and controlled, she gave one the feeling of being comfortable and sensitive. Yet she was just as beautiful in her own way with her clear features and lovely smile.

Marge let me take the lead in questioning Deolinda, "What we are having difficulty with is the idea that Jason was Jeff's son, and the boy went unacknowledged by his father even though they lived in the same house. Can you tell us anything about the relationship between the two men, or the boy and the man?"

"Mr. Amos, if you want me to answer your questions you have to speak in English I understand. What is it you want to know?" Deolinda asked with the slightest smile on her face.

"I want to know how Jason and his father got along," I said, feeling rather foolish.

"When we first saw the boy we all knew that he was Mr. Macomber's son. You'd have to be blind not to see that. He was a cute baby. Everybody loved him, but the father stayed away as if when he looked at him he felt the pains of his sin. Mr. Jeff liked women and they liked him. So Mrs. Macomber's sister loved him too. They had a son. The boy was theirs together. But the old man loved that little boy. He was always bringing him here to the house. When the boy was a baby he didn't know what we all knew. He was innocent. Like the Virgin Mother's baby we see in the pictures. I can see him now, so cute in his mother's arms, but with the mark of sin on his father."

That certainly was a picturesque description and one that my mother would choose. I laughed because it was like hearing my mother come alive. Marge looked at me questioningly and I explained that Deolinda expressed things just as my mother would.

Deolinda laughed and said, "Of course, we are Portuguese and we have our way of talking and thinking."

"So what did you think when you saw that baby?"

"I thought the man needed a good beating for doing what he did. What kind of a man sleeps with his wife's sister?"

"But how did Mrs. Macomber feel?"

"Who knows? She shows nothing. Everything she thinks is deep inside her."

Marge asked, "Did she know?"

"Of course she knew. My lady is not blind or stupid. Of course, she knew.

"And, Mr. Goetzel?" Marge asked.

"He was mad as hell at the beginning. Then, he saw that he had a grandson, and he really went crazy for the kid. He couldn't get enough of him. He would sit with a big smile on his face watching everything the kid did. Then when he started to get older, he would play different games with him. They played cards and chess all the time. He loved him so much," she said this as if she had a vision of Mr. Goetzel in her mind.

"You said he was mad as hell at the beginning. Did he say anything to Jeff?"

"Of course. Mr. Goetzel was not the kind of man to keep quiet and to keep things to himself. What he thought, we knew. When he was mad, we knew right away. As big and strong as Mr. Macomber was, I thought the old man was going to kill him. Mr. Macomber left the house and didn't come back for a year. I don't know where he went, but I do know that he was gone from the house. The baby went with the mother because Mr. Goetzel was ready to kill her too, he was so mad. But she too went away and then when she came back, it was different. He wanted the baby around him as much as could be, but he never got really close to the mother again."

"What makes you say that?" I asked.

"I don't know. I think he lost respect for her. He was always closer to Miss Amy than to Susannah, but this pushed him closer to the one and away from the other."

Whatever tension Deolinda had felt was soon gone and she seemed to relax. The more she talked, the less threatened she felt. She suddenly remembered that she hadn't given us anything to eat and rose from her seat on the sofa and went into the kitchen to return with a tray full of Portuguese mallasadas. These are similar to what the Italians called fried dough and are a raised dough stretched so that they fry thin and crispy and then are dusted with sugar. My mother made these to perfection and I remember them as a special treat on Shrove Tuesday when they were a traditional staple of every Portuguese household. When Deolinda brought out the tray and saw my reaction, she broke into a pleasant giggle. She was so beautiful at that moment, I could have reached out and kissed her.

"Just like your mother made when you were a little boy, am I right?" she asked laughing and poking Marge in the ribs. "Did you ever see anything like it? The men always want to be little boys again. No matter how old they are, they want to be boys in their mother's kitchen."

She was happy now because she knew she had surprised me and pleased me at the same time. Mallasadas were hardly part of my normal diet but I couldn't resist these with a cup of tea. She knew I would eat them with tea and she made sure the tea was piping hot. It was a side of Deolinda Arruda that surprised me.

I think Marge enjoyed the fresh mallasadas as much as I did and she too ate two of them. I knew we would both suffer from heart burn later but it was worth it. It did indeed bring back thoughts of my mother's kitchen. I remember her standing over a little saucepan just large enough to hold the stretched out raw dough and enough lard to cook it in; then carefully turning the dough with a fork until both sides were crisp. Then she would place the cooked mallasada on a brown paper bag to drain some of the cooking fat and then onto a dish towel to soak up the rest. I would eat the almost too hot fried dough eagerly and with great appreciation. A smile would come over my mother's face as well and I remember that she had the habit of rubbing her arms with her hands as she crossed them in front of her. It was the gesture that I remembered most when I thought of my mother as happy.

Before I lost the gist of the questioning and valuable time, I brought Deolinda back with the question that bothered me the most. "As the boy grew how did he feel about his father?"

"That's the question I knew you would ask. It is the one question I can't answer because I don't know. My boys grew up here with their father in the Portuguese way. A Portuguese man didn't play ball or go to Little League games like I see the fathers do today. My husband punished them when they had to be punished and gave them a slap on the back when they did something good. But, they didn't sit around all day loving each other. They went their way and he went his way. It was the same with Mr. Jeff and Mr. Jason. So even when Mr. Jason knew that Mr. Jeff was his father, I don't know what he was thinking because they never warmed up to each other. Did Mr. Jeff punish the boy? Never. Did he slap him on the back? Never. In other words, what I am trying to say is that he never went near the boy. And the boy? He was with his grandfather or with Miss Amy but never with his father. He loved his grandfather and he loved Miss Amy. Everybody could see that."

Marge went back to the question though. "Do you think he had bad feelings toward his father?"

"Of course. The boy was not made of stone. He knows that his father is Mr. Macomber. He had feelings. How would you feel if you were in a house with your father and your father pretended you didn't even exist? You would be pissed off. I would."

At that point I suddenly felt tired. I wished there was some easy solution to the case and that I could go back to the Point, pack my bags and Marge and I could go somewhere for a week or two and relax and forget the whole thing. I hadn't felt that way in a long time but, suddenly, I was out of energy. I always felt that meant I was coming down with something. For me lack of energy normally meant the onset of a cold or the flu or some debilitating sickness that left me in bed sipping tea and hoping for better days. I looked at Marge and Deolinda and I thought that it would be great if I were to walk into the study and read Mr. Goetzel's journals and find a full confession in one of them that would solve the case for us. I doubted that it would happen and I had no faith in the idea that it would, but I still felt tired and was hoping for the easy way out. That wasn't normally my way, but I was tired and I knew it. I decided there and then to take a couple of days off and to get away with Marge even if it meant just a couple of days to ourselves.

I turned to Deolinda and said, "Not good enough and you know it. Something had to go on between the father and the boy. Now help us out. Were there arguments, fights, physical confrontation, yelling matches, anything that would give us a clue as to how they felt about one another. Could the boy have killed his father?"

"How do you know that anybody killed Mr. Jeff? Who told you that? We found him dead in the study with the gun still in his hand. You trying to make trouble here with lies or are you looking for the truth?"

"You haven't answered my question. Could the boy have killed his father? He was a man then wasn't he? Did he have so much resentment toward Jeff Macomber that he would take his life?"

Mrs. Arruda threw up her hands in disbelief. She picked up the empty tea cups and the tray of mallasadas and started toward the kitchen. She turned as if to say something and then continued on her way. We heard her mumbling to herself and we waited silently for her return. Marge sat uncomfortably in her chair, bolt upright, while she waited and looked at me with a look of concern on her face. I winked and she smiled and we waited for Mrs. Arruda to return. We waited for what seemed like five minutes or more until Deolinda emerged from the kitchen and walked defiantly into the room.

"You are trying to make a murder from a suicide. Why? The man has been dead for twenty years. Now you decide to make it a murder. You want to blame that poor boy. Well, you won't get any help from me. I have said all I am going to say to you, Mr. Amos. So, I think you should get up and leave before I call the boys and they help you get out."

"No need to get the boys. We'll leave, but, let's get one thing straight. Mrs. Macomber asked us to find out what happened and, right at this moment, I am sorry I got involved in this whole thing, but, involved I am. I will get to the bottom of it or die trying."

Marge and I left at that point and I admit that not only was I tired, but I was angry as well. I said very little on the way back to Westport Point. Marge respected my desire to be quiet and to think. What was getting me down was the fact that we were dealing in people's impressions which were being filtered through their own personalities. There was no direct evidence. What we learned we learned through other people and who knew if they were telling us the truth or a variation of the truth as they saw it. Who could tell if they were covering up the truth or even lying to us? We read Mr. Goetzel's journals, but they were filtered through what he wanted the world to know about him. He had to have known that those journals were going to be read some day so, it stood to reason that he was going to be careful about what he entered in them.

I told this to Marge over dinner that night. She had been quiet all evening and she knew something was disturbing me.

"You saw Mrs. Arruda's reaction today. It was overblown. There was no reason for her to react as strongly as she did, except that she has a direct connection with Jason and thought that I was about to accuse him of murdering his father or, maybe, even worse, I was going to somehow frame him for something he didn't do. So, she lost control."

Marge laughed and said, "All the smoothness and suavity went out of her. She was like a lioness protecting her cubs. You made the wrong move and she was ready to pounce. Actually, I thought it was rather cute, didn't you?"

"Not really. So, I say we take a few days and get out of here. We need a good break. I know I do. I'm really exhausted with chasing shadows and we haven't even begun really. It is the same problem that I see over and over again. There is no direct evidence. Everything comes at us second hand. I find myself repeating the same phrase over and over again. 'What do you think?'"

"The old retired people need a break from the difficult duties they have taken on themselves. Would you believe it? In all the years you were working did you ever imagine that you would end up doing something like this at your age?" Marge asked and then gave me a nudge in the ribs to emphasize the point. "Here you are at 72 trying to get in a vacation so that you can get some rest. Most of my friends are taking vacations to break the boredom."

"Well, I say let's get away for a few days. I don't want to hear anyone express an opinion about Jeff Macomber for at least a week. As a man who never had a penny and who could never afford the thought of a vacation until recently, it seems wonderful that I have the option to make a quick decision about getting away. But, of course, I wouldn't even consider it without first consulting my romantic interest."

"And, who may that be?"

"My lovely companion, Marge, Marge, Marge who has made my life complete and wonderful."

"For a seventy-two year old man you sound like you have delusions of grandeur, but to be honest with you, I couldn't be more pleased. So, where shall we go?" Marge asked.

"Let's go somewhere where we don't have a minute to think. A big city would be just the thing, I think. Somewhere with a lot of activity, lights shining everywhere. What do you think?"

"New York City. I think we could do whatever we liked. Dinner in good restaurants, a play, the opera, a concert, The Frick or the Metropolitan, just what we need, don't you think?"

"Sounds absolutely great. Let's do it."

I felt relieved almost immediately. Just the thought of getting away was enough to boost my spirits, but even in that I could feel a little of what Jeff Macomber must have felt when he made his escape on his yachts each year. I was not running away, although I had the distinct feeling that he had been. I couldn't get rid of the man. He was with me even as I planned to go away and I determined to leave him behind.

Clarissa drove us to the train station in Providence and we took the non-stop express to New York City. We had made reservations at the Essex House and we spent the first morning in the city at the Frick Museum where, like so many people before us, we were struck by the VerMeers that Mr. Frick had had the foresight to buy for his personal collection. It was the perfect way to spend our first morning in New York and it did do the trick for me. I forgot all about Mr. Jeff Macomber and the Goetzel family. It turned out to be a lovely day in the city, even with all the inevitable construction and noise.Every time I visited, I enjoyed the activity and excitement. The quiet on the Point was wonderful. On any given day, sitting in my kitchen looking out over the water, I could go without seeing another soul aside from my immediate neighbors and friends. Here on the busy New York City streets I was surrounded by more people in one hour than I would see in a year at home. Marge was a people watcher and liked nothing better than to see people from all around the country and the world, for that matter, rushing to and fro on the city streets, being jostled on street corners and rushing across intersections when the lights changed.

We settled into the hotel and I was like a kid on his first trip to Disney World. There was so much to do and see that I could hardly wait, but first I wanted to make love to Marge, and fortunately it seemed, she felt much the same impulse. We are never too old for romance.

We planned for an early dinner so that we could go to the opera to see La Boheme. This was an old war horse that I enjoyed tremendously even after hearing it countless times. It was new to Marge who had taken an interest in opera only after moving into my place with me. I had the habit of listening to opera in the background quite often during the evening. She had listened to it and begun to enjoy it. How many times had I heard it? How many evenings had I spent alone in my house years after my wife left me correcting papers or doing lesson plans and listening to the great lyrical, romantic music. But, in all those years, I had never seen a full production of it. In fact, I had never been to the Metropolitan Opera. It had always been beyond my means.

Again I couldn't help but think of Jeff Macomber as much as I tried to resist him. What would he have done without the money that Amy Macomber provided? I had been trained to be frugal as a child growing up in a household where my father worked as a blue collar worker in a factory. We were never without, but all our money went to necessities. If I hadn't gotten a scholarship the chances are that I could never have attended college. As a teacher I had sufficient money to live on, but I had never been able to afford the luxuries of life. People with money take those things for granted, but those of us without extra money flowing in, can take nothing for granted.

The idea that I would some day be able to take a trip to New York on the spur of the moment would never have occurred to me. To take the express train would be the last thing from my mind and to get a hotel without considering the price was unheard of. Even now that I had more money than I could ever spend, I couldn't help but think about prices on everyday items. Jack laughed at both of us, but we still pumped our own gas at service stations for the few pennies we were saving per gallon.

Here Marge and I were staying at a wonderful "small" hotel in New York City. My poor mother would have felt too intimidated to even enter the hotel lobby, but here we were. My problem in dealing with Jeff Macomber and his wife and the Goetzels, was that I was not in their league. Did they check the prices of the hotels in New York City? When and if Jeff Macomber went to the theater did he ask for the price of the seats? When he sat down at a restaurant did his eye naturally travel to the right hand column to see the price of the entrees? How about Amy Macomber who had been born with money? She had never known a day without it. How important was money to her? Was it something she thought about? We already knew that she supplied her husband with all the money he needed. Did she check to see that he spent the money correctly?

Behind it all was Jack's presumption that the evil that took place in the world had largely to do with money. Was he right in this case? Was there friction between Sam Goetzel and Jeff Macomber that threatened the latter's supply of money? Or was money involved in some other way that we hadn't yet discovered? Certainly, if Jeff Macomber's source of cash was threatened his life would be altered irrevocably. He had never been trained, as I was, to do without. He didn't have to think about money as I did when I was young and through most of my life. He used what he needed. There was no sitting down on Friday evenings to pay the bills that were due or, many times, overdue. That would be done by an accountant most likely. But, suppose his way of life was being questioned and the money was being denied him? Would he have become so depressed that he would have taken his own life? We just didn't know enough about the man to make any assumptions.

I couldn't help but think about any other permutations there might be to the money problem. Could Jeff have been in money troubles and been refused help by Amy and taken his own life? That seemed unlikely. Could someone have been putting pressure on him to repay a loan, for instance? Could he have been gambling and gotten himself deep in debt and been unable to pay off tariffs? Could he have made some bad investments in the stock market and lost heavily? From what we already knew of Jeff Macomber, none of these seemed to fit, so it was unlikely that Jack's premise would hold up. If Jeff Macomber committed suicide or was murdered, money was unlikely to have been the motivation.

I told all of this to Marge and she laughed at me for thinking about the problem while taking a few days vacation to run away from it. She claimed that I had tunnel vision and I had to agree with her. All of my life, my singular good quality was that I had the tenacity to attack a problem like a pit bull and to cling to the problem until I was satisfied that I had the solution. What I realized now, was that I was not trying to escape from thinking about the problem, but rather putting some distance between myself and the house where Jeff was killed or committed suicide. With the paucity of facts we were dealing with, it was unlikely that we could arrive at any conclusions, but distance from the scene would hopefully prove to be useful if for no other reason than it would give me a chance to clear my head.

Then it occurred to me that we hadn't contacted even one of the people who had been to the party that day. We had been busy, but we still had to get that done. At that point I almost regretted having taken the vacation. But then Marge took my arm and hustled me out of the hotel room and we were on the streets of New York in nothing flat. We entered the New York City hubbub the moment we touched the sidewalk outside the hotel and I found myself relieved of every thought except making our way through the usual traffic and pedestrian chaos. We made our way to the street where we hailed a taxi and were driven to a restaurant that Marge had found on the internet and where we managed to get reservations for an early dinner.

Early dinners were always my choice. The late dinner preceded by drinks may have been fashionable for the wealthy and socially elite, but in our working class family, dinner was as close to five o'clock as possible. As a child I was trained to be in the house and washed for dinner at five o'clock. There were no cocktails and my mother put the meal on the table often before the clock showed five o'clock. It was a rare occasion when we ate later than six. Why? I never knew except that I know that at five o'clock my stomach started growling and I knew it was time to eat. There was no reason to have the kitchen clock remind me what time it was.

In our house, unlike Jack's, dinner was a time for talk. It was one of the few times during the course of the day when my father talked and discussed a number of subjects. His favorite during my early years was Franklin Roosevelt, whom he adored with a passion. There wasn't an utterance or a proposal that the President made that he didn't record in his little notebook in his oversized script. He wrote with difficulty because he suffered from arthritis and he had difficulty holding a pen or pencil, but he was one of many ardent supporters of the President among the poor in cities like Fall River. It was one of the most important days of his life when he saw Franklin D. Roosevelt in person in Oak Grove Cemetery when he attended the funeral of Louis McHenry Howe who had been the president's friend and advisor as well as press secretary. I was just a child but the event was so momentous that somehow I can remember certain parts of it very vividly. I remember distinctly my father's excitement when we walked to the Locust St. entrance to the cemetery and he pushed through the crowd with me on his shoulders and my mother in tow behind him. He was beside himself with excitement and even if he had not seen the President he would have known that he was within shouting distance of him. The crowd was big but orderly; it was a funeral and people still had respect for the burial of the dead. Everyone stood in anticipation of the president's arrival and I know my father stood on tiptoes with me on his shoulders trying to get a view. And then finally there was a distinct but controlled murmur that went through the crowd and we knew the President had arrived. I had a glimpse of him in his wheelchair being taken to the crest of the hill where men were all around him. I learned later that they were the Secret Service and he and his wife were being protected. Years later I would learn to admire Eleanor Roosevelt but on that day I cannot remember seeing her.

Of all the special days in my father's long life, the visit of Franklin Delano Roosevelt to Fall River was the greatest day in his life. For years, whenever he had an audience, he would begin telling about the wonderful day by describing the walk to the cemetery from our tenement about a half mile away. He would not skip one detail of what we had seen and done. He must have repeated the story to me at least one hundred times; each time as if it was the first time he had told me. He told it as if I hadn't been there sitting on his shoulders the whole time. He never lied or embellished in telling the story. He had no need to since he thought it was such a wonderful event in itself. On his death bed, he told me that the two proudest days of his life were the day I received my college diploma and the day he saw Franklin Delano Roosevelt. I couldn't help but think that Mr. Roosevelt was unlikely to be admired by Mr. Goetzel and his many rich friends.

We ate at 5 o'clock every evening except Sunday when my mother made Sunday dinner. We went to 9:30 mass at Holy Rosary Church every Sunday without fail and then returned home to eat the dinner my mother made as a special event for my dad.

Our dinners at night were large meals comparable to those Jack had described to me when he was a boy and young man living at home. Chicken was the standard on Sundays along with a roast, but we didn't eat expensive cuts of meat during the week. Our meals consisted mainly of fish which mother prepared to perfection. Meat for meals consisted mainly of body parts and organs such as calf's liver or chicken livers or gizzards. We ate all of the foods that I have since learned were conveyors of large amounts of cholesterol. Kidneys and eggs were my favorites and I take Lipitor now as a consequence of my love of tasty foods. Half of our meals at least, were based on hearty soups of one sort or another. Potatoes were inexpensive and my mother thickened soups with them or rice or pasta. We ate well if not healthily. It was bread, though, that made up a big part of our diet as with most peasant families from Europe. We were a family of three and mother was a light eater, but I still picked up two loaves of Portuguese Vienna bread every day at the Lisboa bakery. The breads came out of the ovens at four in the afternoon and it was my chore to pick up two breads before the bakery ran out for the day. I remember to this day the smell of hot bread drifting into the street as the baker opened his ovens to take the hot breads out with wooden pallets. Standing outside the bakery which was more like a storefront, we stood in line waiting for our turn to enter the shop and get our breads. I am sure that every family in the neighborhood was represented. There were no strangers among us. I knew everyone in line including every one of the little widows who were dressed in widow's weeds and who seemed to dominate the line. They stood in the cold of winter or the heat of summer, always it seemed, dressed exactly the same way. They wore a black dress with black stockings and black shoes with a cross hanging in a pendant from their necks. Over their heads was a black shawl, always it seemed loosely knotted around their necks. They discussed the happenings in the neighborhood. Not much went on that we in the line did not hear about. When I returned home with my breads every day, my mother was waiting to hear the news. We knew who was getting married, who had been laid off from work, who was sick and just about every other event of note in the neighborhood.

The breads were ready at four in the afternoon but the line was filled by three-thirty. Every bread was sold every day and there was never a day that I could remember when all the breads were not sold. I once asked the baker why he just didn't make more breads to satisfy the existing need. He laughed and told me that he needed to make 400 hundred breads a day to make a good living and that he actually made 450. So his basic needs were exceeded by fifty loaves which were enough to ensure that he and his wife would have sufficient money to live on when he finally had to close his bakery. He insisted that making an additional fifty loaves would mean working extra time in a day that was too short already and give very little value for his labor since he did not need the money.

So, we rushed to buy his bread and waited in line for the doors to open. The widows and children didn't carry cash. They had little notebooks in which the owner's wife noted the number of breads they purchased and I supposed a reckoning was made from time to time. It was the Depression and there were many families who the baker carried I am sure. Many of the people in line were buying for their tenement house which might mean ten breads for three families. Multiple purchases were common because the families were big. The breads were put in lunch buckets and were the basic ingredient of most of the diets in the neighborhood.

Our two loaves were only a minor part of the day's business but a part nevertheless. I was always treated with respect and courtesy by the smiling baker who was prone to give children a cookie now and then along with a slap on the back and a laugh because he knew that he had left his telltale sign of a flour imprint on the back of our shirt or sweater. It was a secret wish of mine that Mr. Goncalo would just once do the same to one of the widows who were dressed in black. I could just imagine the stares and smiles as one of them walked past the tenement houses with the mark of the baker on her back or bottom. Needless to say, it never happened.

In all the years I ate at home I cannot remember one meal at which there was not a Bell jar of hot red peppers and pickled onions sitting on the table next to the salt and pepper shakers. Every summer the house would reek and become a bottling factory with a huge pan of boiling water sitting on the stove containing bell jars and lids which were being sterilized in preparation for being filled with long red peppers and small peeled onions along with the spices which were used by my mother and which were unknown to me. I was not allowed in the kitchen for fear the large vat of water would spill on me and disfigure me for life if not kill me outright. But I did have the pleasure of smelling the exotic herbs which wafted through the steamy air. My mother would take the hot quart pickling jars out of the boiling water with tongs and then quickly fill them with the peppers and onion and the vinegary liquid and then as quickly seal them before they could be contaminated by the bacteria in the air. This was repeated over and over again until I thought my poor mother would faint from the heat. She would be standing in the kitchen swathed in the steamy air in a full house dress and a pair of slippers with a bandana around her head to keep the perspiration and hair out of the bottles while she labored unceasingly in the hot summer days. Then there was piccalilli and tomato relish to be made and bottled as well as the summer vegetables. Not everything was good as far as I was concerned. Every year mother put up green beans and sweet corn. The green beans when they were opened were tasteless and stringy and to me almost uneatable. Their only saving grace was that they were green. The sweet corn was absolutely terrible. The color of the corn faded and the corn lost all its sweetness and became almost exclusively some sort of starchy carbohydrate that was tough and unidentifiable. There were other successes and failures, but my father and I ate what was put before us, sometimes with great pleasure and at other times with actual distaste.

The point is that all of this, the bakery, even my mother canning vegetables, played a major role in my life. All of the experiences; the tastes, the smells, the personal contacts and the life in the inner city gave me things that I would take with me all my life. I couldn't help but wonder what experiences Jeff Macomber had had. What I felt did not make me a better man than any other man. What I had experienced was unique to me and influenced my life. What experiences did Jeff Macomber have that were unique to him and had shaped his life? That was the question I could not get answered. We all have events that are important to us and make up a large part of our lives. I knew those that had influenced me. What was behind the man who became Jeff Macomber? Would I ever find out? Perhaps not. But, I determined that I would do whatever I could to find out.

Our short vacation was a pleasure for both Marge and me. We had enough to do to keep us busy and to sharpen our senses.

Chapter XV

Jack came to the house with the complete dossier on Mrs. Desrosiers. It seems that her husband and his predecessor had had her checked out thoroughly and there wasn't much about her that wasn't known. How Jack got the information was beyond me, but he most certainly had it.

"She married her first husband when she was in her late teens. From what is contained here, it seems that she was never a beautiful woman. We can see that in her now. She handles herself well, but beauty is not her great claim to fame and fortune. Her son was born of that marriage, which, as far as the researchers can determine, was a happy one. Her husband was a salesman and real estate hustler. He made a small fortune considering what he was doing. He walked a fine line between being legal and being crooked. Then he had a massive heart attack that took him away in one day. She inherited the whole works."

"So, she did very well," I said. "How long were they married?"

"Ten years, ten deliriously happy years in which he worked himself to death. Not for her, I'm sure, but for himself. I know the type. I've met hundreds of them. They begin making money. Then they get greedy and the desire for money takes over their lives. His income was in six figures for at least ten years. He invested heavily in real estate, so when he went he left her a rich woman by Fall River standards. She was only in her late twenties at the time. And, as we say in the financial world, she had the risk capital she needed to widen her horizons. She began investing in real estate herself and from what I can determine, did very well. The housing market in the city was in a slump and she had the capital to invest. She picked up quite a few properties at heavily discounted prices. In the meantime she became the mistress of one of the most successful businessmen in the city. He was married, but she made no demands on him to marry or leave his wife. He did support her, though, in grand style with a house in the city, one on the Cape and a condo in Florida. Why she needed to be supported is open to question, but support her he did. He was with her until his wife finally threatened to divorce him if he kept seeing her. That threat was sufficient to make him suddenly lose interest in our lady. According to my sources, a divorce would have cost him in the vicinity of ten million dollars in cash and property."

"Did she end up with the properties he bought for her?" Marge asked.

"Absolutely. That was part of the deal she made for her silence. She wasn't about to let him off the hook without receiving more than adequate compensation. She had her hooks into him and she handled him in a highly professional style. Make no mistake about this lady, she is very good."

"The way you are describing her she must have been very good, Jack," I said half joking with my double entendre.

"I don't think Father Sousa at Sacred heart would describe her in quite that way," Marge said.

We met Jack that night at my house for dinner. Marge had prepared a beef stew with wild mushrooms that had been her specialty when her husband was alive and she served dinner for a number of guests. It was delicious with a freshly baked baguette that we formed using Italian bread dough that I kept in my freezer. The dough came from a bakery in Providence and I bought it by the pound for just such an occasion. It was Jack's kind of dish and he made short work of it that evening. Along with a couple of bottles of his favorite beer and two profiteroles with ice cream and chocolate sauce he was a happy man.

"Well, she is a hell of a woman. Marrying her was like sailing into the Bermuda Triangle. Our attorney didn't have a chance. This is her third marriage. The poor jerk was way over his head. She began her life sleeping around and learning her trade. You'll have to excuse me on this Marge, but there is no other way to tell it. She learned to use men at an early age."

"How did you find this out so fast?" Marge asked.

"Oh, she has been checked out any number of times by her previous husbands and other men and women. There isn't much that happens today that isn't to be found on some computer somewhere, unfortunately. In this case it works in our favor."

"I'm sure we have nothing in our backgrounds that would be embarrassing, have we gentlemen?" Marge asked with a smile.

"Well this isn't what I would call embarrassing. It is downright bad. Her first husband was a hustler. When he died he left her with the tools to move ahead financially. Then she became a mistress and that worked well."

He waited for this to sink in. As usual his hands took on a life of their own. That was his most characteristic idiosyncrasy. When he began to talk, his hands began to move as if he were doing a hula dance or some such thing. I once heard an actress say that when she was confused by a role, she would dance through it without words. The dancing made her look inside herself to find her character. I was reminded of that when I watched Jack. His hands were extra large even for a big man and his fingers were long and thin, so the effect was dramatic as his hands waved through the air around him going their own way. Normally a quiet man, Jack became demonstrative only when something was very important to him.

"Well, let's call it what it is. She was very good in bed. The word is that she was not a beautiful woman. She used her wiles to work her way into men's good graces or into their pants, not meaning to offend Marge. But that is exactly what she did. She has the gift of charm and of making men feel wanted and needed. That's what they tell me anyway. I know that when we go to meet her, there is no way in a thousand years that I go alone. Before I walk into that room to meet her, I am sure she will know the contents of my portfolio better than I do. By this time, of course, you realize that it became more and more difficult to find men. For one thing she had more money than the men she was chasing. It isn't easy finding a man who has more money than you do when you have amassed a considerable fortune. Added to that was the fact that she was a woman brought up in Fall River by a poor family and her tastes had never developed. She liked the glitter and she would have liked to have been flashy, but that didn't fit her needs. So from the time our businessman dumped her until her second marriage was a difficult time for her."

"You sound like you sympathize with her, Jack. I see her as the worst of all possible women. She certainly doesn't fit our idea of a successful woman today. We are seeing women emerge for the first time in our lifetimes and they certainly aren't doing it by selling themselves. They are using their education and their skills to make a place for themselves in our society, not using the bedroom to get there," Marge said, and she was very serious.

"She came from a different world, I think," I added. "She is the product of an immigrant family with very low aspirations for their women. I imagine that as a little girl she was trained to take her place in the long line of wives who bore their husbands offspring. Those offspring in the Azores were bred to become workers and to aid the family as they scraped a living out of the land. When they came to this country they did the same only instead of working the land, they took jobs in the factories or anywhere else they could work and brought their money home to their families. Schooling was not part of the overall picture. I ran into it time after time in the schools. Smart boys might be given the option of going on in school, even to college, after they turned sixteen, but rarely was a girl from an immigrant family given that option. It wasn't even considered. Girls were meant to get a job and help the family before they got married themselves. It was senseless for me as a teacher to argue with a parent that if the girl stayed in school and got a profession, she would be far better off and lead a better life. Fathers didn't listen to that argument. Their concern was for the immediate welfare of the family. A pay, no matter how small, helped put food on the table or helped pay a mortgage. When the girl was old enough, it was understood that she would set out on her own and get married, but until then she was a contributing member of the family. If other girls were taken out of school, there was no possibility of one girl being privileged to stay in school."

This was a long speech for me but I thought it had to be made to make us all understand where the attorney's wife was coming from.

"So what you are saying is that she took her training to be a wife and mother and care giver and refined it so that she became a vixen, a woman who would live and thrive off men," Marge said.

"I suppose that's as good a way of describing it as any. She was trained to satisfy men and anticipate their needs so that they felt like they were kings of their homes. I have seen the crudest and ugliest women suddenly turn into gentle loving wives in the presence of their husbands. But what is not imagined by people outside of the Portuguese culture is that for all that outward pose of subservience and submission to their husbands, it is Portuguese wives who are dominant in their households. I am sure it was the same way with our lovely bride."

"Well, Noah it seems you have given this some thought," Marge said.

"Not really. I grew up with it and it was all around me. I often wondered if I had had a sister whether she would have been allowed to finish school or not. Remember I had a loving father and mother but that does not mean that they could overcome their cultural heritage. I had a friend when I was a boy who ran away from home so that he could go to school. He ran away when he was sixteen years old. I met him years later in Boston. He was a professor at Tufts University in Medford. He had gone to Washington, D.C. where he drove cab for years while he worked his way through high school, George Washington University where he earned his B.A. and Georgetown where he earned his doctorate. He was a fabulous success story, but unfortunately he was one out of a hundred thousand. There aren't many like him, and I am sure he paid a heavy price psychologically for his personal victory. So, I think Mrs. Desrosiers probably took the only route open to her in her bid to make something of herself. I don't condone what she did, but I certainly understand why she took the route she did."

"She married again, didn't she Jack?" Marge asked.

"Yes she married an older man. In fact, he was a doctor. One of the doctors who took care of my mother as she approached death. I was surprised when I saw his name on the report. He always struck me as very level-headed. At any rate, by the time he married Mrs. Desrosiers he was in his seventies and she was in her fifties. She had become a successful business woman. She was mainly into real estate and had amassed a considerable fortune. He was a wealthy man who had invested heavily in nursing homes along with his colleagues. So by the time she married him, he was well on his way to becoming a millionaire. He was close with his money though and strict about its use. He married her, but she didn't have the run of his bank book.

"That must have gone against the grain'" Marge said.

I had the distinct impression that Marge was warming to the subject. What Mrs. Desrosiers had done was completely against everything she stood for. She had been raised to the same end probably as Mrs. Desrosiers, that is, caring for a home and raising children and taking care of her husband, but she approached it from a different direction. She was a good religious girl who had been raised and trained to be honest and not to be manipulative. However, she didn't have the same stresses as Mrs. Desrosiers had had in her life. Like many women of her age and social class, she saw manipulative women as both attractive in that they did things that most women would never do and, at the same time, as deserving of whatever evil fate befell them. I could see her fascination growing as she listened to Jack.

"Who knows? One of the skills of this woman is that she never discusses her problems outside of her home. Whatever went on between her and her husband was never known. The one thing that happened was that he became very ill. He was incapacitated for at least seven years and during that time she took care of him or had him cared for in her home. According to the investigators, on more than one occasion, she was loyal to him and stuck by him in his illness," Jack said and waited for a response form Marge.

"That is amazing. Do you mean to tell me that this conniving, intriguing and manipulative woman actually nursed her husband while he was incapacitated? I don't believe that kind of woman would do so."

"Well, she did. She cared for him for a number of years all by herself and then when she was too physically tired to continue, she hired round the clock nurses to tend him. At the beginning he was alert, but as time went on, she could easily have put him in one of his own nursing homes at no cost and had him cared for there," Jack laughed and continued, "That upsets our view of her doesn't it? This is a woman who would be party to stealing her husband's safe with close to a million dollars in cash in it but would not put her husband in a nursing home."

Marge said, "I find it hard to believe. She must have had some ulterior motive."

"I don't. I know it seems preposterous, but it seems to me that it is part of her culture that she would not put her husband in a nursing home unless she absolutely could do nothing else. I remember when my father was ill, my mother would not allow even a mention of a home for my dad. She suffered terribly taking care of him, but she would not even consider it.

When she became ill, I felt I had no choice but to find her a place where she could get decent care. There was no way that I could care for her. The best I could do was to visit her every day. Even then, knowing I couldn't care for her and I certainly couldn't afford around the clock care, I still suffered terrible guilt. We all have this kind of thing in our backgrounds. Young women who feel they have to be faithful to abusive husbands because they are supposed parents of drug abusers who stand by their children no matter what. So, maybe Mrs. Desrosiers was in the same category, a woman who was caught in her background and acted accordingly."

"Oh I think that is absolutely an oversimplification in this case, Noah," Marge said with conviction.

Jack laughed and rose from his chair and went to my freezer for a container of Ben and Jerry's ice cream. He looked at me as if to get my nod of approval and then spooned out most of the container into a soup bowl and came back to sit at the kitchen table where we were seated. He began to eat it by the teaspoonful very slowly, savoring each small mouthful. He was in no hurry and sat with his elbows on the table as if he were pondering some large question of major significance while he looked out of the kitchen windows at the inlet of the Westport River below.

"When he finally died it was a blessing to everyone concerned. He had had no quality of life for most of his last ten years. That life represented what he had fought against so long as a practicing physician. But, his death enriched his widow considerably. By that time I am pretty sure she had more money than he did, but she became a very rich widow when she buried him because he left no children."

"Aside from gaining from her marriages and her years as a mistress, she really couldn't be accused of wrongdoing, could she?" Marge added. "She just took advantage of what she was offered."

"And, from all that has been uncovered about her marriages, it seems they were happy . She was good to her husbands and there was never any problem with her relationship with them. There were no threats of divorce or periods of separation. No matter how good the investigators are or how thorough, no one from the outside can judge what goes on inside a house."

He finished his ice cream and rose from his chair to take the dish and spoon to the sink where he rinsed the dish and the spoon and placed them in the dishwasher.

Marge laughed and said, "That is just the point we are talking about, isn't it? Jack, why did you rinse out the dish rather than just leaving it on the table or in the sink? I think because you were trained to do that as a young man so you wouldn't think of any other way of doing it. Am I wrong?"

"You are a persistent lady, I'll say that for you. No, you are one hundred percent right. My father and I were both snackers, so my mother insisted that when we dirtied a plate, we rinse it and put it in the sink. We didn't have a dish washer in those days, but we never left a dirty dish in the kitchen, Mom wouldn't let us wash the dish ourselves because she didn't trust us, but we had to rinse it and make sure it was decently clean. It is a habit that has never left me."

"Isn't that just Noah's point about Mrs. Desrosiers? We don't put our early training behind us, ever."

"Maybe that's why she married her last husband. Who knows? Certainly she had more than enough money to live on very comfortably and she had more than sufficient to take care of her son. I estimate from what I have seen in the reports and what I can put together, that she was worth well over three million dollars. She married this man in spite of the fact that she knew he was an alcoholic with a reputation all over the City of Fall River and New Bedford for being a nasty drunk. He has been barred from more clubs and restaurants for his behavior than anyone of any professional background in the area. So why would she marry him? I, for one, have no idea."

"Maybe we'll discover that when we meet with her," I said. "In the meantime we have to go on the presumption that she and her son stole the money. That sounds like it goes against the grain of what we have been discussing here."

"Well, I'll tell you gentlemen, for two old men who are supposed to be sitting on their back porches rocking away their afternoons, you certainly have busy lives. You wear me out trying to keep up with you."

Chapter XVI

Nothing of any importance seemed to be coming out of the journals. I wanted to browse through them quickly to see if there was anything of note that would give us some clues as to what we were looking for; some indication of what had happened to Jeff Macomber in that study on that busy afternoon. But Marge had become fascinated by the man who had written them and would have no part of my breaking her thorough reading.

"What I am finding here is a very methodical man who approaches his life and work in very small terms. He is not a big picture guy like my husband was and you are, Noah. He has a little picky mind that we might call anal, but he is much more than that. He is a borer who deals with a problem and keeps thinking about it until he finds a solution that is acceptable to him. Just follow these entries that span about four days."

TUESDAY
...AMY INSISTS ON CLEANING THE PAINTING HANGING IN THE HALLWAY. I THINK IT IS SILLY TO GO THROUGH THE BOTHER. IT HAS NO REAL VALUE. IT IS A STILL LIFE OF SOME ORANGES AND STRAWBERRIES AND IT HAS GOTTEN OLD AND LIKE MOST OF US WRINKLED AND SOILED WITH TIME...

WEDNESDAY
...NO POINT ARGUING WITH AMY ABOUT THE PAINTING. I HAVE CONTACTED AN ART DEALER WHO HAS A MAN WHO DOES RESTORATIONS FOR HIM. WILL MEET WITH HIM FRIDAY MORNING...

SATURDAY

...THE RESTORER WAS HERE AND I DOUBT HE KNOWS MUCH MORE THAN I DO ABOUT RESTORING PAINTINGS. BUT AMY INSISTS. HE WILL REMOVE THE PAINTING AND HAVE IT BACK IN A MONTH HE SAYS...

SUNDAY

...I HAVE BEEN READING ABOUT THE TREATMENT OF OLD PAINTINGS AND THE PROCESS FOR CLEANING THEM. IT IS FASCINATING. IT IS A MATTER OF CHOOSING THE PROPER SOLVENTS SO THAT THE ORIGINAL OIL IS NOT DAMAGED...

MONDAY

...IT WOULD SEEM A MONTH IS HARDLY ENOUGH TIME TO CLEAN A PAINTING. THE MAN WHO HAS IT IS A FOOL. I HAVE CONTACTED THE DEALER AND REQUESTED THAT IT BE RETURNED. HOPEFULY HE HASN'T BEGUN WORK ON IT...

THURSDAY

...I HAVE THE PAINTING BACK IN MY POSSESSION. I HAVE REMOVED THE FRAME AND TAKEN SOME SMALL SCRAPINGS OFF THE EDGE OF THE PAINTING AND HAVE SENT THEM TO ONE OF MY LABS TO BE ANALYSED AND TO DETERMINE WHAT SOLVENTS WOULD BE BEST USED FOR CLEANING. FASCINATING...

"About a month later he picks up the subject again in his journal. I find this all very interesting because it sheds light on the kind of man we are working with here. He is a solitary genius in many ways. He explores, reads and studies and takes on a task that most of us would find too difficult to bother with."

TUESDAY

...FINALLY HAVE THE SOLVENTS TO CLEAN THE PAINTING. I HAVE SPENT QUITE A BIT OF TIME ON THE TELEPHONE TALKING TO SUPPOSEDLY THE BEST IN THE

BUSINESS. HE HAS GIVEN ME THE METHOD TO USE AND HAS SENT ME A SET OF TOOLS THAT I WILL HAVE AT MY DISPOSAL. THE NUMBER OF ITEMS IN THE KIT IS DAUNTING. THERE MUST BE THIRTY BRUSHES AND I AM TRYING TO FIGURE OUT WHAT THEY ARE USED FOR. RIGHT NOW I AM TRYING TO GET USED TO THE MAGNIFYING GOGGLES. THEY MADE ME DIZZY WHEN I FIRST PUT THEM ON. BUT I AM GETTING USED TO THEM GRADUALLY. DR. MORIN, THE EXPERT IN PARIS, SAYS THAT THE PAINTING SHOULD TAKE SIX MONTHS IF I INTEND TO DO IT CORRECTLY. I DON'T KNOW IF I AM UP TO IT...

FRIDAY
...WORKED ON A SMALL SECTION OF THE PAINTING. DIDN'T KNOW THE MAN DID SO MUCH IN INK UNDER THE OILS, BUT THERE IT IS. I AM WORKING ON THE EDGES AND SO FAR THINGS SEEM TO BE GOING FAIRLY WELL. THE FIRST THING IS TO REMOVE SOME OF THE SURFACE DIRT. I AM USING A SOLUTION ONE OF THE CHEMISTS MADE FOR ME AND IT IS WORKING PRETTY WELL. HAVE TO DO A HALF INCH SQUARE AT A TIME. IT IS PAINSTAKING WORK. IF I HAD STARTED THIS EARLIER I MAY HAVE MADE A CAREER OF IT. IT IS COMING, THOUGH, AND I FEEL PRETTY GOOD ABOUT IT. AFTER THE FIRST LAYER OF PLAIN DIRT, I'LL HAVE TO START WORKING ON THE OILS THEMSELVES...

Marge stood then and closed the journal. "Amazing isn't it? Here is this very rich man who is willing to learn something completely new and to take his valuable time to work at it. I would love to have met him. He must have been quite a man."

"I think I would have been jealous of him to tell the truth. You would have been gawking at him in admiration I suspect. It is certainly revealing. Reading his words you get to feel as though you know the man. But, aside from being interesting, we haven't uncovered anything that would lead us to believe that he would have harmed Jeff Macomber."

"If it is in the journals it will come out," Marge said. "In the meantime I am eager to know how he made out with the painting."

Chapter XVII

Jack had compiled his dossier on Mrs. Desrosiers and was ready for a meeting, but first he had to visit Attorney Desrosiers so that he could set out what he was proposing for a solution to his problem. He approached the meeting with trepidation because he knew that what he was proposing wouldn't go down well with the attorney. Per usual in this kind of thing having to do with money, I went along only for the ride.

When we arrived at Attorney Desrosiers' office, we were met by an alarming sight. He was drunk and in desperate shape. His clothes were rumpled and dirty looking like he hadn't changed them in days. His shirt was half out of his pants and there was some sort of girdle showing through under his shirt. He was a big man with a big girt and like a bald man trying to hide his baldness by wearing a cheap toupee, so it was senseless for Mr. Desrosiers to be wearing a girdle to hide the size of his stomach.

One glance told us that he was in despair. He had a wild, frightened look in his eyes as if he had just awakened from a nightmare. He was visibly shaken and, as we entered his office, I was only thankful that he did not have a gun. He looked like he would have used it. Jack was calm. He walked to the desk where the attorney was sitting and poured a shot in a tumbler that he had on his desktop.

"Easy, now. Just take a few sips of this. Don't gulp it; just sip it very slowly." he said modulating his voice so that it was just above a whisper. "We're going to take care of you. Now come over here to the couch and lie down. Relax, everything is going to be fine. Okay, just sit quietly now and relax."

"I can't move. I can't move. I can't move," he cried louder and louder each time.

I realized that he literally couldn't pull himself out of the chair to stand and walk. Jack immediately walked around the desk and took him by one arm and tried to pull him out of the chair. He couldn't manage it by himself, so I took the other arm and we got the man to his feet. He was a dead weight. It wasn't easy to move him to the other side of the room and to the couch. He had wet himself, so the combination of the smell of liquor and urine was revolting. It was hard to feel sympathy for him at that moment. I wondered why we should have to deal with it. My instinct was to call an ambulance and to ship him off to the hospital or a rehab center and let professionals deal with the problem.

He sat on the couch and began sobbing. It was as if he had been holding everything in and suddenly he was melting right before our eyes. He lifted his hands to his jowls and said over and over again, "They will kill me."

His body was shaking with fear. He was sobbing uncontrollably and I went to the washroom attached to his office to get a towel so he could soak up some of the tears that were running down his face. His face was so wrinkled that it became drenched in no time. The tears were dripping off his cheeks and jowls and falling on the rug in front of the couch. It was not a pretty sight.

Jack dropped his quiet approach and in a little stronger voice said, "My God man. Pull yourself together."

That had no effect and seemed instead to increase the sobbing and the repetitions, "They are going to kill me. They are going to kill me."

He kept that up for about an hour and then gradually began to slow down his diatribe until he was barely audible and then gradually he sank back on the couch and slipped off to sleep.

I turned to Jack and asked, "What do we do now?"

Jack moved to the chair in front of the desk. He sat with an exhausted groan and stretched out his long legs. He was a tall man with an angular slim body so that when he moved he reminded me of a puppet hanging on a string, moving in all directions at once. In this case, he truly seemed to unwind. For the first time since I had known him, he looked his age. He was tired and I sensed that he was in anguish looking at this man lying on the couch looking like he had been in an automobile accident or run a marathon with his business clothes on.

"What do we do now?" I asked again.

"I have no idea what to do. He has obviously been drinking for quite some time. If we leave him here, he is liable to have a heart attack or a stroke. On the other hand there is no way that we are going to move him now. If we call for an ambulance, they may very well refuse to treat him. They do not treat alcoholics at the hospital. They will want to put him in a rehab center to dry him out under supervision. The problem is they won't take him in without his request or a family member's application for admittance. Bloody mess we've got here."

"So, what do we do?" I asked and I was afraid of the answer I was sure I was going to hear.

"Well, I don't know what to say. We know we can't leave him in this condition. I think we have to keep watch over him to make sure he doesn't go into some kind of a fit or something. Let him sleep it off. He probably won't sleep too long. I'm sure his stomach is a mess and is probably growling for food now. What do you think?"

Jack said this and stretched his legs out in front of him to their full length. I was wondering if he was preparing to go to sleep himself. I was more worried about him than the drunken man on the couch. I had never seen him looking so defeated and despondent in all the time I had known him.

"I think you are right," I said. "I'll call Marge and tell her what we have run into. Then we can stay here until he comes out of this sleep. Are you hungry?"

"Starved," he said. "Absolutely starved."

"Okay, I'll go to KFC for a bucket of chicken and some biscuits and some drinks. That should hold us for at least a few hours. Hopefully he'll wake up by then. In the meantime you get some rest. You look beat. I'll run out and be back in three quarters of an hour at the latest."

When I returned Jack was sitting in the chair in the same position in which I had left him. He was dozing off. I knew he couldn't sleep for very long in the position he was in, but at least he was getting a little rest. I looked at him very closely and I was pleased to see that the color was returning to his face and hands. He had been almost gray when I left, and it had caused me some concern. I have always linked an ashen complexion with heart problems and Jack, although he wasn't ashen, was not himself. Seeing him sitting there snoring slightly with the color coming back to his face gave me heart. Desrosiers was breathing heavily and snoring on the couch. I was surprised that he hadn't awakened himself.

I called Marge to tell her what was going on and then took a look around the office hoping that I could find something for Desrosiers to wear other than soiled clothes. He had been staying in his office overnight, and I had hopes of finding some clean clothes somewhere in the small confines of the office and the adjoining bathroom. As it turned out, the bathroom contained a shower stall and I thought that would come in handy to get the man cleaned up when he came out of his drunken stupor. In a small closet I did find some clothes including a change of underwear which was a Godsend as far as I was concerned. I had visions, probably too optimistic, of getting the attorney to take a shower and to change his clothes.

With both men sleeping I had nothing to do but to sit at the attorney's desk and wait for someone to wake. I opened a window to get some fresh air in the room and then sat at his desk and waited patiently for Jack to awaken. I found myself dozing off as well, and I began to wonder if there was something in the room which would cause us to go to sleep. Then I decided that the thing that was in the room was three old men who were tired. One was drunk. The other two had gone through an emotional upheaval of sorts and were mentally exhausted.

Jack woke in a half hour or so and immediately looked for food. The bucket of Kentucky Fried Chicken was on the desk He opened it and dug right in. He picked up a napkin and since we had no plates of any kind, used the napkin to hold the chicken that he started to eat almost immediately. Jack was hungry and when he was hungry he had no time for words. He didn't gorge his food or eat quickly. He ate slowly and deliberately, but he concentrated his full attention on his food and had no time for anything else. From time to time he stopped to eat a potato wedge which he had spread out on a number of napkins and sprinkled with salt. Then he would take a sip of soda that I had brought in the largest container they had. I joined Jack in eating several pieces myself, but it didn't take long before I could feel heart burn and I decided that the great taste of the chicken was not worth the after effects.

It was some time before Jack finished and sat back to let his food digest. He finally rose and went to the bathroom to wash his hands and to rinse his face. When he returned his color was back to normal. I felt relieved.

"Well, this is a mess. He seems to be sleeping well," he said.

"I found some clothes and there is a shower in the bathroom so maybe we can get him to clean up and get some food into him. He certainly is a mess."

I said this and we both looked at the attorney who was sprawled out on the couch. He hadn't improved in appearance. The perspiration was actually running from his forehead. There were huge sweat blotches on his shirt. It was difficult to imagine anyone married to him and respecting him in his present condition.

With the window open the sounds of the traffic and the voices below came up to us. Living in the country, I had forgotten how noisy the city can be. An ambulance rushed by and the attorney turned slightly but didn't come fully awake. In a short time he was back asleep. Jack and I sat looking at each other wondering how long we were going to be there.

It was fully two hours before he finally woke. It took a few minutes for him to become acclimated to his location. Without thinking, we had neglected to turn on the lights. When he became aware of us, he cringed in fear, but Jack spoke to him and he seemed to recognize Jack's voice and lost his fear. I turned on the lamp on his desk and a lamp in the corner of the room which shed enough light, so that he could see without being hurt by the glare. He sat up and put his hands to his face in despair. He wasn't fully sober, but at least he had his senses. He looked around. Jack knew he was looking for something to drink and he said, "No booze now. You have to pull yourself together. Can you stand? Take your time. Noah found some clothes. I want you to go into the shower when you think you're able and clean up. We have a fresh change of clothes for you."

He said this in a matter of fact way that left no room for discussion. He wasn't asking him to shower, he was telling him and the attorney recognized it and didn't have an answer. Had he said one word in way of argument I think Jack would have left the office. He was in no mood for any problems at that point nor was I. In my view the man was hardly worth worrying about. No matter what we did that night for him, it was evident that it would have no lasting effect. He needed treatment and he needed it badly, but by professionals and under medical supervision. I had seen our neighbor, Joan, undergo treatment. She had changed her life after many years of alcohol abuse. I knew it was possible, not easy, but possible. The attorney would have to want to go through the difficult times of rehabilitation. From the looks of Mr. Desrosiers at that moment, I felt it would be a monumental job if he chose to go in that direction.

The chance that Jack was going to have the opportunity to have a serious discussion with him at that time was very slim. Our job was simply to get him on his feet, cleaned up and sober. There really wasn't much point in bringing up the settlement that Jack was proposing to offer his wife.

It took some time before we managed to get the man on his feet, undressed and into the shower. He almost fell several times but fortunately managed to hang on and finish the job of washing. He sobered up fairly quickly in the shower but even after he emerged from the bathroom with his clean trousers and shirt on, he looked like a wreck. He was too weak to bend to put his socks on. I did that for him, kneeling on the floor in front of him, while he sat on the couch. I couldn't help but wonder how many times his wife had been put in that humiliating position. With each passing moment, I felt more and more sympathy for her and more antipathy for the attorney.

While he was showering, Jack scoured the office for hidden bottles of liquor. He found none. The question in my mind was what were we going to do with him?

I asked Jack exactly that question.

"Well, I would say we get him dressed and out of here and see if we can get some food into him and take him wherever he wants to go. If he wants to go home, then we will take him home or he can stay here. But, one thing I do know is that he is on his own once we feed him."

We did exactly that when he was finally dressed. We ended up at a diner where he managed to force down some meat loaf and mashed potatoes that looked absolutely revolting to me. Even Jack passed on it and had a cup of coffee and a grilled corn muffin. I passed in favor of a decaf since I had no intention of staying up the rest of the night if I could help it. He was speechless from the time we left his office to the time we finally brought him back.

When he finally did speak it was in a deep rumbling voice that resonated throughout the office. It was his professional voice that he had obviously worked on over the years.

Jack wasn't interested in his affectations at that point in time. We were both tired and had had enough.

"We've got you here safe and sound. You really should check yourself into a rehab somewhere and dry out, but that is for you to decide. In the meantime we are going to go home. If you are stupid enough in your condition to get some booze and to get potted again, that's your problem. I came here to talk about a proposal I want to make to your wife, but that is going to have to wait. Right now, Noah and I are going home before we both fall over with fatigue. I'll be in touch."

Attorney Desrosiers said, "Tell me about the proposal right now."

"You are in no condition to hear it," Jack said and without any hesitation took the Kentucky Fried Chicken bucket containing the remaining chicken and moved toward the door. "I'll be in touch."

We both breathed a sigh of relief when we reached my car and I was very happy to be on my way home.

The next morning, for the first time in many years, I found myself sleeping until after ten o'clock. Even the smell of coffee brewing did not wake me up. When I finally did wake I felt like I was carrying a weight on my brain. My mind was foggy and my body wasn't responding to my efforts to get out of bed. It was a sensation that was new to me. It was a bit frightening until I finally managed to swing my legs out of bed and plant them on the floor. Marge heard me and shouted up the stairs asking if I was all right. I answered, put on a light robe and made my way down the stairs. I wondered for a moment what our friend the attorney must be feeling this morning assuming that he hadn't found a cache of liquor or gone out for a bottle.

Marge had coffee ready and I sat at the kitchen counter where I could get a view of the sailboats in the water below. It was a lovely morning with some large cumulus clouds blocking the sun from time to time as they billowed across the bright blue sky. But the sun shone through and, even in my kitchen, I could feel its heat.

I explained fully what we had been through the night before in Attorney Desrosiers' office. It had been an exhausting process. The terrible influence of alcohol on the man was new to us. He had lost all his dignity. No one wants to be witness to such a complete collapse of another person.

"I think I have had enough of our friend the attorney for a while. As far as I am concerned at this moment, I would not even bother pursuing this whole affair. Let his wife keep the money however she obtained it as far as I am concerned. What difference does it make?" I said and I know I sounded frustrated. "The man is in a shambles and I am sure he has put his wife through hell. We haven't met her, but from what Jack told us the other day, I don't think that she deserves any bad treatment from him. My kids back in seventh grade would characterize him as a jerk. I do the same."

The kitchen door suddenly burst open and Jack rushed into the room. "He's dead," he blurted out. "I can't believe it. He's dead."

Jack stood at least six foot three and at that moment with his wild stare and blush red face, he looked dangerous. Marge jumped out of her chair and grasped me by the shoulders. She was actually frightened not so much by Jack I think, but waiting for him to tell us who was dead.

"Who's dead?" I asked.

"The police just called Patrick to tell him that they found him. One of the secretaries in the office found him and called the police."

"Who?" I asked again.

"Attorney Desrosiers, of course," Jack said and he looked for a moment like he was losing his balance. I got up and held him by the arm and asked him to sit down for a moment before he continued.

"Settle down Jack. You are much too excited. Calm down before you say another word. Let Marge get you something to eat."

She went to the refrigerator and took out a bran muffin that was left over from her own breakfast and she quickly sliced it and put it in the toaster oven. Then she poured Jack a glass of orange juice and placed that on the table in front of him. He quieted down for a moment when he picked up the glass and took a sip. He seemed to settle down then and looked at the toaster oven as if he wanted the muffin to jump out and land in front of him. Marge caught the look and rose to get him the muffin and a dab of raspberry jam which she knew he liked.

He ate slowly and silently, bit by bit. He had the habit of tearing little pieces off the muffin which he held in his left hand and then dipping the broken pieces into the jam rather than spreading the jam on the muffin. When it came to eating habits, he rarely changed.

Finally he said, "They found the attorney dead in his office. He had been shot several times. It is murder from the looks of it. Patrick is on his way now and he will call us when he gets back."

"Had he been drinking?" I asked.

"We won't know that until Patrick calls us. I told him to call us as soon as he has something. I would think we'd hear from him this afternoon."

The fact that Desrosiers was dead came as a shock to me. I had just been considering washing my hands of the whole messy affair when Jack appeared to tell us that he was dead. Now I was awash in guilt. I had to ask myself whether I disliked the man or the fact that I had seen him drunk and in terrible shape. I had to admit that it was the latter. I was absolutely repelled by the sight of the man who had acted and looked so dreadfully the night before. Now he was dead and I knew he was better off than continuing to live in the way he had been living.

Jack knew what I was thinking. He had been quiet and he seemed to have pulled himself together.

"Regardless of how we felt about him personally, no one deserves to have his life snuffed out by a killer. He certainly doesn't deserve to be shot to death. No one deserves that. No one has the right to take someone else's life. But in the meantime, let's wait to see what Patrick has for us."

It was later in the afternoon just as we were thinking about dinner that Patrick called and said he would see us at the house at 5:00 when he got home. Even though I lived across the road from Nelly and Patrick, I hadn't seen much of them since Jack and I started on the Macomber case. I missed both of them and Peggy who spent more time with her grandchild as each passing day went by. The baby was consuming all of their time and both Peggy and Nelly rarely did anything else but take care of her. Marge saw more of both of them than I did and was taken with the little girl, I think, as much as they were.

We saw Patrick's car pull into the drive at about 5:10 and Jack gave him 20 minutes before he called. Patrick asked us to come to the back porch so that we wouldn't wake the baby, and that he would be waiting for us.

We arrived a few minutes later to find him sitting on the porch with Peggy. There was a platter containing fruit of different kinds and a plate of cheese and crackers with Jack in mind I am sure. There was also a pitcher of lemonade and Jack and I settled into the swinging porch settee while Marge went into the house to talk to Nelly and Peggy.

"Well," Patrick began, "He was shot from very close quarters. I would have to guess that the killer wasn't more than two feet away from him. Whoever it was came up from behind him and shot him in the temple and then again in the back of the head or vice versa. It is hard to tell which shot was made first, but I am sure that the coroner will be able to tell us."

"So, there is no question that it is murder, then?" Jack asked.

"No, no question at all. As best as we can figure, he was sitting at his desk and the killer came up from behind him. He must have known the person or he wouldn't have allowed him or her to have the run of the room. It was a small caliber pistol that was used, from what we can guess. The wound is clean and the cranium is whole."

"Was he sober?" I asked.

"I can't say. The room smelled of liquor and there was an empty fifth in his bottom drawer. He certainly stunk and his clothes were a mess. The coroner will tell us definitely after he checks the contents of his stomach."

We explained that we had been with Desrosiers the night before, and we told Patrick all about waiting for him to sleep for him to become partially sober and taking him out to eat. We also told him that he had been frightened that someone was going to kill him.

"Did he tell you why he thought someone would attempt to kill him?" Patrick asked.

"No," Jack said. "We thought he was just drunk and being paranoid. We had no way of knowing whether there was an actual threat of any kind. Maybe there was. He just kept repeating over and over again when we first got there something like 'they are going to kill me.' He was so drunk that he couldn't get out of the chair, and he had soiled himself. He was a mess, so we just assumed he was delusional. Bad mistake on our part, obviously."

"We had no choice. He wouldn't even listen to entering a rehab, and I knew that the minute we left him that he would begin looking for booze again. He was disgusting and I think we did pretty well in getting him cleaned up and getting some food into him. We couldn't even talk to him, he was so bad."

"When you left did you lock up behind you?" Patrick asked.

Jack answered, "We didn't lock up. His office is down the hallway from the elevator so I don't know how you would lock it. The only thing would have been to lock up his office directly, but that would have been unlikely. We would never have considered locking him into his office."

I added, "We were both pretty much exhausted mentally and physically when we left him. I, personally, just wanted to get out of there and get home. It wasn't a pleasant experience to say the least."

"What was your connection to him?" Patrick asked.

"I don't think you want to hear it. It had to do with some money that was missing from his office. We were trying to figure out some way to get it back. Now that he is dead it doesn't make a difference, does it?"

"Only if the loss of the money is directly related to what happened to him during the night," Patrick said. "I think it will probably turn out to be, so I think for the good of our pursuing the killer, you should tell me now."

"I think he is right," I said. "I can't imagine how it would not have some relevance or at least the odds are in favor of it."

Jack thought for a minute and then sat back with his hands behind his head and explained everything to Patrick. He was not judgmental, but he laid out the case pretty much as we knew it.

"I was going to try to make a deal with the Mrs. I was going to offer her half the estate including half the money in cash in the safe for a clean divorce with no legal hang-ups. She could have been free and clear with half of everything the guy owned in a month the way I figured it. This way, of course, she gets the whole thing unless he left a will," Jack said.

"Was there any indication that he was being threatened?"

"Well, when we got there he was so drunk we couldn't take him seriously," Jack said. He sat quietly for a moment sipping on his lemonade. "But he kept saying 'They are going to kill me.'" He said it over and over again. We just dismissed it as drunken paranoia, but who knows?"

"Did he mention any names?"

I answered, "No. He just kept repeating over and over again that "they" wanted to kill him, but he never said who "they" were."

"What time did you leave him?" Patrick asked.

"After midnight. He slept for about four hours, I would say, and then we had to get him cleaned up and dressed and then we went out to eat. So it was after midnight before we left him," I said.

"Were there any phone calls while you were in the office?" he asked.

Jack didn't hesitate to answer, "No. There was not one call in the time we were there and there were no secretaries on duty. Any calls would have come in directly I would guess, but I don't know how the phone system works in the office. There are a number of lawyers who share the suite of offices, so they must have some sort of system to record in-coming calls."

'Well, we have a murder on our hands and I am putting all my available resources on this one. Any ideas on where we should start?" Patrick asked.

"I would think the obvious place would be with the widow and her son. The attorney and his wife were on the verge of splitting up, so there was no love lost between them. Why she would do this or want it done is beyond me, but who knows," Jack said. "The whole thing is bizarre if you ask me."

"I would love to meet her and her son," I added. "She has to be quite a character."

"Same goes for me," Jack said.

"Well, okay. As soon as I set up an appointment with them, I'll call you. I see no reason why you can't take part in the interview. We'll do them separately of course. Let me set it up. In the meantime I would love to have the two of you work on this case with me. Renew old times. Nelly misses you too since she has been so busy with the baby."

We left him then and went back to my house where Marge and I had to put together a meal in a hurry since we had nothing prepared in advance. I fell back on one of my mother's quick dishes which was a frittata made with Portuguese chourico, potatoes, onions, green peppers, garlic and beaten eggs. Marge put some packaged corn biscuits in the oven and in no time at all we had a meal on the table that Jack would find reasonably filling and yet tasty. All the time we were working and preparing the meal and the table setting, Marge raved about the baby. I regretted then that we were too old to have any ourselves and that she had never been able to have one of her own. On any number of occasions she had said to me that had she the chance to do it over again, she would have adopted a child. Having had so many children as a teacher, it never occurred to me that I would have wanted to adopt, but, Marge realized better than any one else that we have to take what we have at hand and not live with regrets for things we never did.

Chapter XVIII

I was happy to get back to the Macomber house to get away from the Desrosiers case. Jack was embroiled in it, but I wanted only to meet with the wife and son if for nothing other than curiosity. What kind of people were they? I was getting a mixed message on her, but basically nothing on the son. Would she be capable of killing her husband or did her son do it under her orders or on his own accord? It was interesting, but I found the whole case difficult to deal with.

The Macomber study had become a comfortable respite for both Marge and me. She was fascinated by the man who had kept the journals and looked forward to reading his entries day by day. I found much of what he had to write very anal and far too detailed for me to find interesting.

WEDNESDAY

THE PEACE ROSE ON THE SIDE OF THE HOUSE NEXT TO THE CHIMNEY THAT EMMA PLANTED YEARS AGO IS STILL BLOOMING. THIS MORNING I WENT OUTSIDE AND SURE ENOUGH THERE IT WAS IN FULL BLOOM. YELLOW WITH JUST A TOUCH OF PINK IN A BIG BLOSSOM THAT MAKES IT SO BEAUTIFUL. THAT HAS TO BE TWENTY YEARS AGO AND I THINK WE PAID SOMETHING LIKE $5.00 FOR IT AT A ROADSIDE STAND. I CAN'T GET OVER IT. EMMA LOVED THAT ROSE BECAUSE IT WAS THE ONLY THING SHE EVER PLANTED THAT LIVED. AMY COULD GROW ANY PLANT SHE WANTED TO ON A ROCK, BUT POOR EMMA HAD A KNACK FOR KILLING

EVERYTHING SHE EVER PLANTED. I MISS HER MOST WHEN SOMETHING LIKE THIS REMINDS ME OF HER. SOME SILLY THING BRINGS HER TO MIND AND ALL OF HER FAILINGS. I USED TO SAY SHE WAS A SILLY THING, BUT SHE WASN'T ALWAYS THAT WAY. SHE BECAME SILLY ONLY WHEN I MADE ALL MY MONEY AND SHE FELT I DIDN'T NEED HER ANY MORE. BUT THE ROSE IS IN BLOOM RIGHT NOW. I SHOULD HAVE AMY TAKE A PICTURE OF IT SO THAT I CAN HAVE IT HERE ON MY DESK AS I WORK.

"Don't you find that charming?" Marge asked.

"I suppose. He certainly seems to have loved his wife." I said.

"Yes he does. It just seems to me that he expresses so much in so few words. None of it seems to have been contrived. He is writing from the heart," she said.

Evangelica came in at exactly that moment to clean the study. I thought she might have been in her early fifties. She had a little weight on her but she was still a handsome woman. She had the look of her mother and she exuded sensuality in the same way.

Marge said, "We won't be in your way, will we? If we are we can move to the desk."

We were working at the table. My chair sat close to Marge's so that we could read the pages together. I thought that was a very inefficient way to work, but Marge insisted on it. I still felt we could do the job just as well by reading and skipping pages. Most of what was recorded was pretty dull stuff about a man's everyday life.

Evangelica said, "Are those the books Mr. Goetzel wrote in every morning?"

"Yes they are," Marge answered.

"What does he talk about?" she asked.

"Oh just little things about what goes on in the house, how he feels about things, nothing very big and important."

Marge had caught an unexpected interest from Evangelica, and I thought that if she had anything to say that she might feel more comfortable talking to Marge, so I excused myself on the pretext that I had left something in my car and left the room. I happened to catch a glimpse of Jason doing some work in the shed outside the back entrance and I meandered over to him in the hope that we could talk.

He cut me short. "I don't want to seem rude," he said, "But I am mixing a spray for the rhododendrons and I don't want to make any mistakes in my measurements, so I really can't talk now. Maybe I'll take some time later. I am truly sorry."

He smiled and I knew there was no point in staying. I went back to the car and picked up a manila folder which I tucked under my arm and made my way back to the study. The women were talking when I entered and Marge gave me a surreptitious sign to leave again. I put the manila folder on the table and then left the room. Marge had moved to the leather chair in the far end of the room and Evangelica was continuing to dust and clean. I left immediately and found my way to the kitchen where I hoped to rustle up a cup of coffee. There was no one present so I found myself drifting outside and looking for the Peace rose that Mr. Goetzel had written about in his journal. I walked around the perimeter of the house until I came to the chimney that I associate with the fireplace and there, still growing, was the rose that had been planted at least forty years before. It was as Mr. Goetzel had described it and it was in bloom; a large cabbage style rose which had faded to white with little touches of pink and yellow faintly visible. Another bloom seemed to be ready to open and this was almost wholly in a bright yellow with pink along the edges of the petals that would be open in a day or two. I laughed to myself when I saw it and I felt like saying a word or two to Sam Goetzel to let him know that the plant was still alive.

I couldn't find anyone to talk to and decided to make my way back to the study in the hope that I wouldn't be disturbing Marge and Evangelica. When I did get back I found that Evangelica had left. I also found a smiling Marge.

"Very quickly, I'll tell you that the girl of twenty years ago was very much in love with Jeff Macomber," she began. "She is almost breathless when she talks about him."

"That's interesting. What makes you so sure?" I asked.

"Oh there is no question about it. The girl was head over heels in love with him. She does everything but sigh the minute she focuses in on him. Her eyes take on a misty look. No, she is in love with him still, although she insists that it was not reciprocal," Marge said.

140

"Can you be sure?"

"Absolutely. We used to use the word 'gaga' when I was a girl. She is gaga over him. She keeps saying that he always treated her like a gentleman and that makes me wonder. How many times can she say it? Is she trying to convince me that he was a gentleman. We've got to find a way to follow up on this."

She sat in the brown chair for a moment, deep in thought.

"Another thing has occurred to me that I think is interesting," she said. "We have been reading these journals for any number of days now and do you notice that not once does Mr. Goetzel refer to his son-in- law? Not once have I seen the name of Jeff Macomber in any of this other than the time he mentions Amy naming her azaleas. Doesn't it seem strange that Mr. Goetzel would have so little to say about the man? It is as if he doesn't exist. I wonder if we will see any mention of him at all here."

She looked to me waiting for an answer and I had nothing to say. I hadn't thought about the paucity of mention of Jeff Macomber. I hadn't thought about what it could mean. I wasn't sure what it might mean.

"I'm at a loss on that one. You're right. The idea that he doesn't mention him at all is surprising. He certainly is anal about other things. While I was outside I did search out the rose he mentioned, the Peace rose. It is growing next to the fireplace outer wall just as he said. That makes it well over forty years old. For the $5.00 they paid, I would say they got a pretty good bargain."

Marge laughed and went back to the large table where the journal was laid out. She sat with her back as stiff as a board, slipped her reading glasses on and began to studiously approach her work. At that moment she looked as beautiful to me as she had ever looked. The lights shone on her from above and her hair picked up the light and accentuated the softness of her lovely face. It was hard for me to believe that the lovely woman sitting in front of me was in her late sixties, but I knew that to be the case. But I also knew that much of what I felt had to do with what she was. I have noticed over the years that how I perceived the beauty of a woman had to do more with my feelings about her than with her appearance.

It was then that Jason came looking for me in the study. He had removed his work boots and stood in front of us in his stocking feet. He apologized for not talking to me and said that he had about an hour before he had to get back to work. I introduced him to Marge. We sat in the comfortable leather chairs that appealed to me so much. He expressed no surprise that his grandfather had kept the journals, but showed no curiosity about their contents. He knew about them and said they were part of a mental exercise his grandfather set out for himself.

I hesitated to ask the question that had been on my mind for some time, but I decided to ask it straight out.

"We have been asked to look into your father's death by your aunt Amy. How do you feel about that?" I asked.

"Well, we might as well get this over with. Anything having to do with my father is very upsetting to me. So, having you here looking into his death is not easy for me," he said.

His manner was always rather remote and casual and he appeared that way now. He sat back in the soft leather chair and seemed to relax. He was in no hurry and his mind seemed to be somewhere else as if he were with us physically, but was thinking about his beloved rhododendrons.

Then he looked directly at me and said, "Let's get this out of the way. There was no question in anyone's mind that I was his son. I loved my mother. She lived in Italy most of the time, so I had the great opportunity of being raised there. It was lovely growing up in Tuscany and I was the apple of everyone's eye, the young, golden haired boy who was so easy to like. By the time I was five years old I was speaking Italian like a native."

He was smiling as he said this as if he was taken back to those times of his carefree youth. He sat quietly thinking for some time before he continued.

"It was a reciprocal love affair. I loved the people and the area and they loved me. I had come back to the States on a number of occasions and my grandfather took a liking to me and vice versa. And, Aunt Amy showed me great affection. I was surrounded by loving and caring adults. My mother was unique. She was what would be called a "flake" today. She was flighty and foolish and she was a complete narcissist. I used to tell her that her greatest friend was her mirror. But she loved me with all her heart. I loved her in return. I had a wonderful special childhood with all the privileges that could possibly be provided."

I felt that was a long speech for him. He was not a man who talked very much and I had the feeling that he was reluctant to talk about himself. He struck me as a self-effacing man who would avoid any unnecessary reference to himself. Marge was listening quite intently and she was leaning forward to hear every word. She was a little hard of hearing, and I knew that she did not want to miss a word of what this man was saying. I didn't ask any questions because I felt that Jason Goetzel was telling us the story as he wanted us to know it first hand.

"So, of course, you want to know about my father. Those who saw us in the same room knew that he was my father. There was no question about that. I was given the name Goetzel because my mother was never married to my father. Before she died she explained to me that she had been in love with my father for many, many years and that they had been lovers. Poor Aunt Amy had to hear the same thing, and here I am every day working next to her reminding her of my father's perfidy."

He stopped as his voice noticeably cracked. He was uncomfortable and I could sympathize with him. The revelation he had made was not easy for him. I am sure Marge, like so many other women before her, had to be struck by his appearance. He was dressed in work clothes, but there was something almost regal in his stature. He was a powerfully built man. His chest was broad and his upper arms were muscular where they showed beneath his cut off sleeves. His arms rippled with muscles, and one felt that the strength flowed down to his hands as well. And yet, he was deceptively handsome. He stood and sat upright and his blue eyes and blond hair were an attraction that not many women could resist. Add to that the fact that he was a multi-millionaire and he became irresistible.

"I say perfidy because it is not very often that a man has a child by his wife's sister. I have had to deal with this all my life. If he was so in love with my mother, why didn't he get a divorce from Aunt Amy and marry her? No matter how many times I ask the question, I always come up with the same answer. He didn't want to take a chance on losing his money. It certainly wasn't to protect Aunt Amy. In the few talks I have had with her about the subject, she claims that she had long since ceased to love my father. Had he divorced her, the realization would have come earlier, but I am sure she had realized by then that she no longer loved him. So, even though he was having a long-term affair with my mother, he refused to acknowledge it until I was born and then only because he had no choice but to acknowledge the obvious. It is ironic that both Aunt Amy and I deal with the dominant genetic characteristics that make our work possible and it was those very genetic dominants that betrayed my father. I am the mirror image of him. What were the chances that that would happen? The odd thing though is that even though I was his son, he never dealt with me personally and more often than not, ignored me completely."

Marge couldn't sit still for this and said, "You mean he actually ignored you? That seems rather cruel."

"Oh, no he wasn't being purposely cruel I don't think. I don't know what he was thinking. We had very little to say to each other. It may seem weird to you as an outsider, but he was indifferent to me and oddly enough, I didn't need him. Grandfather was crazy about me. He took me everywhere and we had a wonderful time together. He took an interest in the things I liked, and we were more like father and son than most real fathers and sons. Aunt Amy was just as much fun. We spent hours together, as we do now, working and discussing everything from world affairs to Italian art and opera and classical music. We read books together and shared them. We had something very special going. And then, my real father was away most of the time."

He sat back in his chair again and crossed his legs. He seemed more relaxed now that he was telling his story. Marge was still listening intently and was leaning forward in the same position she had assumed quite some time ago. I found the man very interesting. He was obviously bright and gave me the feeling that he was quite worldly, and yet here he was hidden away on a small farm in Middletown, Rhode Island breeding rhododendrons. One had the feeling that he should have been the CEO of a large firm or a foreign diplomat or an art critic. Somehow, he seemed wasted here in this large house by the sea. Then it occurred to me that people must have felt the same way about his father. We knew already that Jeff's family had felt that he was wasting his great potential spending his life sailing. Was this man doing the same thing? Was what he was doing worth all of his energy and time?

"Basically, I think we had nothing in common. His interest was in sailing. He had no interest in music, art, literature. I don't think he ever read anything that wasn't required reading. Amy has told me that he was a very successful student, but he had no intellectual interests whatsoever. He had an interest in anything to do with the sea. He would walk for hours along the shore looking at the shells and the life along the shore. I know he often went to Newport to walk the rocky shoreline where he could view the different forms of life that settled in the inlets and shallows formed by the ledges. But these were solitary occupations and didn't involve me. Other than that and his love of sailing, he really had nothing to share with me. For some reason, he never chose to share any of that."

"Were you aware of it at the time?" Marge asked.

"Not really. He was a solitary man living most of his life in his head. If anything, I have a vision of him standing on the deck of a sailboat alone and looking out to sea. What his thoughts were, if he had any, I cannot even venture to guess. He didn't communicate well with anyone, least of all, with me. I will try to explain it to you as best I can. Let me get my thoughts together."

He again sat back and I could see that Marge was very much interested in what he was saying and the way he was saying it. He was an intense man. He did not waste words. I suppose he worked in the same way, making every movement count for something.

"From the time I was a little boy, I loved my grandfather. There was a special bond between us. We would take long walks together and for much of the walk we wouldn't speak because, as I look back on it now, there was nothing to say. But then when Grandfather did say something, I knew exactly what he meant even though he often spoke in short incomplete sentences. Did you know that that is why he kept these journals?" he asked.

Marge said, "I don't understand."

"He kept the journals because he practiced putting together whole sentences and thoughts. He didn't speak that way. He spoke in half sentences many times and his words would trail off so that he seldom finished a spoken sentence."

"So what you are telling us is that he kept the journals as an exercise, a discipline to help him communicate more correctly?" Marge asked.

"Exactly. Grandfather was determined to overcome his speaking problem. I think it had to do mainly with the fact that he was very shy. He would begin fumbling for words and then stop speaking. Communicating verbally was a problem for him and even at work, I understand, he wrote much of what he wanted to communicate to his subordinates."

"Reading his journals, one would never get that impression.," Marge said. "He gives the impression of being completely in control."

"He was in control in his mind. But, the point I was trying to make is that from the very beginning he had no need to talk to me. I understood everything he was trying to say. He would look at me and I would say, 'they lost 3 to 2.' I knew he was going to ask me how the Red Sox made out the day before. The same went for me. It was amazing and the two of us and Aunt Amy laughed about it all the time. We didn't need to speak half the time. Aunt Amy was part of our little game. We thought exactly alike. Isn't that funny? I looked exactly like my father. My mother was a silly fluttering butterfly, but somehow I had the mind of my grandfather and my Aunt Amy. Something in my chromosomes determined that my physical makeup would be my father's and those same chromosomes gave me the brain of my grandfather and my aunt. It was as if there was to be no mixing. My body type, my color, stature, facial appearance, eye color, shape of head, every physical attribute is my father's. But inside, I have nothing in common with him. I find it absolutely amazing."

He waited for this to come home to us and smiled. He was enjoying himself now explaining something, I think, that was dear to him. He was explaining something he had kept to himself but had never had reason to divulge. Now he was unburdening himself.

"So what it comes down to is that I never understood my father. I could not fathom his mind at all. Where I only need to look at Aunt Amy to know what she is thinking, I had no idea what that man had in his mind. And that was why there was never a connection between us. I am sure he felt the same way about me. We had nothing in common. It is as simple as that. So, initially, we began this conversation asking what my relationship was to my father. I think I have given you the answer and I hope it makes sense. Did I miss what would normally be called a father-son relationship? Not for one minute. I tried to avoid contact with the man who was my father because I was embarrassed when I was with him. I didn't know what to say to him and he didn't know what to say to me. On the other hand grandfather and I got along swimmingly. I loved nothing better than being with him. So, I hope that settles that once and for all."

He said this and smiled. I think he certainly told us what we wanted to know and his explanation was enough to make me understand why the two men could live together in the same house and not acknowledge one another.

Chapter XIX

I had been remiss in not checking on the numbers Amy had given us to call. I finally sat down and began calling. I had planned to have Marge do the calling since a woman would be less frightening to strangers and elderly people, but she had enough to keep her busy just reading the journals each day.

I was trying to locate people who would have been contemporaries of the couple when they celebrated their fiftieth wedding anniversary. I gave the list back to Amy with the idea that she would mark off people who were approximately her age. Older people at the time of the celebration would most likely have passed away by now, twenty years later. The list came back with about fifty percent of the names marked. I set to calling those people.

I had no luck with the first fifteen names on the list. I was just about to give it up for the session, when I did contact a woman who had been at the party and who was reasonably lucid and quite verbal. I had Marge talk to her and to set up a date to visit her in her home in Barrington, Rhode Island. Marge suggested that she call Amy if there was any question. We set the meeting for the next morning at 10:00 A.M. and we both felt that we had finally accomplished something outside of the Macomber house. I called Jack to give him the news that we would be visiting the elderly lady, but he was too involved with Patrick and the Desrosiers case to accompany us. He did invite himself to the house for a "late night snack" since he claimed that his cupboard was bare and that he was starved.

Marge put on a pot of decaf, saying, "Even Jack shouldn't be drinking caffeinated coffee at this time of night."

I put some bacon in the microwave and then made a quick omelet using some fresh parsley that grew outside the kitchen door. I remember my mother making that dish for a quick snack for me when I was a young boy and would return from school in the afternoon hungry enough to eat something light. Together with bacon and two toasted English muffins I thought that would be sufficient for even Jack before going to bed for the night. With Jack, however, one never knew.

I enjoyed cooking for Jack because even though he had an enormous appetite, he relished what he ate. He approached his food as it were nectar of the Gods. The simplest dish was something to be enjoyed and he never under any circumstance gulped down his food. He ate slowly and thoughtfully, giving his full attention to what he was eating. He did not pretend to be an epicure, but he enjoyed every morsel of food to the fullest. Tonight he ate the simple omelet with pleasure and as he dabbed some jam on his English muffins he did so carefully and attentively. We waited for him to finish before we began conversation. I had discovered long ago that there was no point in talking to him while he was eating because he could not concentrate on food and talk at the same time.

When he finished and was beginning his second cup of coffee, he said, "I can't understand for the life of me why anyone would want to shoot that man. His wife and stepson had his cash from the safe. So what would be the point of them trying to kill him? That's what I don't understand. Well, we should know more when we get to sit down with them. The funeral is set for tomorrow. There will be no wake. Patrick had the autopsy done and there doesn't seem to be evidence of any other foul play. He was definitely drunk when he was shot. He had very little food in his stomach and the alcohol level in his blood was exceptionally high. He must have started drinking the minute we left him. We know he didn't eat much, and he was drunk enough as it was. Whoever killed him had an easy target."

After this speech, I half expected him to start looking for food again to refuel, but he just sat back and sipped his coffee.

"The temptation is to say that he was better off dead than living the life he was living, but who are we to make that judgment?" he said, and he raised his hands to his temples and brushed his hair back. I liked Jack but I especially liked him in the contemplative mood in which I now saw him. It was then that I saw the real man that I knew. In a sense he had come from nowhere. A city like Fall River had to be considered nowhere in the larger scheme of things, but he had made a life for himself by using his intellectual skills to his advantage. Those skills were not in philosophical or abstract thinking but in the technical and mathematical applications to the stock market and the making of money. His was a kind of qualitative analytical mind that I hadn't encountered in my lifetime. He was not flashy or intuitive. There was no Sherlock Holmes here. But his mind stripped everything down to the mathematics that was so much a part of his being. Things were expressed in numbers for him and whatever thoughts went through his head were his and his alone. The only person I had met with the same kind of mind was Clarissa and, of course, the two managed to communicate with each other in their own special way.

"Whether he should have died or not is none of our business," I said. "I disliked the man intensely and that is something I rarely do. I found nothing about him that made me feel anything but contempt for him, but that is not why we are in this whole business. Our job is simply to figure out what happened and who did it. Correct, Jack?"

"That sums it up very well. So you two guys go to see the lady you talked to, and I will go to the banks and see if I can get some sort of lowdown on our rich friends, the lawyer and his wife as well."

So the next morning Marge and I were off to see Mrs. Durfee in Barrington. Barrington is a lush little community of the rich and professionals mainly from Providence. It may not be as rich as some of the famous bedroom communities across the country but it certainly is one to be admired. In this area of southeastern Massachusetts and eastern Rhode Island it is the shining star of all the communities. I had been offered a teaching position on a number of occasions in Barrington, but I felt I owed it to my kids to stay in Fall River. The kids of Barrington didn't need me, the kids in Fall River did.

We drove to Barrington on the old road that led from Fall River through Somerset and Swansea and into Warren and then finally into the seaside town of Barrington. The town had an impressive cove which was home to any number of picturesque sailing vessels. The town looked like a picture postcard version of what New England towns were supposed to look like including the white, steepled church on the main street.

Mrs. Durfee lived in a bungalow on a tree shaded street in a remote, untraveled part of town. She had told us that the house had a brick wall in front of it which was covered with rambling roses. We found it almost immediately. It was an attractive house in a surprising shade of bright golden yellow which didn't fit our image of an elderly lady living out her days alone.

A nurse answered the door. We suspected that she had been waiting for us because we no sooner rang the bell than she opened the door and welcomed us into the house and directly into the parlor where she asked us to make ourselves comfortable while she went for Mrs. Durfee.

We waited for at least twenty minutes before we saw Mrs. Durfee entering the room using a walker while her nurse stood anxiously beside her in the event that she lost her footing. She was very feeble and I wondered about having asked her to meet with us until she began to speak. Her voice was controlled and clear.

"I am sorry to keep you waiting. There was a time when my delay in entering a room had to do with my appearance. Today it has to do with getting my body in motion," she said with a smile on her face that made us smile in return.

She struggled to sit after letting the walker go and the nurse was right by her side.

When she was safely seated, she turned to her nurse and said, "You may leave us now Helen. I'll call you when I need you. Thank you dear."

She gave us her full attention then. "I'm sorry I can't serve you anything but I can't do it myself, obviously, and I do not want to treat Helen as a servant. She is a trained nurse and I feel she should be treated as such."

Marge, I suspect, trying to add her woman's voice as a calming influence said, "We have no need of anything. We understand."

Then Mrs. Durfee said, "If you have questions you had better get started as soon as possible. I may just fall asleep before you finish."

"Well, can you tell us anything at all that would give us a clue as to what happened that day? Do you think Mr. Macomber committed suicide, for instance?"

"I would be shocked if he did. He enjoyed life too much and even at his age there were women to be charmed and drawn into his bed. He loved women and he loved life and he loved sailing. There is no reason to believe that he would give that up."

She laughed. "That got your attention young lady," she said. "Nothing like a hint of sex to get people to sit up and pay attention, I always say."

We all laughed. I could see that this woman was one to be relished, she might have been old and feeble, but her outlook on life was unique. There was none of the self-pity that some of the elderly deal with. She had the capacity to laugh and that was worth a hundred doctors.

"Now I am really going to shock you. I was one of the many women who had an affair with Jeff Macomber. I repeat, one of the many. Maybe it will help you to know that he was the most charming, romantic man on the face of the earth. With him, romance was food. He had the capacity to find something wonderful in every woman he ever met and when he set his sights on you, you didn't stand a chance. He would romance you with love letters, poetry, flowers, perfume, gifts, everything imaginable. He swept me off my feet and I was married to a wonderful man."

"May I ask when this happened?" Marge asked, and I could see that she was overwhelmed with curiosity.

"It happened in the summer of 1952; the most wonderful summer of my life. It was more than 50 years ago, and I can remember every moment like it was yesterday. He was teaching me to sail and, my goodness, he taught me a lot more than that."

She had the devil in her eyes when she looked up and said, "I am afraid your lovely lady is blushing. Don't let an old lady embarrass you, dear."

She was in no hurry. She was enjoying the fact that she had company and I, for one, was having a good time listening to her. Marge was a little taken back by her bluntness, I think, but had heard a great deal worse in her lifetime even among her Sacred Heart ladies.

"Poor Amy always knew too. He didn't try very hard to hide his affairs from her although he didn't flout them in her face either. But, I knew that she was aware that we were having an affair. I felt terribly guilty about it. I felt that I was betraying her, but the experience was so delightful that I couldn't stop it. It didn't last long and when it did end, I wanted it to end. I didn't want regrets or guilt or a jealous husband to ruin one moment of it. I knew it was going nowhere, but I didn't care. I had had the experience and no one could take it away from me."

"So it would seem that your point is that he was a happy man doing the things he did and that under no circumstances would he take his own life," I said.

"Exactly. The only reason I could see was if he found out that he had a fatal sickness that would curtail his life style. He had an unending supply of money, his boats and all the women he wanted in his life, and he definitely wasn't the type to give it all away or deny himself what he loved most."

"Did your husband know him well?" I asked.

"Oh, yes. They were social acquaintances but not very close, not what you would call friends. My husband thought Jeff was a foolish playboy wasting his life on sailing and women and drink. My husband was a wonderful man, but Jeff's lifestyle was the direct opposite of his. My poor husband never took his eye off the big prize, and he died without ever having spent a day of leisure in his life. A heart attack took him at work. It was ironic justice that he should have been taken doing what he spent all his life doing, working."

She sat still, but not waiting for a question. It was obvious that she had her own thoughts which were occupying her at the moment, and both Marge and I respected her time. She was easy to like. There was a lightness about her that was pleasant at any age. Growing old is difficult especially when we lose our joy of life. I had the feeling that this woman could be bedridden for the rest of her life and still manage a smile.

"Who was right? My husband who was driven to work or Jeff who had one good time of his life? The older I get, the less I understand of such things. Was I wrong in having an affair? I can tell you now that I was not. It gave me one glamorous, adventurous moment in an otherwise mundane existence. Is that too high falootin a way of saying it? Then let me say that I had a hell of a good time, one I will never forget. I wish my husband had had the same. I wish that he had let himself go just once, so that at the moment he was dying, he could have said, 'It was all worth it'. Isn't this awful talk from a doddering old lady? I should be ashamed."

Marge laughed and said, "But you're not."

"Right you are."

"You are one of our few witnesses to what happened that day. Can you tell us how you felt when you heard about it and what other people were saying?" I asked.

"Before I forget, Michael Earle was there too, and he is still alive and kicking. Before you leave, I'll give you his number and address. He was as close to Jeff as anybody. He has his wits about him, so he may be helpful to you."

We thanked her and waited for her to go on. She was enjoying herself and was in no hurry. I wished that I had brought some bits of pastry along with us so that she might enjoy something to eat while we were talking.

"Well those of us who were still there were really shocked. I couldn't believe it. At first we heard that Jeff was dead and that he had been shot. I was amazed. I thought I was going to faint. Then we were told that he had committed suicide. That was even more shocking. I didn't believe it then and I don't believe it now. Naturally everyone was excited and people were chattering away, so you couldn't hear yourself think. Fred wanted to leave immediately to avoid any chance of publicity or notoriety, but I made him stay as long as we could."

The nurse appeared in the hallway then. She signaled us that it was time for us to leave, and Mrs. Durfee was perfectly aware of it.

"Helen wants me to go take my insulin shot and that means that I will have to rest afterward. I am sorry to curtail this wonderful opportunity to talk. It is a rare pleasure for me. Do you think you could come back again tomorrow?" She looked at Helen who nodded yes. We said that we would be there the same time tomorrow.

"One more thing," Mrs. Durfee said. "He was seventy-two when he died and I'll tell you he looked not a day over 60. The rumor was that he had some girl pregnant even at that age, although I don't know if that was true or not, or just wishful thinking on some mother's part."

She said this with her mischievous grin. All of us laughed including Helen who had come forward now to take her to her room. We stayed only long enough to say goodbye and to ask her for Mr. Earle's address and telephone number so that we could call him. She and Helen went into another part of the house. We waited until Helen came back with the information. It was unlikely that, at his advanced age he would father a child, but that would not be a first for men of his age. We began the drive home to the Point and I asked Marge what she thought.

"Could he have fathered a child? Of course he could. There is no question about that. He would fall into a long line of men who have done

153

the same. But what is more important is how do we find out if it was true, and, if so, what relevance does it have on this case?"

"Maybe our Mr. Earle can shed some light on that. We'll call him when we get home and see if we can set something up for tomorrow afternoon. Does that sound all right to you?"

It had definitely been a successful morning as far as I was concerned. We had heard from another party that it was highly unlikely that Jeff Macomber would take his own life. According to Mrs. Durfee he had everything to live for. We had heard the same from other people and even Jack had expressed the same idea. I was becoming convinced that we were probably dealing with murder.

One thought would not leave me. Why would they have an elaborate and expensive party to celebrate a marriage that existed in name alone? That question dogged me. It would be normal to have a celebration for a couple that had been married fifty years. I had been to several of them myself. Friends and family were brought together to honor the married couple and to share in their good fortune. But in this case there didn't appear to be much sense in celebrating a marriage in which the husband was a known philanderer, a marriage that had long since turned out to be anything but a continuing love affair. Then to make things worse, Amy's sister, the mother of Jason had been invited. She was the known mistress of Jeff who had obviously fathered Jason. In my neighborhood that alone would have been a mark of shame that would have branded the family for years. Here they displayed the truth by having Jason attend the celebration as if to thumb their noses at society.

Had Mr. Goetzel planned the murder of his son-in-law? Had he in his meticulous fashion decided that he would celebrate, not the fiftieth anniversary of his daughter's wedding, but the death of his son-in-law in the midst of a noisy, happy crowd? Did Amy herself have anything to do with the murder? If so why would she want it investigated now? Did Jason happen to stumble upon his father in a drunken state and decide to make up for all the years of neglect he had suffered at his hands? Was there another motive for murder that had gone unseen and unnoticed by us? And then the little shred of doubt entered my mind. Despite everything we had heard, could this possibly be a suicide? Was there some reason unknown to us and hidden from his peers, that caused Jeff Macomber to end his own life?

Chapter XX

We had to cancel the meeting with Mrs. Durfee because Patrick, through the District Attorney's Office, had arranged a meeting with Mrs. Desrosiers, even though it was before the funeral. She was not playing the role of weeping and mourning widow, but was anxious to get the investigation into the murder on its way so that she could go to her condo in Naples, Florida. She, in fact, was the one who called the District Attorney's Office to set up the meeting. She had tried to arrange for her son to come in at the same time, but Patrick had insisted that they be interviewed separately. Jack and I were allowed to attend the meeting along with one of Patrick's trusted lieutenants.

I was quite surprised when I saw Mrs. Desrosiers. She was by no means a beauty. Whatever she used to attract and to hold men had nothing to do with her physical beauty as far as I was concerned. We associate women who are successful in dealing with men as being beautiful, but there was no question Mrs. Desrosiers was not beautiful and I suspected that she had never been so. She was dressed in black, but not the black that I had seen Portuguese ladies wear for years. This was a stylish looking dress that was knee high with black stockings and black pumps with no jewelry except for a wristwatch. I say the dress was different from those I had seen because it made the mourner, Mrs. Desrosiers in this case, look like she was about to go out to a cocktail party. My ladies in the bread line would not have been happy about her outfit, but I also had the feeling that Mrs. Desrosiers wouldn't have cared one way or the other how they felt. I was a little surprised that she would even wear black considering what we knew about her marriage.

She was surprised to see Jack and me at the meeting but she accepted our presence without saying a word. She looked both of us over very carefully before she took her seat in front of Patrick's desk. Patrick introduced us. He told her we were associated with his office in the past as volunteers. She accepted us without any question. From her initial look I would have guessed that she knew we had met with her husband the night he was killed.

"Before you waste a lot of our time with your questions," she began in an authoritative tone like a woman who was used to having her way, "let's get a few things on the table. First off, the guy was a drunken bum who was abusive. He was, I think the term is, verbally abusive. He had no respect for women. He was tolerable when he was sober, but he was awful when he got drunk, and he was drunk most of the time. So, just so you know, I had seen a lawyer and I had kicked him out of the house. He wasn't living at home. He was living in his office."

Patrick interrupted by asking, "How long has he been out of the house?"

I noticed that she seemed to be directing her answers at Jack. I found that rather strange. For a few moments I thought she was making a play for him. I couldn't believe it considering the location and the circumstances, but she was not too subtle in her manner. I even wondered if she had checked out his financial status.

"I guess around six months. He has been drinking all that time. He has been pretty much out of his head. Among other things he becomes very paranoid when he drinks. Better put that in the past tense. I still can't believe he is gone. It'll be years before I get over him."

Patrick said, "Thank you for your candor. Now that we have the status of your relationship out of the way, when was the last time you saw or heard from him?"

"He was always calling. He claimed that I wanted to kill him. Nothing was farther from the truth. I was going to divorce him," she said looking again at Jack and keeping her eyes directly on him, "I had every right to anticipate that I could legitimately get at least half of what he owned if not more in terms of money. So money was not the object. Why would I want to kill him? But, that's what he had in his head and I couldn't change that, and I didn't care to, one way or the other."

Jack leaned forward in his chair and asked, "What would have happened to your own money had you divorced him? It seems to me that you probably have more money than he had, so how did you think you could walk out of a marriage getting half of his money? It seems to me that you were actually in danger of splitting your funds with him as well as his with you."

She smiled at Jack and said, "You are a very perceptive and wise man to have picked that up. How did you know that I had money of my own?"

She didn't take her eyes off him for one second. It seemed to me that she was trying to get the measure of the man sitting so tall and quiet in front of her. She was playing her own game now and Patrick and I were merely onlookers.

"Your husband asked me to help him out. Noah and I were looking into his affairs for him. You were included, and I did a background check on you. I think you know that, so we might as well get it on the table now. Without hesitation, I would say that you had more money than he had. So how did you cover yourself?"

"You're not being too subtle here Mr. Crawford," she said with a smile. "I think you already know the answer to your question. Do you want to tell me or shall I tell you?"

It was as if the two of them were in the room alone as far as she was concerned. Jack seemed unperturbed by the attention. I wouldn't have been the least surprised to find out that he was thinking about where to go for lunch.

"I'll defer to you for an answer, Mrs. Desrosiers," he said.

"Marguerita," she said, still smiling. "The truth of the matter is that I had a pre-nuptial agreement protecting my personal money in my son's name. In other words, my husband had no legitimate right to any of the money I possessed on entering the marriage. All of my property and money was out of his reach. Do you think that was wise, Mr.Crawford?"

Jack smiled back and said, "Considering what happened to Mr. Desrosiers, I can't see that it made any difference at all."

Patrick sensed that the interview was getting away from him so he intervened by saying, "The point is that you are saying that there was no way, given a divorce, that you would lose your money?"

"That's right. My money was my own, and it was locked tight and protected from my former husband."

It was clear to me as I looked at her more closely that she must have had a face lift to take the wrinkles out from around her eyes and lips. Her hands as she held them in her lap were wrinkled and looked just as one would suspect the hands of a seventy year plus woman would look. Her face was unlined and smooth and wrinkle free and that did not go together with her hands. It made no difference as far as I was concerned, but it did give me evidence that this woman did care for her appearance and didn't just use her wiles to attract men. From my point of view I didn't think it added one iota to her appearance to have smooth skin, but it did give her the look of a woman who was not what she appeared to be.

"How about Attorney Desrosiers' money? Did you sign an agreement protecting his money?" Patrick asked.

"Of course not. I would not have married him if he asked me for such a pre-nuptial agreement," she answered.

Jack entered the questioning by saying, "I have to ask this question for the Disrict Attorney's elucidation if you don't mind. How did the attorney protect his money if not by a written agreement between the two of you?"

"He hid his money. He always dealt in cash with his clients as much as he could. He was a defense lawyer you know and most of his clients were crooks, roughs, and drug dealers. These kinds of people were more than willing to pay cash for his services because they are hiding their money too. He was a bum dealing with bums if you want to know the truth. He would even brag about hiding money to me when he was drunk. So I took his safe where he kept his cash. Imagine. He was so dumb that he kept his cash in his office. He wanted it near him because he didn't trust the banks or a safety deposit box."

Jack said, "So you admit that you stole the safe?"

"How could I steal something that was legally mine to begin with? The money in that safe was half mine by law. I had a carpenter tell me that one day he was in my husband's office fixing a door that my husband had broken in a drunken fury, and my husband suddenly opened his safe and started bragging to him about how much money he had. That's all I had to hear. I figured that he would open it up one day and somebody would end up stealing the money from him. So, I took the money to make sure that it was safe with me and was out of his hands. Now, I know he thought I stole it, but like I said Mr. Crawford, how can I steal something that belongs to me to begin with?"

"I agree. I think you are a very clever lady." Jack said.

"Coming from you I take that as a high compliment," she said smiling.

Patrick rose from behind his desk and walked to the water cooler in the corner of the room. He turned to Mrs. Desrosiers and asked if he could get her a cup of cold water and she nodded. He carefully selected a paper cup and filled it. I could see that he was stalling for time so that he could get the interview on different ground now although I thought we had learned quite a bit about the woman sitting in front of us. She was nobody's fool and she knew it.

Patrick returned to his seat and asked, "Can you think of anyone who would stand to gain from your husband's death?"

She sat for a moment and seemed to be thinking about the question. Again she was looking at Jack and not the District Attorney as she contemplated her answer.

"I can't think of anyone who would gain by his death. I can think of a lot of people who were upset with him. I don't know how many phone calls I received at home asking for him. The men who called many times were really upset. When he was sober he was a good lawyer, they tell me. But once he started drinking, he was pretty poor. He promised clients the world and then many times he couldn't deliver. When that happened we had some very unhappy people. He caused a lot of pain for quite a few people, but he had a way of wheedling up to them and winning their confidence. Then he would deliver the goods or fall flat on his face. With the people he was dealing with, falling on his face could be very dangerous. So, if you spend your time looking for the people who went to jail because of him and have recently been released instead of chasing widows around, I think you'll be a lot better off."

Patrick smiled and said, "Maybe you are right. Would you like to start working with us?

The moment he said it he knew he had made a mistake.

"I would actually like that if I could work with these two handsome gentlemen," she said and looked directly at Jack.

Jack was not in the least perturbed. I suspect he had heard it all before.

Mrs. Desrosiers uncrossed her legs and placed her feet solidly on the floor in front of her. She then leaned forward and looked directly at Patrick and she said, "I know how people look at a woman who has been married three times and become wealthy as a result. You think of me as a money grubber who married men to take advantage of them and to get their money. That is not true. I loved my first husband and he killed himself working. He didn't do it for me, but for himself. My second husband I loved very much. We had a good marriage. He was a lot older than I was and when he got sick I took care of him until he died. This last guy was a big mistake. I never should have married him. Now that he is dead, I can say good riddance. That sounds terrible, but he was a terrible man. I can't live without a man so I will start looking for another man; but, for himself, not his money. I am sure that telling you this makes no difference, but that's the way it is."

She sat quietly after her long speech and then said, "So, if you have no more questions for me, I'd like to leave. You have my number at home and can call me if you have any more questions. I plan to leave in two weeks for Florida unless there is any reason why you think I can't go."

With that she rose and without waiting for a reply smiled at each of us in turn and rested her eye on Jack for a moment longer, turned on her heel and walked out the door without so much as a look back.

Patrick laughed quietly and said, "Quite a lady there and she took a shine to you Jack without question."

"Hah," Jack smirked, "She is too shrewd to be that obvious. She was trying to prove something. I am not sure what. Maybe she was trying to distract our attention. I don't know what she was doing to be honest, but she was not making a play for me. She has done her homework and realizes that I am the only eligible man here since you are married and too young, and Noah has a woman living with him. That left me. When I come up with an answer, I'll let you know. But what she said about her money makes sense. She admits to taking the safe, but justifies the theft by saying she was protecting her own property. She is right in that respect. It was as much hers at it was her husband's."

"But, just as her husband was harboring illegal money, so is she. The money he was hiding from the government is as illegal in her hands as it is in his. She'll have to account for that sooner or later. I can't turn a blind eye to it. You know that, don't you Jack?" Patrick said.

"I wouldn't think much of you if you did to be honest with you."

"I don't think she gave us a bad lead there," I said. "W hen she said we should be looking for someone who was recently released from jail and might have reason to revenge him or herself for being poorly represented by Attorney Desrosiers."

"Certainly one avenue for investigation, I agree with you there," Patrick said. "Let's see what we get out of the son. He is due in here tomorrow afternoon at two. I don't think he will be as much of a challenge as his mother was."

Jack laughed and said, "For a while there I was wondering who was in charge. I will say one thing for her. I wouldn't want her for an enemy."

We visited Mrs. Durfee again and I brought her some little sugar free tea cookies that I thought might at least give her something to nibble on while we were at her house. Her nurse okayed them and Mrs. Durfee was quite thrilled with the idea of having something new and special. It was like a young man bringing his date a box of chocolates.

She was warm and quite voluble. She enjoyed our company. Marge liked her and it showed, so Mrs. Durfee responded to her in turn.

"I have been trying to remember who the girl was that Jeff was supposed to have gotten pregnant and for the life of me I can't remember who it was. It is somewhere in the back of my mind, but I haven't been able to come up with a name yet. But, I will."

"The last time we met," Marge said, "You weren't sure about the pregnancy. Are you saying now that that was definitely the rumor?"

"Yes, I think so. But remember those kinds of rumors float around all the time. How many are true, you can guess. But, I think, in this case, it was true. Too many people were talking about it."

We sat and talked for another hour without there being any great revelation. We had planned to leave Mrs. Durfee's house and drive to Little Compton where we would visit Mr. Earle after lunch. We understood that he had been Jeff Macomber's best friend, so we were eager to sit down with him. She was hesitant to let us go, but she understood that we had made plans to visit Mr. Earle

He was waiting for us when we arrived. His home was on a pond and he brought us to his back screened-in porch which had a view of the pond and a welcome soft breeze which cooled us as we sat. Mr. Earle had prepared lemonade which he poured over ice cubes. Marge was grateful for the lemonade but looked at me questioningly because she knew that it had enough sugar in it to cause me some problems. I didn't say a word but held the glass in my hand and from time to time lifted it to my lips for only the slightest sip.

We introduced ourselves and then I began the questioning after I explained again why we were there.

"We understand that you were Jeff Macomber's best friend. Is that right?

"If there was any such thing. He was very close to the vest. He wasn't a man who had many friends. He was more of a woman's man than anything," he said with a shyness that was surprising.

Mr. Earle was not the least bit frail. He must have been a very strong man in his day. I was struck by the knots of muscles in his biceps and forearms that showed under his short-sleeved shirt. Even now in his nineties he looked surprisingly vigorous and strong. I imagined that Jack would look about the same if he made it to his nineties.

"I don't quite understand what you mean by that," I said.

"Well, you must know by now that JM loved the women. Women were his thing. No matter where we went, at home or on a sail, he was sure to be looking for someone to bed down. Sorry, Mrs., if I offend you."

He looked at Marge and she laughed and said, "Well sir, you certainly haven't said anything to offend me yet."

"So, he spent most of his time doing that. If I was his best friend it was only because he didn't have any others. The other thing is that we sailed together all the time. When he left the ship or had a woman on board, he could trust me to take care of things for him. He paid me, of course, so I was really a hired hand although he didn't treat me that way, I will say that."

"You mean you were part of his paid crew, so you weren't just a companion," I said.

"That's right. JM didn't take much for being a boss. He wanted his crew working as a team even though we were being paid. A few of the young kids came along for the fun of it, but most of the crew had to make a living, myself included."

"Mrs. Durfee tells us there was some talk about Jeff Macomber getting some girl pregnant just before he died. Do you know anything about that?"

"I heard about it. It wasn't one of the rich ladies from what I hear. That doesn't surprise me. The guy couldn't leave women alone. To be honest he wasn't even that fussy. He just had to have a woman all the time. I wasn't that way. I know it is hard to believe but I had a wife here at home that I loved very much. She was a hard worker and we both came from absolute poverty together. We didn't have children and she always blamed herself, but who knows, maybe I was sterile. But I couldn't cheat on her no matter what. So I was a perfect companion for him on his boats. He would go ashore sometimes for two or three days and meet some floozy and get drunk and he knew I would always be back at the vessel taking care that nothing was stolen. Understand me when I say that he paid me more than he would have paid three men together, so it was worth it for me. But friends, we were hardly friends, don't you see?"

He seemed to want to make his relationship with Jeff Macomber very clear. There was no doubt that he wanted us to understand that he was an employee and not a friend. He sat quietly sipping his lemonade as if he was giving us time to digest what he said.

"If you are looking for someone who might have killed him, I would look for a jealous husband or lover. He ruined his share of marriages. There weren't many women in the area he didn't take a shine to at one time or another. Most of the time they walked away without ruining their lives or their marriages, but there were some that went sour. Make no mistake this guy was a great lover with his flowers and love notes and romance. He was good at what he did. Some women couldn't handle going back to their dull, fat husbands."

"My guess is that you didn't like him very much," Marge said.

"Well to tell you the truth, I didn't. Everything was too easy for him and he didn't care what he left behind. Not many men could compete with him. He had all the money he needed. He didn't work so he had loads of free time on his hands. He was a handsome devil and smart as a whip. They didn't make them any better equipped for what he wanted to do. Even with his reputation, he was hard to resist and I can't think of one woman I know that didn't fall for him once he set his sight on her. Those on the sailing vessels were easy pickings. Those on shore took a little more work, but that made it all the more fun for him. No, I didn't like that part of the man at all."

"Was he as good a sailor as we have heard, or was that just part of his reputation?" I asked.

"No better man ever stepped on the deck of a sailing vessel. He was the master. I don't care how bad things got he had that ship completely under control. There are no words to describe it. That part of the man had my complete admiration. I loved that in him. He was made for the sea. I have seen him come on deck dead drunk and be sober the minute he started moving that sailboat through the water, I don't care how big the ship or under what conditions. He should have been in the America's Cup Races, but he never wanted the competition. So, that's about all I have to say. Probably said too much already, but who knows?"

He stopped talking now and both Marge and I had the feeling that he had said his piece, and there was not much more we could get out of him.

He wasn't finished though because he said. "You know I have done a lot of thinking about the man. If you will listen I'll tell you what I think."

He looked at both of us as if he was waiting for a response and I said, "Of course, Mr. Earle. That's why we are here. Please go ahead."

"Well, the man had everything going for him. He was handsome, rich and healthy. He was very smart. He went to Harvard Law School and became a lawyer. And yet he never practiced law. He threw his education away and never used it. He never used his money for any great purpose or any purpose at all except to satisfy his lust. He was truly a gifted sailor, born to the sea, and he wasted that talent sailing on little trips to amuse the ladies or himself. His big gifts were wasted. How many of us even have one little gift? How many of us have ever had his opportunities? I look back, at my age, and I realize the one gift I had was that I was a hard worker and was a steady man. And you know what? With my very limited gifts I probably did more than he ever did. I found one woman to love, who loved me. He didn't even have that."

He finished the statement and then said, "One more thing. He wouldn't have killed himself because he was having too good a time living and that meant more to him than anything else."

We spent another half hour or so with Mr. Earle who reminisced about the "good times" when he was young and vigorous. Both Marge and I felt that if we looked like he did at his age we would both be very happy. His wife had been dead close to ten years now he said, and he still missed her.

He thought about her every day. I couldn't help but think that he indeed had accomplished quite a bit in his lifetime in his love for his wife and her love for him. He was to be envied.

Chapter XXI

Marge complained that she missed her journal reading after being away from the house for several days. I had long since given up any hope for some startling revelation but she was very deep into the personality of Mr. Goetzel and she thought that that was where the solution to our mystery lay.

"Considering that Jeff is such a presence in the house, how can Mr. Goetzel write in his journal every day and yet fail to even mention him? Would you believe that? After all, the journal was a place where he talked about almost everything that affected him and yet he never mentions Jeff Macomber. Here is an entry that is interesting, for example."

WEDNESDAY

I HAD MY ANNUAL CHECKUP YESTERDAY AND THE DOCTOR HAD A FEW CONCERNS. MY HEART IS WORKING AT ABOUT 60% EFFICIENCY. SEVERAL OF MY VALVES ARE CLOSED AND HE THINKS THAT I MAY END UP HAVING OPEN HEART SURGERY. THE THOUGHT FRIGHTENS ME. WHAT WILL HAPPEN TO EVERYHING WHEN I'M GONE? I HAVE TO START MAKING PLANS NOW FOR THAT POSSIBILITY. AMY IS TAKEN CARE OF AND THE BUSINESS WILL CONTINUE WITHOUT ME WITH NO DIFFICULTY. JASON WILL COME IN FOR MOST OF THE INHERITANCE IN THE LONG RUN AND EXCEPT FOR HIS PROPENSITY TO HAVE TOO MANY WOMEN AND NOT SETTLE DOWN WITH ONE, HE IS A GOOD MAN.

"Now wouldn't that have been the ideal time to mention the boy's father and his son-in-law? The perfect cue. You would expect him to say 'like his father' or 'like Jeff'. But he doesn't mention him at all. It is inconceivable that having written that much that he wouldn't immediately be reminded of Amy's husband. But no, not a single word. Don't you find that odd?"

I nodded my agreement while we continued reading the entry.

I DO WISH HE HAD TAKEN SOME INTEREST IN THE BUSINESS. I WOULD FEEL A GREAT DEAL BETTER IF I THOUGHT THAT HE WAS TAKING OVER THE BUSINESS AND FOLLOWING THROUGH ON WHAT I BEGAN. I KNOW HE WOULD LEAD THE COMPANY IN DEVELOPING NEW PRODUCTS. WE HAVE LONG SINCE REACHED THE POINT WHERE MONEY IS SECONDARY AND AS I HAVE GOTTEN OLDER I THINK I HAVE LOST MY RESEARCH EDGE. IT WOULD BE WONDEFUL TO HAVE SOMEONE LIKE JASON MOVE THE COMPANY IN THE RIGHT DIRECTION AGAIN. BUT IT ISN'T GOING TO BE. TOO BAD.

"Again, not a single word about his son-in-law. As careful as he is and as methodical and precise as we now know him to be, it cannot be by accident that he doesn't mention Jeff Macomber. Did he anticipate that these journals would be read and purposely left out mention of Mr. Macomber? Or did he refuse to acknowledge him in life or in his own intimate thinking? I find it a fascinating question. It goes against his way of thinking. I would have thought that having Jeff Macomber in his home would have been a source of constant irritation. He couldn't have liked the man, and I am sure that he couldn't have dismissed him so easily."

"Okay, so what are you driving at, Marge?" I asked.

She sat looking at the entry as if she was rereading it or trying to solve the mystery of what wasn't there.

"I'm not sure what it means. But this man is too clever to do things without a purpose. If he does not mention Jeff Macomber, then I think he is doing it purposely. He has a motive. What could that motive be? I have no idea. But I know there is a reason behind the whole thing, and I will discover what it is before I am finished. It has become a contest between us now between this dead man who I never knew and me."

I laughed at those words and the challenge she had just issued. I knew she was absolutely convinced that she was right. Somehow she felt that the answer to what happened to Jeff Macomber would be found in the journals. I couldn't approach the problem with any degree of certainty. We were learning a great deal about the man who had been found dead on his fiftieth wedding anniversary, but we were not even getting a hint as to what had actually happened. We began our search trying to discover whether he had been murdered or had committed suicide, and, as far as I was concerned, I had uncovered not a bit of evidence to confirm anything.

In the time she had been working on the journals, she had not changed her approach in any way. She had arranged them chronologically and read them in the exact order in which they were written without skipping a single word or rushing ahead. She was thorough in her reading and I knew she would find out whatever was behind the journals, if there was anything at all. I sat next to her and I admit that at that very moment of seeing her look so beautiful and so intent on her work I was more than stirred sexually. Seventy-two year old men aren't supposed to think or feel that way, but without the aid of Viagra or any other artificial stimulant, I found myself excited enough to want to close the door and make love to her in that room at that moment. If Marge sensed my feelings, and I had found that she was good at reading my moods, she made no sign of it, and I joined her at her work.

We read for about an hour. I could see why she was interested in the man. He didn't say anything of any great moment and he didn't attempt to be cryptic or wise, but merely expressed some thought that had occurred to him the day before.

SATURDAY

AN ARTICLE APPEARED IN THE NEW YORK TIMES YESTERDAY DUSCUSSING THE FACT THAT AMERICANS FIND THEMSELVES TRAVELLING MORE AND MORE. THEY TRAVEL NOT ONLY IN AMERICA BUT OUTSIDE THE COUNTRY AS

WELL. THE ARTICLE CLAIMED THAT MORE THAN 50% OF THE TRAVEL IS TO WARMER CLIMES LIKE THE BAHAMAS, MEXICO AND THE CARRIBEAN. I GAVE UP ON TRAVEL YEARS AGO. I PREFER TO STAY HOME RATHER THAN TRAVEL BY AIR. I HAD ENOUGH OF THAT WHEN I WAS OUT HUSTLING CUSTOMERS FOR THE BUSINESS. I DON'T UNDERSTAND WHY PEOPLE THINK IT IS SO CONVENIENT. EVEN WITH MY CHAUFFEUR DRIVING ME TO THE AIRPORT THERE IS THE MATTER OF CHECKING BAGS IN, GETTING TO THE AIPORT AN HOUR AHEAD OF TIME OR SO, WAITING FOR THE PLANE TO TAKE OFF, THE TERRIBLE AIR IN THE PLANE, WAITING FOR BAGS AT THE OTHER END AND GETTING THROUGH CUSTOMS. I FIND IT ALL TIRESOME AND SOMETIMES IRKSOME.

THEN THE MATTER OF LODGINGS IS VERY IMPORTANT. IN MOST INSTANCES MONEY PAYS THE WAY, BUT ONE NEVER KNOWS. AND OF COURSE THERE IS THE FOOD. OUTRAGEOUS DISHES SERVED TO A MAN WITH VERY SIMPLE TASTES LIKE MINE ARE NOT VERY WELCOME. THE JAPANESE WERE THE WORST. THEY WERE SO POLITE AND TRIED SO HARD TO BE COURTEOUS AND HOSPITABLE AND PART OF THEIR HOSPITALITY WAS TO SERVE ELABORATE DINNERS TO GUESTS, BUT OH WHAT TERRIBLE MEALS I HAD TO ENDURE. SO LET ME STAY AT HOME HERE IN MIDDLETOWN OR IN MARYLAND.

BUT MOST OF ALL IT IS THE ROUTINE THAT IS SO DISTURBED THAT I CANNOT OPERATE. EVERYTHING IS AT ODDS AND ENDS. NOTHING IS WHERE IT IS SUPPOSED TO BE AND MY CLOCK GETS ALL MIXED UP. IN JAPAN MY INTERNAL MECHANISM DIDN'T KNOW IF IT WAS MORNING, NOON OR NIGHT. I COULDN'T PLAN MY WORK AND I COULDN'T SLEEP. SO WHAT IS THE POINT? TRAVEL AROUND HALF THE WORLD TO DISCOVER THT THE PLACE YOU LEFT WAS THE PERFECT PLACE TO BE AND TO LIVE.

JOSEPH RODERICK

JASON LIVED IN FRANCE AND IN ITALY AND HE LOVED IT.
HE LOVED THE LANGUAGES, LEARNING THEM, AND I THINK
I MIGHT LIKE THAT TOO. THEN HE LOVED THE PEOPLE AND
THE ART AND THE FOOD. MAYBE I WAS TOO OLD WHEN I
STARTED TRAVELING OR I HAD TOO MUCH ON MY MIND. I
WOULD GO TO GERMANY AND BE OUT OF THERE IN TWO
DAYS WITHOUT SEEING MUCH OTHER THAN MY HOTEL
ROOM AND A RESTAURANT. EVERYTHING ALWAYS SEEMED
TO BE TURNED UPSIDE DOWN. ONCE I GOT AWFULLY SICK
AND I SWEAR I HAD FOOD POISONING. ANYWAY I'LL STAY
HOME WHILE THE REST OF AMERICANS TRAVEL AROUND
THE WORLD ON THEIR WONDERFUL VACATIONS.

"I don't see anything very wicked here," I said laughing. "There is
certainly nothing beneath the surface that I can see. Just as Jason says, he
may just be practicing writing full sentences. Remember Jason said that
he didn't speak in sentences and used this to practice thinking that way.
To me he sounds like an old man who has lost the sense of adventure that
travel gives many of us. He wants to stay home and be comfortable. I can
imagine my father feeling the same way."

"And yet, here he is writing about traveling and his dislike of it when
in his own household is a man who spent his life doing just that. He
doesn't say what most of us would say, 'My son-in-law has spent his
whole life sailing, and what does he have to show for it? He is none the
wiser or happier from it, from what I can see.' Isn't that an obvious
connection?" Marge asked.

"Could it just be, Marge, that he refused to think about the man? He
was a strong personality and it could be that he rejected Jeff Macomber
completely and refused to even let him enter his thoughts."

"No. That's too easy. This man was a very successful and rich man. He
came from humble beginnings and worked hard to become a success. He
is a strong and determined man. Along comes a man who marries his
daughter, a man with great promise who throws everything away. What
are we to think? He accepts that unequivocally. I doubt it. Then he sees
that same man make a farce of his wedding vows. Do you think that Jeff
Macomber led the life he did with women and his father-in-law knew

170

nothing about it? Then, he goes and has a son by his other daughter. Does Mr. Goetzel accept that? And, he admits having a long term affair with her. Do you think that while that was going on, Mr. Goetzel knew nothing about it? I think that is asking a bit much."

"Even if he knew all of this, and I am sure he did, what is the point?"

"The point is that I can hardly accept the fact that Mr. Goetzel refuses to acknowledge that the man exists. I can't imagine such a lame response from a man of such power and influence."

"So, are you suggesting that he killed him?" I asked.

"No, I have no basis for saying that. But don't you see that it is not his nature to lose control. Every word he writes here tells us that he controls whatever comes within his reach. He doesn't like to travel, for instance, in the section we just read because he loses control of the situation. His food changes, the time changes, his methodology changes. He loses his routine and control. So now he has a son-in-law who is a bad one. He cannot sit back and let it ride. That much I am sure of. The question does not become a question of whether he acts or not. It really becomes a question of how he acts."

"So, you really think he plotted his murder, don't you?" I asked.

"I'm not ready to answer that but I think that is where I see this going. Why this rubbish in these journals? You mean to tell me that a man with his drive and his brilliance suddenly is reduced to writing this sort of thing? The dribble that he turns out every day. Suppose I am right and this is only an elaborate smoke screen. It could very well be that what he says here is true, but, on the other hand, it is untrue because he avoids the burning issue of his relationship with a son-in-law he cannot help but be in despair over. Why would he avoid any mention of him? You say he wants him out of his mind. I say it is hardly likely. I think Jeff Macomber was a burning issue for him, and he couldn't just dismiss him."

"So what do you think it all leads to? Murder? You keep saying it is incomprehensible, but you give me no indication of what could have happened. Let's put it together. Jeff Macomber enters the library in a drunken state to get away from the crowd for a few minutes. He sits down and goes to sleep. Mr. Goetzel enters the library and finds him sleeping. He goes to his desk, takes out his pistol and comes back to shoot his son-in-law in the temple. Then he places the gun in his hand and leaves. A little later someone finds the body and calls the police who then call it suicide. Is that what you see?"

"I don't know, but I just can't imagine this man allowing the situation to exist over such a long period of time without doing something. I insist he would have to have done something. I can't imagine him sitting by and doing nothing. Okay, so I don't know what. But let's give it time and we'll discover what he was thinking. For instance, why did he have a celebration of a marriage that was no marriage at all? That is an unanswered question as far as I am concerned."

We left it at that for the moment. I determined that I would ask Amy for an answer to that question and would not be satisfied until I had one. The question had come up and she had merely stepped aside without giving us an adequate or satisfactory answer. Now in the light of Marge's feelings about Mr. Goetzel and his possible motivation, I felt I needed an answer.

Chapter XXII

Patrick set up a meeting with Mrs. Desrosier's son. He was the son of her first marriage and his name was Martin after the father. Roger Martin was fifty-four years old when we met him, but whereas his mother carried her age well, he looked like life had treated him badly. His face looked ravaged and he was much too heavy for his short stature. There was something unhealthy about his looks as if he were a drug addict or alcoholic. His eyes were shifty and he seemed to be looking at everything around him without letting his eyes settle on anything for even a moment.

Patrick introduced him to us and he said immediately, "These are the two old geeks that Desrosiers hired to dig up shit on me and my mother, right?"

Jack said, "These two old geeks were hired to try to recover the contents of the safe that was stolen from him. He thought you did it or arranged to have it done."

"He must have been hard up to hire two old men," the man said with a smirk on his face.

Patrick said, "We'll have plenty of time for personal recriminations later, I'm sure, but right now I want to get down to business. So let's get right to it. You have a record that is nothing to be happy about, multiple arrests for drunken activities from driving under the influence to hit and run. Then there are all the drug abuse arrests and retentions. You are a public nuisance. And now, there is the very serious business of murder that we have to deal with."

Patrick waited for a response but got none. The man sat quietly and seemed perfectly content to wait for Patrick to continue.

"So, tell us why you did it," Patrick said.

"Fuck you. You have to be out of your mind, crazy bastard."

Jack suddenly stood up and walked to Patrick's desk. He sat on the edge of the desk with his long legs crossed and looked at Roger very carefully. The man kept shifting his eyes from one place to another until Jack said, "Look at me."

Roger Martin seemed to be uncomfortable and shifted in his chair.

Jack leaned forward and said again, "Look at me."

Roger was truly uncomfortable now, and I knew that Jack had him.

"The truth is that Desrosiers told me that he was putting some of his friends on you. That he was going to have you eliminated if he didn't get his safe back. I told him to hold off. Did you know that he was looking for someone to put you away? You and your mother."

"Yeah sure. Elephants fly too, asshole."

Jack leaned very close to Roger and said very quietly in a voice just above a whisper, "The District Attorney is a gentleman and he is in a position where he has to control himself. I am not a public official and can walk out of here at any second. Look at me now Mr. Martin. If you call me another name like that, I am going to get up and knock you on your fat ass. Do you hear me? Let me say it again just in case you didn't hear me. If you call me another name or swear at me, I am going to get up and knock you on your fat ass. Is that understood?"

Now Jack leaned back and I could see that Roger Martin's face turned crimson. I wondered if we were about to have a confrontation, but I had faith that Jack knew what he was doing. Martin took a handkerchief out of his rear trousers pocket and wiped his face. He was sweating profusely now, and I knew that with that one action that Jack had him.

"Now, did you know that your step-father wanted his friends to put you away? He had friends on the Hill in Providence he asked for a favor. He figured they would be happy to do the job for him. The only thing I didn't know was if he meant to get the two of you or just you. Which was it?"

"I don't know what you're talking about."

Roger was squirming now and I knew that Jack had guessed right again. He had the amazing capacity to make a wild guess and to be as close to right as he could be. In this case he was right because Roger Martin became extremely nervous and uncomfortable.

"So, you heard what he was up to and then brought in your own guys to do the job. You couldn't do it yourself. You are too gutless. How did you know what he was doing? Did you have his office bugged?"

"No."

Patrick saw that Jack had the edge so he let him continue undisturbed. I'm sure he was preparing follow-up questions of his own but he kept those to himself while Jack continued his questioning.

"Then how did you know who we were? The minute you walked into this office you knew exactly who we were. How come? Not only did your mother know who we were but she had me checked out top to bottom. How come?"

"I don't know," he said. But he was shaken now and Jack knew it.

"You don't know anything. You don't know how you knew who we were. That's a good one. Who are you kidding? You knew us the minute we walked in this door, didn't you? You better start giving me some straight answers."

"Okay. I saw you two going into his office the other day. Then when I saw you just now I knew who you were. He told my mother he was going to have us wasted so I wanted to see who was going in and out of his office."

"Where were you when you were watching us?"

"I was on Main Street across the road from the office building."

"Did you follow me to Kentucky Fried when I went out?" I asked.

"Yeah I did."

"How about later when we took the lawyer to the diner?" Jack asked.

"Yeah I saw you."

"Did you follow us?"

"Yeah, I wanted to know what you were doing," he answered.

I signaled Patrick to let him know that Martin was lying. Jack sat very quietly looking at him as if he were exasperated and was about to do something. I could see Roger Martin cringe, but Jack didn't move a muscle. He sat motionless and stared at Roger Martin. The man didn't know where to turn.

"You are a liar," Jack said finally. "You are nothing but a scoundrel and a liar and I have nothing more to say to you."

He turned to Patrick then and said, "If I were you I would read him his rights and arrest him right now for the murder of Mr. Maurice Desrosiers."

"Hey wait a minute. I didn't kill that jerk," he managed to say.

Then Patrick said, "Then you had better tell us what happened because Mr. Crawford has given me the best idea I have heard all day. I need an arrest on this one. Do you have a lawyer you can call?

"I want to go," he said and he started to get out of his chair.

"Sit down," Patrick said with a sternness of voice that made Roger visibly fearful. At that moment he wished he were anywhere but in that office facing this questioning.

"Let me make it easy on you," Patrick said easing his voice a little. "Tell us how you knew what was going on in your step-father's office. How did you plant the bug?"

"Some guys did it for me. He was always drunk and we were afraid that he would de something crazy, so the only way we had to know what he was doing was to listen in on what he was saying in the office."

"And we, is your mother and you right?"

"Yeah. He could have done anything he was so crazy. So we wanted to know what he was doing."

"So you heard him order a hit on you right?" Jack said.

"No."

"So you figured that before you got hit you might well take care of him right? But before you had it done, you needed to get that safe out of there with all the money in it. He told us it was three million dollars. That's a lot of money."

"No way. He was lying."

"So, you admit that you took the safe," Jack said.

"Yeah, like Mom said, it was our money and the way he was drunk all the time, someone could have snatched it from him, no trouble. That money was as much hers as it was his."

Jack laughed and said, "And a lot of that money belonged to Uncle Sam because he never paid taxes on it. I hope you are ready to face charges of tax fraud when the District Attorney here notifies the Internal Revenue Service."

"Shows you how smart you are. Mom's lawyer has already contacted them and they are looking into the payment now."

He looked very proud of himself that he had tripped Jack up. He had a grin on his face that I suspected Jack would have liked to have erased with a good slap but Jack managed to control himself.

"You outsmarted me on that one, you and your mother, I'll give you credit. You guys are pretty smart. So, how did you bug his office or did you just bug the phone?"

"I ain't going to tell you that, and I ain't going to talk to you any more," he said. He turned to Patrick now and asked, "Do I have to answer his questions?"

"Let's skip that for now," Patrick said. "The important thing is for you to tell me when you decided to have your stepfather killed. Who did you hire to do it?"

"You are as crazy as he is. I know my rights. You want to arrest me go ahead. I'll call my lawyer. You can't make me stay here and listen to this shit all day."

Patrick knew then that we had lost him. Jack didn't fail very often when he decided to take a direction and a forced line of questioning, but he had lost this man. Patrick saw it and gave him a quick exit. He just said that he wanted him to stay in town and that we would be getting back to him and he let him go.

As soon as he had left Jack said, "Well I screwed that one up. Sorry about that."

"Not really," Patrick said. He picked up the phone and called one of the officers in the outer office to come in. He talked to him quietly and the officer left without hesitation.

"We are going to sweep the office and find out if it was bugged. I think we'll find that it was. Then, we have to find out who did it. I think we have to agree that neither the son nor the mother is capable of doing it. If we find out who did it and we know the best in the business and the tools they use, then we can hope to get the complete tapes of all the conversations that took place in the office."

I laughed and said, "You've made quite a jump from guessing that the office was bugged to having a record of everything that was said."

"I trust Jack and his jump of imagination. I think almost certainly the office was bugged and I would make another leap of imagination and say that that character we had in here just now was the man who hired a professional to kill his stepfather, with or without his mother's permission."

"Well, good luck but I still think you are making some big leaps into the unknown," I said.

It was very unlike Patrick to act precipitously. I couldn't figure out what he was thinking and I finally came to the conclusion that he must have known something about the case or Roger Martin that I didn't. It was also unlike him to keep things back from us so he had me totally confused.

I spoke to Jack about my feelings and he admitted that he was as surprised as I was.

"It is not like Patrick, I think we both agree. We were the ones who jumped to conclusions and he was always the one who proceeded with caution. We almost had to have proof in spades before he would even listen to us. Now this sudden switch in methods is a puzzle greater than the crime itself," Jack said and began laughing at our quandary.

We both had a good laugh. We must have looked strange to onlookers who saw two old men leaving the District Attorney's Office laughing uproariously. One normally did not see people leaving that particular office in a happy mood and here we were having a wonderful old time.

Chapter XXIII

The next morning at ten o'clock we were waiting for Amy Macomber to come into her sun room. I thought it was important that we confront her with the rumor of the pregnancy. Jack agreed that we were being too nice in not raising the question and that we would have to bring it to her attention sooner or later.

She entered the room slowly and deliberately.

"Arthritis is really acting up this morning gentlemen. I can hardly move without terrible pain. Jen wanted me to stay in bed, but at my age staying in bed is too much of a luxury that can become habit forming. I can do without it. I fear that once I take to my bed I will never get up again. But I don't have arthritis in my jaw and I can talk."

Jen helped her into her chair and even helped her to lift her arms so that her forearms rested on the sides of the wicker chair. It was evident that she was in a great deal of pain.

When she was completely settled in and Jen had placed the blanket over her legs, she said, "What's on your mind gentlemen?"

I began by saying, "Are you sure you want to talk to us this morning? You seem to be very uncomfortable."

"It's okay. As I said, my mouth doesn't have arthritis and talking might take my mind away from the pain. You know my friends in Japan don't have arthritis and they sit right on the ocean. It has to be the diet. I wish I had known the trick of it at an earlier age. This is very unpleasant. I have had it for forty years and it grows worse."

"Then we have a few tough questions to ask you," I said trying to figure out how to broach the question of the pregnancy.

"Ask ahead. There is nothing too hard for me at my age. Believe me I have seen and heard a great deal in my time and I doubt if there is anything you can ask me that will embarrass me or offend me."

"Well this has to do with a rumor that was circulating at the time of your husband's death that he had gotten some local girl pregnant. I am sure you were aware of the rumor."

Amy Macomber's face became downcast and I regretted having asked her the question. She didn't answer immediately, but seemed to be thinking about her answer. Jack and I waited patiently for her to talk. I had the feeling that she would like to have moved her hands but she knew it would cause her pain, so she sat absolutely still. She finally looked at me without flinching and said, "One of many. You have to understand that Jeff had a fatal attraction for women. Women absolutely adored him. The fact that he would get a woman pregnant never surprised me."

"The rumor we have heard is that he got a local girl pregnant. Did you know about that?"

She hesitated before answering and then said, "I heard of several cases over the years. I paid a few angry parents a substantial amount of money to placate them. Jeff was incorrigible, but I couldn't let the mothers go without taking care of some of their financial needs. We all knew, and you certainly know by now, that Jeff was no angel. The local girls hoped to get him for themselves by allowing themselves to get pregnant by him. Foolish girls. Once he had his way with them, he lost interest in them. Then I had to pick up the pieces. It wasn't very nice."

Jack said, "I have to ask you again why in the world you put up with him. I went on sailboats with him. I saw what he did there, at least he was out of sight. How could you let him subject you to the humiliation you must have felt dealing with this sort of thing? I don't understand it."

"Jack and Noah, I know it is hard for you to comprehend. It was hard for father too. He often badgered me about it. But I think I have tried to explain my position to you before. Jeff had great promise. Not only was he a handsome man, but he was extremely intelligent and believe it or not, he was a hard worker. He did well all the way through school and he learned to be a great sailor. When we were young he said to me that he had worked very, very hard for everything he had accomplished. He put a great deal of pressure on himself. He often described himself to me as being in a pressure cooker. He thought of himself as what we used to call a 'grind', that is someone who worked very hard at his studies and everything he did. Then he married me and I adored him. I wanted to satisfy him in every way, including giving him all the money he needed. Why not? I had all I would ever need.

She stopped then. That was the first time I noticed that she was short of breath. It might have been the pain she was suffering, but whatever it was she suddenly turned very pale and seemed to be gasping for breath. I began to move toward her but she lifted her finger to signal me to stop. She did not move for what seemed like an eternity to me and then said, "This will pass. Give me a few more minutes."

"Then it happened overnight. We came back from Japan. I was all aflutter about the azaleas and as happy as a new bride should be. We were home for about three weeks and he said that since the ship was in tip top condition that he would take it for a short sail down the coast. We had settled into this house and although I knew I would miss him, I gave him my okay. I was busy trying to locate azalea breeders and growers around the country. From that day he decided that he had no need to work and, in fact, that he did not want to work."

Her eyes filled with tears as she told the story and I was sorry to do this to her. She was a sweet woman, and it isn't good to drag up the past under any circumstances, but this had to be hurtful to her. She had had her share of hurt and it wasn't fair to take her through it again. I knew that this woman sitting before me was as strong as they come and that making her relive the past was difficult for her and possibly unnecessary.

"So, what was I to do? I loved him. I understood it when he said that he had been under so much pressure all his life that he needed some time to pull himself together and that I had given him a new perspective. He needed time. He would take a year off, and then take the bar exam and get back to work. Well, needless to say it never happened and I was partially responsible for that because I gave him the wherewithal to continue. He was a weak man after all, for all his physical strength. I came to realize that as time went on. It was like being married to an alcoholic. The habit grew on him and he couldn't bring himself to break the inertia. I continued to provide him with money. I was too weak to deny him."

The tears were rolling down her cheeks now and she didn't have the physical strength to wipe them away. I reached forward and with a paper napkin which was on her tea tray began to wipe her face very slowly and as gently as I could while Jack rose to call Jen to our aid.

When Jen did come back with Jack, Amy motioned her away, which surprised me.

"Then the women started and that hurt very, very much at the beginning. But even that pain gradually passed and I turned my mind and eyes away. The man I married was quite different from the man he became. I realized that I had loved not him, but my vision of him. So, what was I to do then? Nothing. In a sense he had become what I had encouraged and allowed him to become."

My heart went out to her and yet I realized that she hadn't answered the one question I had asked her and I began to wonder if the long answer she was giving us wasn't just a way of avoiding the question.

"Did you know about the rumors of the girl he was supposed to have gotten pregnant? Did you know who the girl was and did you have to pay her off as well?" I asked.

"No, I didn't know who it was and no I did not pay her off to use your terms," she said this very quickly and with no thought. I knew she was lying. I have heard enough students lie in my years of service to know when I am being lied to. I knew that Amy Macomber was lying to me and I wondered why. She was very forthright about everything else no matter how much it hurt. But now she was lying to me for some reason which I could not fathom. Suddenly, all of the pity I felt for her was gone. Now she became a part of a puzzle to be solved. I needed answers to some questions now and I knew I would not be getting them from her. But now, I had an idea that what I was looking for was not far away and that a solution to what started out as a simple problem and had grown more and more complicated was near at hand.

Marge was in the study when I arrived and was following her thorough study of the journals. Evangelica was with her doing the cleaning. When I saw her I immediately saw the opportunity to pursue my questioning about the girl Jeff Macomber was supposed to have gotten pregnant.

"Did you work here long before Mr. Macomber died?" I asked.

"Oh, I was here about ten years, I guess. My whole family worked for Mr. and Mrs. Goetzel. Then I think I was about twenty when I started working full time. I haven't ever worked anywhere else in my whole life you know. This is like home to me."

"Did you like Mr. Goetzel?" I asked.

Marge looked at me with a questioning look on her face, but I continued talking to Evangelica. Marge knew I was after something, but she wasn't sure what.

"Oh, yes he was a very nice man. Always treated me like a lady. He never said a single nasty word to me in all the years I worked here. He was very particular about everything too. Nothing could be moved out of its place. When I dusted for him, I picked things up and then put them back exactly where I found them. He always gave me nice Christmas and birthday presents too. He always gave me special, nice things."

"How about Mrs. Goetzel?"

"Oh, I didn't work for her very long. She died very young you know. I was only here a few years when she went. But, she was a nice woman even when she was very sick. She died of cancer you know. Mr. Goetzel felt very bad about that for a long time."

"How about Miss Amy?"

"Oh, she is very nice. She is a lot like her father. Everything has to be left exactly where it was when you started cleaning. She worries about things getting broken too. You have to be very careful. If anything does get broken, she can get very angry at you. Once I broke a vase, and I thought I was going to get fired. But, most of the time she is very nice."

"How about Mr. Jason?"

"Oh, he is a nice man. I like Mr. Jason. He doesn't say much, but he is always polite and never has a bad word to say to anybody. I like him."

She said this and continued to clean. While she was talking she walked slowly dusting everything she came across including every one of the book shelves and the tops and front of the books. She didn't take them off the shelf but dusted them very carefully. From what I could see she was extremely methodical and, if not painstakingly slow, at least efficient. She didn't stop to talk but kept moving all the time so that I had to strain at times to hear what she had to say as she turned her head or turned her back to me.

"Jen is nice too. She is young, so she doesn't pay much attention to what I do, but she is nice to have in the house. I miss her when she isn't here because she has an early class or she goes to visit a friend."

"How was Mr. Jeff?

183

"Oh yes, he was very nice. He was always sweet and nice to me. Always, he acted like a gentleman. He never had a bad word to say and always had a smile on his face. He gave me nice presents too."

"He was a ladies man though, I hear. Is that right?"

"Oh, I guess. He was very handsome, like Mr. Jason. He was like a movie star."

As she talked about him she took on that dreamy look, so I suspected she must have had a terrible crush on him when he was living in the house. I could imagine her as a young girl in her twenties looking at the tall, blond tan man and seeing him as Amy Macomber had first looked at him at Harvard.

"The rumor was that some local girl was pregnant by him. Do you know who it was?'

At that she suddenly whirled around and said, "What Mr. Jeff did was none of my business. That is a terrible thing to ask me. What is the matter with you? Are you sick in the head or what?"

"No," I persisted, "Mrs. Macomber asked us to find out what happened to her husband and we are trying to find out. So, you don't know who the pregnant girl was?"

"I won't talk to you about this. You are not being a nice man now. I have to finish my work. You can talk about anything else, but I won't talk about this."

I knew she was serious and would not continue answering my questions. For the first time I recognized that the girl was mentally deficient. I don't know why I didn't see it earlier, but I knew now after listening to her that she was not possessed of a high I.Q. I would have guessed that she was below normal in intelligence and that probably explained why she was employed in cleaning out this one room.

Her beauty covered up her deficiencies. Over the years I found that beautiful people with handsome or beautiful features have a leg up on the rest of us. As much as the rest of us like to deny it, it is a fact of life. We have a natural tendency to like people who we find attractive. This may not hold true over a long period of time, but at first meeting we like people who are pleasing to be with and who please our version of beauty. Evangelica was one of those people. Even at her age she was quite lovely. Her mother was sensual, but Evangelica was lovely. Her face was angelic with big brown eyes and perfectly shaped lips on a face that would have served as a model for Boticelli. When I met her, I was swayed by her appearance and didn't pay attention to the way she talked or what she said that would have given me the tip-off to her mental slowness.

I thanked her and left her with Marge so that I did not add to the discomfort I had already caused. How I could have missed the obvious is beyond me, but I certainly did. It came from not listening to people and taking their appearance as an indication of what they were rather than listening to them. It was an unforgivable mistake for a teacher to make. I could have kicked myself as I walked through the garden outside the house and down to inspect the rhododendron and azalea introductions in their own gardens.

I had never paid much attention to rhododendrons in the past. I knew about the large specimens that grew on large properties in the area. There was a church in the city that had remarkable specimens growing on the property. As I learned from Jason, these were the old standards that were so successful in the northeast and which the nurseries pushed to their advantage. They were hardy, colorful and almost one hundred percent sure, planted by even the most novice gardener. Lately there had appeared a whole group of rhododendrons that also fit the climate and growing conditions of the northeast. These had been developed by an English hybridizer named Dexter. He had created any number of outstanding but large plants in Sandwich, Massachusetts at the entry to Cape Cod. His most famous plant was called Scintillation and it was making quite a stir in the New England area and in other sections of the country conducive to rhododendron growth. Many of his hybrids have been rediscovered and brought back into cultivation and distribution and have made a great hit among growers. But, they all have one thing in common aside from their beauty of flower and hardiness and that is that they are all huge. Jason's new introductions would be much more in keeping with the size of urban gardens in the crowded northeast. The ones in his gardens in the back of the house were not in bloom, but the markers at the base of the plants had names, crosses and dates written on them. The oldest was only seven years old and that was a good looking plant with grayish undersides to its leaves and was only three feet in diameter and two feet tall. From what I could see there were any number of buds at each of the junctures of the leaves and it looked like the plant would be heavy in bloom come May. There was no way to determine the size of the blooms from the buds that were showing but if they were anything like he described to me, I felt that Jason certainly had a winner. It was a handsome plant in its own right and I could see that it would not get out of hand size-wise in any garden if its size after seven years was any indication. I had seen much younger Nova Zemblas, a vivid red rhododendron, grow to five feet tall in as little time. The same held true for the other dwarfs that I located and I knew that he had produced plants that were almost perfect for the cities like Boston and Providence and Portland in the northeast.

Would these plants satisfy a man? Would these be enough to justify a life's work? It wasn't for me to say. I thought of the man who introduced two azaleas in the northeast that have become as ubiquitous as the marigold. These are the PJM azalea which is found everywhere in New England, and I am sure in other parts of the country as well. Every planting it seems has at least one and their lavender flowers greet one everywhere one turns in May in New England. The same can be said for its sister plant, Olga Mezzitt which is almost as popular with its great show of small pink flowers. Now, I suspect that Mr. Mezzitt were he alive today would be glowing with pride if he saw his introductions in bloom everywhere he looked. It could be that the same would hold true for Jason Goetzel in years to come.

Chapter XXIV

The bombshell hit that afternoon when we got back to the Point. Patrick had left a message on my machine telling me to call him immediately and to contact Jack if he hadn't been able to get him. It certainly sounded important to me and I was in the process of calling him when Jack came rushing into the house.

He could hardly contain himself and said in a loud voice, "It was suicide or accidentally self-inflicted, one or the other."

"What was?" I asked.

"Desrosiers' death. The doctor claims that he was dead before he got shot. The shots came after he had died of an overdose of sleeping pills. He must have taken the sleeping pills by accident or on purpose. If by mistake, Patrick calls it accidental death. On purpose, it is suicide. So how are we to know?"

"Where is Patrick now? Can we see him?" I asked.

"He wants us to meet him at his office right away. We should get into town as fast as we can," Jack said.

The drive to New Bedford took about twenty minutes from the Point and we parked in a space reserved for the District Attorney. A policeman came by and told us that we couldn't park in the reserved space. Jack told him that we were meeting with the District Attorney and that we worked for him. He laughed and said something to the effect that he must be pretty desperate to hire two old men. Jack laughed as well and invited him to come into the office to check with the District Attorney to see if we did, in fact work for him. He took Jack up on the offer and accompanied us into the office and was rather taken aback when Patrick met us and asked us to come right in. The policeman didn't say a word. He was gone before Jack could turn and make a comment, much to Jack's chagrin.

Patrick asked us to sit and then took out the coroner's report and began to read sections from it to us. The first thing he read was a summary that said, "Without a second opinion I hesitate to say that I am 100% sure, but as closely as I can tell I would venture to say that death was caused by an overdose of sleeping pills, rather than by the gun shot wounds to the head. The injuries done by the damage to the skull and head were after the fact. I have requested a follow up autopsy by one of my fellow doctors in Suffolk County to verify my findings."

There was more that followed, but it was justification for the same conclusion. It was a stunning finding as far as I was concerned. Suddenly a murder became something quite different.

Jack said, "Where are we then Patrick?"

"Well if the coroner is right, then we are over and done with the case. We can't very well take someone to court for shooting a dead man. It is a terrible thing to contemplate. I can't imagine shooting a dead man at close quarters, but there it is. Can we prosecute someone for contracting the death of another man if that other man is already dead? I don't think we have a crime. This is certainly the weirdest thing I have come across."

Jack began to laugh and it became contagious. I have been in situations in which people began laughing when there was really nothing to laugh about. That was the case here. There really wasn't anything funny about this whole situation but here we were three grown men actually tittering and laughing hilariously.

Finally, Jack said, "Who would believe it? First they steal his safe that contains close to a half million dollars or more in cash. And, as his wife says, she is not stealing anything that does not belong to her already. She is merely protecting it. Then he threatens them with a hit man or hit men which they must have picked up by bugging his office. Then they turn around, I am sure, and put a contract out on him to beat him to the punch. They may even have hired the same guy, but upped the ante. I say, they, but I am sure it was the son who did all this. Somehow I can't imagine his wife acting in that way. It is too transparent. I think she is a little more subtle than that."

Jack was still smiling when he finally got out of his chair and began pacing the floor. Patrick sat back in his swivel chair with his hands behind his head and I sat in the chair in front of the desk trying to find any loopholes in what Jack was outlining. There really didn't seem much to say unless we were overlooking something obvious. Still, it all seemed too simple to me. Jack looked at me questioningly. I nodded to him to continue.

"So, now our friend sits in his office stewed to the gills and has an attack of paranoia. We heard him going through it when we were there. He was scared out of his wits. He must have been warned that something was going to happen. He kept repeating that someone was going to kill him. No question about that is there, Noah?" he asked.

"No."

"As drunk as he was, he must have remembered that he had a bottle of sleeping pills somewhere. Maybe they were in his desk drawer. So he takes a few and then a few more and then maybe the whole bottle not knowing what he was doing. Or maybe he is so frightened that he wants to end it all. Who knows? What do you think Noah?"

"I think he could very well have gotten himself into a state. He was trembling at times when we were there earlier. And Jack is right. He kept repeating that they were going to kill him. We never asked who 'they' were because we thought he was going through some sort of drunken delusion, but he was probably referring to his wife and her son. Did he attempt suicide? I just don't know. He was certainly in despair. Could he have made the mistake of taking a whole bottle of pills? I think that is definitely a possibility. When we left him, we assumed that he was going to sleep it off, but he must have found a bottle of liquor he had stashed somewhere and started right in again. It wouldn't have taken much more liquor to have him incapable of any thought whatsoever." I said all of this, knowing full well that it was all conjecture on my part, but that was what we were working with from the beginning in this case.

"Then, whoever it was who was contracted to kill him comes into his office," Jack continued, "finds him with his head on the desk stinking of alcohol and assumes he is sleeping and has passed out, and thinks it is the perfect opportunity to do what he has been contracted to do. He takes his pistol complete with silencer and shoots two bullets into Attorney Desrosiers' head and walks out the door, having accomplished what he set out to do with a minimum of fuss and effort. One of the secretaries comes in the next morning and finds the body and there we are trying to solve a murder case."

It seemed to me that he had presented the case as it might have happened in his usual logical manner and there wasn't much more that could be said.

Patrick sat up in his swivel chair and putting both hands on the desk in front of him said, "I think you have pretty well summed it up for us, Jack. What do you think Noah?"

"I agree. I can't see anything wrong with what he said as long as the coroners agree that the man was dead before he was shot."

Jack said, "The only question I have is that if you call it suicide his loving wife won't get the insurance payment, if he had insurance. I think, even though she didn't have much of a marriage, that she deserves whatever insurance he had if for no other reason than that she deserves it for putting up with him. He couldn't have been an easy man to live with."

Patrick said, "I hadn't thought about the insurance end of it. I was just so glad to be relieved of chasing down the perpetrator that I wasn't even thinking."

I couldn't help but add my little bit since I had been fairly quiet. "Isn't it strange the way things happen? As far as I was concerned this man was vile. He was a stingy, greedy, bad-tempered man who drank to excess and probably took drugs. He was a man who liked to throw his weight around. I can just imagine how he treated his clients. I bet he was one of those ambulance chasing lawyers. Then after years of being single, he marries a woman who actually has every intention, from what we can see, of taking care of her husband and being a good wife."

Patrick said, "That's a bit of a stretch isn't it? What's make you think she wanted to make him a good wife and wasn't just after his money?"

"That wasn't her style. Remember, as Jack says, she has more money than he had. Now, I know and you know that she would never have married him if he hadn't had money. Our friend is not a woman who is in the habit of supporting a man. But, at the same time, I feel she would have done everything possible to make his life a good one, just as she had done for her first two husbands. It was her style. We think of her as a gold digger but it would seem that her history is more than that."

I waited for a cryptic response from Jack and since none was forthcoming I continued, "Now she marries a complete heel. So what is she to do? It certainly isn't her style to allow him to run all over her. That, she won't do. She might be willing to be a dutiful, obedient wife, but she is not a fool. So, Jack, take it from there."

And he told the story, as we knew it, when we came along. He was laughing now at how we had escaped chasing this all down and having to prove anything against Mrs. Desrosiers. He knew she was clever. He had no desire to pit his wits against hers.

"She was right you know about protecting what was as much hers as it was his. Now she has all the money that was in the safe. We cannot even prove how much money there was. How do you report her to the feds, Patrick, if we don't know how much money she had? All we have is what her husband told us and that isn't even in writing. It is only a guess on his part. So, do you report her?"

"Definitely. I have no choice. Let them figure it out. All I know is we were told that there was cash in the safe and I have no choice but to report. That has to be her problem. I am sure she will handle it very well, thank you. At any rate, once we decide on whether it is suicide or accidental death, I am pleased to say we are out of it. You can now go back to Middletown and figure out that twenty year old problem."

We shook hands and left the office quite pleased with ourselves, not with what we had accomplished but rather relieved at what we didn't have to do. Marge was as pleased as we were because she wanted us to put all our energies into the Middletown problem.

"So, you've had a murder that turned into a suicide. That's interesting. Wouldn't it be something if our suicide turned into a murder? It wouldn't surprise me one bit. In fact, I would bet on it," she said.

She had prepared an old-fashioned meal of spaghetti and meat balls which she claimed was her favorite dish growing up. Jack sat at the table waiting for the sauce to be ladled over the bowl of freshly cooked spaghetti. I couldn't remember the last time I had had spaghetti and meat balls and I looked forward to eating as much as Jack did, which was certainly unusual.

With freshly grated Parmesan Reggiano cheese and a freshly baked loaf of Italian Vienna bread and a glass of red wine, my day was complete.

It had been very satisfying as far as I was concerned and the meal topped it off. How many years had I eaten by myself, sitting in my kitchen? Now I had the best male friend that I had ever had and a lovely female companion who had fallen like an angel into my life. Life seemed pretty full to me. I thanked my lucky stars and enjoyed the rest of the day.

Chapter XXV

Early the next day while Marge kept up her diligent work on the journals, I managed to corner one of the Arruda boys who worked the fields and greenhouses for Jason and Amy. I was curious what they would have to say about Jeff Macomber. I guessed they were a year or two older or younger than their sister Evangelica, but I couldn't be sure. There were three boys and the one I talked to looked to be in his late forties or early fifties. He was a hard looking, brown haired man with three or four days of beard growing roughly on his face. I couldn't tell whether he was growing the beginnings of a beard or just hadn't bothered to shave. A few minutes after I had introduced myself he told me his name was Freddy and that he had been working for the Goetzels ever since he was a boy.

"My two brothers are Fernando and Francisco. My mother and father liked F names for boys. I'm the second and Frank is the oldest. I got work to do. Can't stand around talking."

"Okay, I'll get right to the point. What did you think of Jeff Macomber?"

He stood still for a moment and then shuffling from side to side said, "He is part of the family and we don't talk about the family. They have given us a good living, so we don't talk about them."

"It was Miss Amy who asked us to get as much information as we could about the death of her husband. I think she would want you to talk to us. I see no reason why you shouldn't."

"I don't care. You want to know anything else, I'll tell you, but I won't talk about the family. That's it."

With that he began to turn away from me and I said, "Do what you want. I can't make you talk so I'll ask Miss Amy if she gives you permission to talk to me about Jeff Macomber."

I said this and turned from him and went toward the house.

From behind me I heard him say, "Makes no difference."

I had no answer to that so I made my way back to the study where I found Marge at the table under the bright lights. I told her about Freddy's reaction and she was quite surprised. Evangelica made no qualms about talking about the family nor did her mother. Why should one of the sons feel that he was being disloyal in talking about Jeff Macomber?"

"I have no idea, but there it is."

Marge found a few lines that she found interesting and pointed them out to me.

WEDNESDAY

I GROW TIRED. I SIT HERE AND MY LEGS ARE ACHING. EVERY MORNING WHEN I GET OUT OF BED I AM HURTING. EVERY MUSCLE SEEMS TO BE ACHING. MY TIME IS GETTING SHORT I THINK. I HAVE TO BRING MYSELF TO FINISH WHAT I HAVE TO FINISH AND STOP PUTTING IT OFF.

The entry stopped there. For Sam Goetzel it represented a very short entry.

Marge said, "It is as if he has gone too far and stops writing in order not to reveal too much. I have gone back over all the entries and this is the shortest I have come across. It is hardly worth his effort if he is telling the truth that his legs are aching. What did he do that morning? Do you think he sat at his desk drinking his coffee that Deolinda brought him and did nothing else or did he have business to attend to while he sat there?"

"I have no idea, but I agree it is an interesting entry. Of course, we all feel some of what he is feeling in the entry. How many times now do I get out of bed in the morning and feel like everything is hurting? First I have to stretch my back muscles or my lower back kills me. Then I have to get my balance. I start making my way to the bathroom hoping the pain in my legs will go away. The rest of the whole business can get very discouraging. I know what he means."

"Then for me there is the matter of what I do with my money when I pass on? I have to start doing something about that. Harry Miller left me a great fortune and I have to be sure that it is passed on to those who will get as much out of it as I have. It is not so much that I have spent much of it. According to Jack I have more than I started with. In my case it brought my lovely house, some wonderful friends and you. That has been pretty wonderful. But, then, like Sam Goetzel, maybe I have unfinished business to attend to. So, you see, I understand exactly what he is saying."

"Except that you are not thinking about leaving your daughter with a worthless and disloyal husband. Could it be that that is the business he needed to clean up?" Marge asked with that little mischievous twinkle in her eyes.

The weather turned dry as the humidity seemed to leave the air and a cold front from Canada moved into the area. The humidity that was so good for the rhododendrons and azaleas caused Amy Macomber great pain. A series of days of cool dry air even on the rise above the water leading to Newport, on which the house sat, followed.

The day we met with Amy to talk about her father's journals and what we had discovered, she looked absolutely jaunty. She used her walker to enter the room, but she needed no help in sitting and when she did sit, she swung her right leg over her left and rested her hands on her knees. She laughed when she saw the look of surprise on my face and waved her hand at me as if to shoo me away. It was difficult to imagine that the woman sitting in front of us was in her nineties.

I had asked Marge to sit down with us so that she could give Amy her view of what she had been reading. She had spent more time on the journals than I had and Jack had barely looked at them.

Amy hadn't met Marge even though Marge had been spending almost every morning in the study. It struck me that her father had probably had as much privacy when he was living at home, so it was highly likely that she had no idea what he was up to when he was in his study.

"So, have you learned some terrible things about Papa?" she asked.

"Not really," Marge answered with a smile on her face. "He was a very likable man. For a man who was as successful as he was, I find him very sensible and down to earth. That doesn't surprise you, I am sure."

"Then there are no terrible revelations that I would be shocked to read?" Amy asked seriously.

"Rest your mind there. No, there is nothing I would be ashamed of if it were my father and certainly nothing shocking. He is a very likable, sincere man who deals with the matters of every day life in a genteel and gentlemanly fashion. So put your mind at ease."

"That is a relief. You know I knew my father as well as anybody could. And yet, we never really know people, do we? So much of what we do is performance for other people. The secret self remains a secret. We hold things back even from our closest friends and relatives. There are people who are married for years and years and then, suddenly, one of them discloses something that the other had no idea about. So who knows what my father really thought except my father himself?"

Marge smiled and said, "I copied a piece of the journal and then made a copy for you, so that you can see a typical entry without getting into the journals. Unless I come across something wholly unexpected, I would certainly recommend that you read them. At any rate here is a typical entry."

She gave us each a copy. Se had gone through the trouble of copying it, which rather surprised me. Marge had obviously been thinking about what she would tell Amy and she had come up with a presentation much like I would have in a classroom.

THURSDAY

THE FIRST SNOW OF THE SEASON HAS FALLEN AND EVERYTHING AROUND THE HOUSE HAS SUDDENLY BECOME WHITE. FROM MY BEDROOM WINDOW I COULD SEE AMY'S AZALEAS IN A ROW ALL COVERED WITH A LITTLE CAP OF SNOW. KNOWING HER SHE WILL BE OUT WITH A LITLE WHISK BROOM DUSTING THEM OFF. THE SNOW WON'T LAST LONG. IT IS TOO WARM TO STAY. IT FELL EARLY IN THE MORNING OR DURING THE NIGHT WHEN IT WAS JUST COLD ENOUGH, BUTAS SOON AS THE SUN REACHES IT, I KNOW IT WILL DISAPPEAR. I LOVED SNOW WHEN I WAS YOUNG, BUT NOW I FIND I AM TOO UNSTEADY ON MY FEET. I AM ALWAYS

EXPECTING TO FALL AND AT MY AGE A FALL MEANS A BROKEN HIP OR SOME SUCH THING. BUT FROM MY BED ROOM WINDOW OR FROM THE STUDY HERE THERE IS NOTHING QUITE AS LOVELY AS SNOW COVERING THE WORLD.

JASON RETURNED LAST NIGHT. I LOVE THAT BOY. AND I LOVE TO SEE AMY WITH HIM; HER FACE GLOWS WITH LOVE WHENEVER HE IS ABOUT.

I WILL BE GOING TO DELAWARE TOMORROW. THERE ARE A FEW PROBLEMS AT THE PLANT THAT I HAVE TO DEAL WITH AND YET I HATE TO LEAVE NOW THAT HE HAS ARRIVED. I HAVE NO CHOICE BUT TO TAKE A DAY OR TWO AWAY, IF NOT LONGER UNFORTUNATELY. HE HAS GIVEN ME SO MUCH PLEASURE THESE PAST FEW YEARS THAT IT IS HARD FOR ME TO RECONCILE HIS BIRTH WITH THE BOY. BUT I DON'T LIKE TO DWELL ON THAT, DO I?

THE FIRST SNOW MEANS THAT THE COLD IS NOT FAR BEHIND. I SHOULD GO SOUTH BUT I ENJOY AMY AND THE BOY SO I WILL COME NORTH AND FREEZE I SUPPOSE. AMY SUFFERS FROM ARTHRITIS AND SHE IS THE ONE WHO SHOULD GO SOUTH, BUT THERE IS NO TEARING HER AWAY FOM HER WORK HERE ON THE FARM. IT IS JUST AS I WAS WHEN I WAS YOUNG; MY WORK CAME FIRST BEFORE ANYTHING ELSE.

Marge waited until we had read the sample and then said, "I think Noah would agree that that is a typical sample of what you will find in the journals. Jason says that his grandfather used the journals to practice using full sentences in his speech and thinking. If so, you can see that he is not overly verbal, but says things in a simple, direct way."

Amy laughed and said, "This is so much removed from his normal speech pattern that it is remarkable. Normally he spoke in broken sentences. He would say things like, 'the weather…it is cold…bitter…too cold…time to go in and warm up.' Here we have him writing sentences, which is totally foreign to me. It doesn't sound like my father."

"At any rate, you can see that he is writing about what he observes from day to day and listing whatever happens the day before. There are no revelations here and certainly nothing that you would be ashamed of," Marge said.

Jack said, "For your more serious concern, they have unearthed nothing that would link your father in any way to your husband's death. I think you should know that. I also think you should tell us why you wanted this case investigated. I suspect it was to make certain that your father had nothing to do with the death, is that right?"

"You are blunt Jack. Yes, I was deeply worried that Daddy might have killed Jeff. There was no love between them, and although I doubted that Daddy would do anything like that, I still was concerned. I wanted closure and I still want it. I have lived with this for twenty years and I want to put it to rest. It is as simple as that."

"Well, I think I can talk for all three of us when I say that there would seem to be no indication that he was involved in Jeff's death," I said. "Not for one moment would I suggest that we know what happened, but at the same time, there is no apparent connection between his death and your father."

Jack said, "Per usual I pursue the money line. We have spent enough time on this case to realize that we have a lot of half truths to deal with. If we are going to make any progress at all, we need to get to the core of a few things. Now, what was the arrangement you had in the event of your death? Would Jeff inherit any money? What would Jason receive?"

"Is this really important?"

Jack looked at Amy and then reached out and touched her arm and said, "I know this is difficult, but we have to have all the cards on the table if we are to make any progress at all. I just want to make sure there is nothing in terms of money that might lead to Jeff's death, either by suicide or murder."

"Well, the way my will was written was simple enough. One hundred thousand dollars was to go to the University of Rhode Island to further studies in azalea genetics. Then there were a number of charitable contributions which have no bearing on this. My husband was to receive a stipend which would allow him to continue the life he had been leading as a member of the household. That would mean that he would be given a monthly allowance much like he was given by me. In other words he would have enough money to maintain his life style which was quite extravagant," Amy said.

"In other words," Jack said, "he would be given enough to live on but he would not be given a lump sum as an inheritance. Would such a stipulation hold up in court in Rhode Island? Wouldn't he have been entitled to half of what you owned by law?"

"According to my accountants and lawyers they had worked that out and he would have had to settle for the provisions of the will. I have no knowledge of the details of how it worked. The rest of my money would have gone to Jason with no provisions whatsoever. He would inherit everything I had of my own and all that was due to me from my father," Amy said in her usual monotone.

"Was your husband's share enough to make a considerable difference to Jason?" Jack asked.

"No. At best it was a pittance. My trust fund and the money that would come to me when my father died was in the millions. Jeff's share was in six figures. Then of course, as it turned out, my sister left most of her sizable fortune to Jason too. All in all, he is extremely wealthy and will be even more so at my death."

"So, in fact he had nothing to gain by his father's death," Jack said.

"Absolutely not. There certainly was no need for him to hurt his father for money. What his father would take from him was hardly a drop in the bucket to him."

"How did Jeff feel about the money he would be given when you passed away?"

"He didn't care as long as he had enough to keep up his life style. Remember, he was in his seventies and even he was slowing down a little. The amount of money he would have received was at least one and a half times what he normally got from me in his monthly allowance. There was also a provision in the will that the trust managers would take care of any extraordinary expenses that he assumed as long as they were within reason. Believe me, he had nothing to complain about."

"So, what you are saying is that Jason had no reason to do him harm. He had no reason to complain about his financial future if anything happened to you. Is that right?

"I've already told you all of this without all the details," she said.

"Amy, I know that, but I want to go over every detail to make sure we haven't missed anything. Again, I know it is difficult but we have to pin this down and you are the best source we have."

"I understand."

"Now I have a question that I think needs an answer. I hope I don't hurt your feelings by asking it. It seems to me that yours was a failed marriage. We have heard enough to know that your husband was not faithful to you and that he didn't pretend to be," I said and waited for some reaction. Amy did not give any indication that she was surprised or offended in any way.

"Your father was more than aware of the situation. Now, I understand that he was the person most insistent on your 50th anniversary party. I find that hard to understand. I know you have answered the question before, but I would like you to answer it again since we are trying to get to the bottom of this. I would think it would be embarrassing to have a celebration and to invite people to the affair who knew full well what was going on and with whom, in some cases, your husband carried on an affair. I, too, know this is difficult, but can you explain that please?"

"I can't," Amy said looking at the far wall behind me. Normally she looked whoever she was talking to directly in the eye, but this time her eyes drifted away. For the first time since we had begun talking to her, I saw a visceral reaction.

"That is exactly why you are here. That question has haunted me for twenty years. Let's get it out in the open. Did my father plan the murder of my husband? Was my father so upset by the way Jeff was treating me that he planned to do away with him? Did he somehow lure him into the study and then, after drugging him somehow, kill him so that it looked like suicide? That is the question I have asked myself over and over again these twenty years? That is the question that has kept me awake night after night. And during all that time I am no closer to an answer than I was twenty years ago."

"I am afraid we don't have an answer yet either," I said, "But maybe we are getting closer."

She looked at me then and I could see the pain and anxiety in her face. I felt sorry for her, but at the same time, I did not want to make anything that sounded like a promise. I wasn't sure what we were dealing with and

I needed to come up with something, but nothing seemed to be breaking for us.

"If you have no more questions for me, I am getting a bit tired. I don't think I will go outside today."

I said, "I do have another question and it is an important one. If you are too tired we can wait until tomorrow. If not, I'd like to get it out of the way."

"I know what it is, so let's get it over with now."

She moved her legs slightly and adjusted the throw that covered her lap and legs. Now, she looked directly into my eyes and I knew too, that she knew exactly what I was going to ask.

"I would like to know who the girl was who was pregnant," I said. "Unless I am wrong, I think I already know."

This surprised Jack and Marge and they looked at me inquiringly.

Amy's face did look tired and I was almost sorry I had asked the question. It wasn't my intention at any time to hurt her, but I knew right then that I had hurt her terribly and brought up something she didn't want to face. She suddenly looked her years and I thought that she might break down, but she managed to slowly pull herself together and to make an answer to my final question.

"Okay, Noah, let's put it into words. The girl my husband got pregnant was Evangelica Arruda. There it is. By now you know that she is a simple, defenseless soul who was nothing less than putty in his hands. It was terrible. I could forgive him his unfaithfulness, his constant adultery, but to think that he took advantage of that girl was even beyond his perfidy. When I found out I was shocked. I was so angry that for the first time I threatened to cut off his allowance and all of his money. Is that what has been bothering you Jack?"

Jack sat quietly and took his head in his hands and didn't say a word.

"Yes I was furious. I could not believe that he could stoop so low. I was so angry my poor father had to suppress his anger and take me aside to quiet me down. I asked Jeff to leave immediately and I didn't see him for at least two months after that. I would not even hear about him coming to the house. I even went so far as to have my lawyers look into a divorce to determine the financial repercussions in the event that that happened."

"So, he did have concerns about money, then?" Jack asked.

"Not at the time of his death. By then, I had pretty much worked out my fury. Although I was no longer talking to him, my lawyers had advised against any action whatsoever. So his financial setup was just as it had been previously."

"What was the basis for that advice, may I ask?" Jack said.

"It all had to do with the fact that I wanted all of the money as I have already explained to you to go to Jason. By staying married, my lawyers claimed that the process would be simple and straightforward. They felt that divorce brought on a whole other aspect of complication that wasn't necessary."

Jack seemed satisfied, and I was glad to get Amy back to the main subject which was Evangelica and her pregnancy.

"So, you were angry about the fact that he had gotten Evangelica pregnant," I said.

"Yes, very angry, and for the first time, I was very ashamed. I can't tell you how ashamed I was. The birth of Jason and the resulting revelation that he was Jeff's son was hard for me to take, but by then I had stopped loving Jeff and the boy was a wonder for Dad and for me."

She stopped talking. I felt she was going to fall forward in a faint. I leaned forward to support her, but she pulled herself up quickly and said, "I cannot go on right now. I am sorry, but you are going to have to be satisfied with this much. Please, Marge can you help me to my room, or get Jen if she is about?"

Marge rose and stepped forward to take Amy by the arm and lead her out of the room. Amy stopped and reached for her walker which Marge had forgotten in her anxiety. She stood next to her as Amy made her way very slowly out of the room and into the hallway leading to the sun room where we were sitting.

Jack sat with his hands on either side of his face and his elbows on his knees. He hadn't said a word and I sat as still wondering how to evaluate what we had just heard. I wasn't sure what to think of it. It would require some thought to try to weave it into a whole, but I knew we were far ahead of where we had been two hours ago.

We waited for Marge to return. Then Jack signaled us to leave. He was stolid and for some reason didn't want to speak in the room we were in.

It was not like him to be secretive. I wondered for a moment whether he thought the room might be bugged. The moment we were outside the house, he said, "Let's get out of here. I find it stifling. It's like an evil spirit is hovering around me. Let's go someplace where we can have a decent breakfast and then we'll talk."

I looked at Marge. She had no objection. We drove to Newport which was only a few miles down the main road looking for a spot to eat. It was early. We found a Newport Creamery nearby and Jack seemed content.

"I remember dropping in here for a drink called an 'Awful Awful' which if I remember correctly was an extra thick milk shake. I wonder if they still serve them."

Marge laughed and said, "Please Jack, not for breakfast. Not even you."

We sat in a booth and Jack searched the menu and said, "Here it is. I'll get one just to see if it is the same as I remember."

Jack ordered his usual high cholesterol breakfast, while Marge and I settled for orange juice.

Before his meal arrived Jack said, "I feel I am surrounded by liars. There is just too much that comes out in dribs and drabs. Nothing seems to be above the surface. Do you think that Jeff was worried about money? I asked that question at the outset of this case. The answer came back, 'He had all the money he needed. There was no question about money.' Now we find out that Amy was considering cutting off his supply of money. She tells us that she changed her mind and at the time of his death he was back in good financial graces. Can I believe her? I'm not sure now."

"I do find certain things very strange," Marge offered. "On the one hand you are being asked to come up with some answers as to what happened. Why even ask you to get involved if everyone is playing loose with the truth? Even in the journals, as I have told you, Noah, there is a sense in which Mr. Goetzel is holding back. There seems to be so much false pride here that I find it in direct contradiction to the facts. How can anyone be overly proud and protective of a family that has such terrible sexual travesty involved in it? Here is a man who has an affair with his wife's sister and has a child by her that is living in the house with his aunt and his father and grandfather. He has very little to do with his father, but is the favorite of his aunt and grandfather. It is a travesty by any measurement. How many times have you heard about a more ludicrous arrangement? And yet we are dealing with pride. It is ridiculous."

Marge was beside herself with indignation. She was actually red in the face as she finished her little statement of dismay.

By then Jack's food arrived and he began the process of putting away his omelet and home fries and sausage along with his Awful Awful and a double order of toast. He didn't say a word as he was eating his breakfast, but ate slowly and with pleasure. Marge looked at me and we both began to laugh at the man and his amazing appetite. He didn't even notice, he was so preoccupied with his meal and his unbelievably thick and heavy milk shake. Marge signaled the waitress to bring us coffees and we sat sipping our coffee until Jack had finished his meal and was ready to talk.

Jack turned to me and said, "Now, Noah, what have you got to say?"

"Well, from my point of view the truest thing we have hard so far is the actual disgust that Amy showed for her husband for having impregnated Evangelica. That was a real moment. There was no cool there, no reserve. She actually had disdain for him when she discovered what he had done. It was one thing, as she said, for him to have his affairs and flirtations and quite another for him to take advantage of that poor, simple soul. Have you talked with her Jack? She is a brainless, but beautiful woman. She is sweet and gentle, but hardly the kind of woman for a man of the world like Jeff Macomber.

It reminded me of the relationship between a student and a teacher. Nothing disturbed me more when I was teaching than to see a male teacher take advantage of a young girl or, more often than not, a female teacher doing the same with a young male. As far as I was concerned it was an unforgivable transgression and one which should have resulted in the dismissal of the teacher. There was a thin line between taking advantage of a student and acting in "loco parentis", that is, in place of the parent. I particularly enjoyed bright students, and I tried as much as possible to have a positive influence on them, but there is a big difference between having an influence and attracting them sexually. Crossing that line between influence and sexual attraction disturbed me every time I saw it happen, and I felt obligated to report any such activity to the people in charge. It was the one area in which there was no question about being loyal to ones fellow teachers. What Jeff Macomber had done was much the same thing. From my point of view, here was a tall handsome man with golden yellow hair and tanned body, gleaming white teeth, charming, and talkative and always gentle and nice, paying attention to a young, innocent and naïve girl who had seen nothing of the world. I could just imagine him sweet talking her and bringing her little presents, whispering to her how lovely she was, and making her the object of his version of love with which he was so good and so practiced. How could she resist him? She didn't have a chance.

I can just imagine the pain she must have felt sleeping with him, the terrible guilt that followed. Everything she had been taught, I am sure, mitigated against her doing anything so foolish as to sleep with a man without marriage. Then, when she became pregnant and her mother found out, it must have been devastating for her and her family. I had seen this scenario so many times, I hated to think about it. The Portuguese are not noted for quiet discussions of traumatic events. Deolinda would have been wailing and wringing her hands and covering her head in a wet towel to aid her breathing. The wet towel was par for the course, and I always wondered precisely how it helped women to breathe. Evangelica would have been sitting in the kitchen with her head in her hands weeping and emitting huge sighs that carried all the sorrow of the world in their wretchedness. Of course, her brothers would be outside the kitchen door swearing and threatening to kill whoever had done this to their sister. The story would come out in screams and cries and sighs and sobs and weeping. Evangelica would hold her head down in shame and disgrace while her mother prodded and dug to find out the essentials of what had happened.

I could even imagine the disbelief when Deolinda discovered who it was. I could see her collapsing into a chair in complete astonishment and disgust at Jeff Macomber and what he had done to her daughter. It would have taken her some time to take it all in and to try to digest what she had been told. She would have asked if Evangelica meant Jason and not Jeff. It would have seemed more plausible had it been Jason. But, Jeff was an old man. The question in Deolinda's mind was not only his age as a lover, but the fact that he could still father a child. She couldn't believe that her daughter might have had other lovers or was using Jeff as a cover for her baby's real father. Did someone else father her child or was it truly Jeff?

Deolinda had to be happy that her husband had not lived to see this day in his daughter's life. But Deolinda had to face the three boys and tell them the whole story. How could she keep them under control was her first thought. Anger at Jeff Macomber made her want to make him suffer, wanted him to be dealt with by the boys who she knew would want to kill him. But her first task was to keep the boys under control until she could plan what to do. The fact that Jeff Macomber had done this to her daughter meant that he would have to pay. The question was to make him pay so that her daughter would come out ahead of the game. Certainly she knew what the boys would want. They would want to kill the man who had done that to their sister.

When the boys did discover what had happened to their sister, they acted just as she knew they would. They shouted and screamed and ranted. They put on a terrible display of anger mixed with mystification and disbelief as well. Their attack centered on the poor girl who cringed and cried and sobbed. They shouted that shame would be brought down on the heads of the family, that they would not be able to go to church with their heads held high but would be walking down the aisle in shame. Deolinda waited out the onslaught and stood stoically by her daughter, soothing her and rubbing her back with her hand. Then her brothers shifted their anger to Jeff Macomber when they discovered that he had done the terrible thing to their sister She waited for one of the men to go searching for a weapon to be used on Jeff to make him pay the price for treating his sister so badly. When it happened she was ready and stood in his way and then forced the three men to be seated and to listen to what she had to say.

I could see the whole thing in my mind's eye as sure as if I had been there. In my years in the schools and in my old neighborhood as a young man I had seen the scenario played out many times. The difference between then and now is that for all the turmoil and guilt the young girl was almost always taken back into the family where she could get the help she needed in the absence of a husband. Today, the young girls, unprepared for motherhood and all that it requires and lacking most of the skills that are so necessary to run a home, find themselves alone and on welfare trying to survive. The most difficult part of the latter scenario is that the poor girls are seen as outcasts in society and with their backs to the wall find themselves in even direr straits as everyone turns against them. One girl said it to me very concisely, "When I got pregnant my family threw me out of the house. The bum who did it to me took a walk. Every one said that I shouldn't get an abortion because I was a good Catholic. The day after I had the baby they looked at me like I was a welfare bum. Screw them all."

Deolinda had the problem of making the most out of a bad situation. She needed no more trouble than she had. To turn her boys loose on Jeff Macomber would serve absolutely no purpose at all. She would have tried to settle them down and then to reason with them to determine the best course to follow.

"The first thing we have to do is to have this girl have an abortion," she said and when she said it there was an immediate reaction from the boys and from Angelica who burst out in a scream that carried with the sound of the pains of hell. "Stupid girl, you are not going to have this baby. Are you crazy? It will ruin your life to carry the baby of a rich man. No. I will not see that man's baby born into my house. We will not talk about it. Mr. Goetzel will arrange for you to have the best doctor they can find,and we will have the operation done in a hospital."

When I was a young man and had learned about such things, I knew that abortions were done by a woman in the neighborhood. This was usually an old lady who doubled as a doctor in the community. I thought of them as witches. They did things like set bones. They learned their craft setting the legs of sheep and animals in the Azores and carried their craft over to the United States and to the immigrant neighborhoods where some of the poor, ignorant people had great faith in them. Once, I broke my index finger and my mother took me to one to be set. She lived in a tenement in dark ill lit rooms that smelled of stale cabbage and old soup. I was scared to death but my mother told me to be brave, and she would take care of me with no trouble at all. This particular woman was in widow's weeds and was tiny and I thought smelled horribly. But she was efficient. She saw that I was frightened so she got right to my finger, touched it very gingerly and quickly put it in a splint. She set it very quickly and painlessly and then tapped me on the head and sent me out the door while she settled the bill with my mother. I knew in a vague sort of way that she performed abortions on girls who found themselves "in trouble" and delivered babies at home for women who could not afford or wish to go to a hospital. How much damage such women did is hard to estimate, but I am sure they were the cause of a great deal of hardship and suffering in later life for those women they "treated".

The odd thing for me was the fact that the people with whom I grew up and lived with in the tenement sections of Fall River were frightened to death of hospitals and thought of doctors as only wanting their money. Doctors were quacks who took advantage of poor people. Visiting a doctor was akin to asking for trouble. They would rather have dealt with a quack and a fraud with very little knowledge of anything especially hygiene than visit a real educated medical person. On my poor mother's death bed, she was afraid of what the doctor would do to her and wanted only to see a priest before she died. She begged me to forbid the doctor entrance to her room and sick bed. Deolinda was not one of this breed for some reason and realized that the best of doctors could be had by Sam Goetzel to perform the abortion on her daughter.

I was deep in my own thoughts sitting in a booth in Newport Creamery and not listening to Jack or Marge when suddenly Marge poked me in the ribs and said, "Noah, where in the world are you?"

Jack said, "Good God man, come back to earth."

I apologized and then explained where I had been. I ordered more coffee and told my thoughts to Marge and Jack.

Jack said, "That would explain the house wouldn't it? Sam Goetzel wasn't the kind of man to hand out money just because he had sex with a woman, no matter how much he might love her. That must have been the deal. Pay Deolinda and Evangelica with the money to provide them with a good home for their future and there would be no questions asked by the general public. Noah, I buy that much for sure. It makes absolute sense in something I couldn't figure out. I couldn't understand why he gave her the money for such a lavish house. Now it follows."

"Now that we are doing all this speculating, can I bring up something I have been thinking about since we found out about the pregnancy? This is going to sound absurd, but bear with me; it is a woman going wild with her imagination," Marge said and I was surprised because it wasn't like Marge to go off on flights of fancy.

"Supposing the baby wasn't Jeff's at all. Suppose the baby was Jason's. And Jeff, in his first decent action for his son, was willing to act as the fall guy to protect Jason from recrimination and possible physical harm from the brothers of Evangelica. This may sound absurd, but the one thing we have seen repeated in this whole mess is that nothing is what it seems or what we are told it is."

Jack said, "It is a long stretch if you ask me. The Jeff Macomber I knew was hardly the type of man to sacrifice himself for anyone. He was too much into himself. I can't believe this one. I can't imagine it would even occur to him to do anything for anybody else."

Marge laughed and said, "Let me push this one step further. Supposing Jen was the baby born out of wedlock, not to some unknown woman, but to Evangelica and then taken into the family. I know it sounds pretty far-fetched but I don't think it is out of the question. I suggest we press Jason to determine who Jen's mother is and end my question."

Jack laughed and said, "Marge I never would have guessed. You struck me as practical and down to earth. This is absolutely shocking coming from the stolid Marge I have known. I am having a hard time buying this one to be honest and I come back to the same problem. Here is a guy living in a house with his son and yet having very little to do with him. They rarely speak, if ever and have nothing in common. Then suddenly, he turns around and in a sense, gives up his reputation, no matter how little he had to begin with, this man puts his life and his financial security in danger, all supposedly for his son. What do you think Noah?"

"Well, it makes as much sense as anything else we have. My biggest problem is that I think Jason is too smart to do something like that with that girl. I would have a hard time coming up with the occasion that would lead him to have sex with Evangelica. But who knows? Maybe Marge has hit on something."

"My goodness, guys," Marge said, "I only threw it out as a possibility, not as a fact."

Chapter XXVI

I expected to get very little out of Deolinda. I knew she was much too clever for me, but I had to meet her once head-on if for no other reason than that I wanted to see how she reacted when I told her that I knew about Evangelica. We showed up at her door unannounced, and I half expected that she would turn us away. Jack, Marge and I stood on her doorstep on a cool morning that presaged the beginnings of fall. The weather was drying and the cool air was a wonderful and welcome relief from the heat of summer and the dog days of August. We were close to the water, and there was still some humidity in the air, but nothing like we had felt a month before.

Deolinda opened the door and stood for a moment looking at us before she swung it open in full and invited us in. Aside from her hesitation and surprise when she saw us she showed no signs of concern. We were ushered into the parlor and sat in our accustomed places now. It is odd how we tend to sit in the very same chairs when we visit someone else's home, as if those chairs had become our personal property. It is like sitting at the dinner table when we take the same chairs each time we sit down.

Deolinda left the room after we were seated and came back shortly with a plate of Portuguese tea biscuits which she knew now that I enjoyed so much.

She laughed at my expression and said, "The tea will be ready in a few minutes. I wish I had some mallasadas for your hungry friend, but I am afraid the boys ate the last of them." She turned to Marge and said, "You will have to learn to make these for Mr. Amos. He loves them. They remind him of when he was a boy at home. I will give you the recipe if you want. They are very easy to make."

She may have been just chattering to appear to be cool and collected, but she carried it off very well.

She disappeared into the kitchen again and we just sat and waited. Jack couldn't resist the food set out in front of him, so he reached out and took a biscuit off the plate, broke off a piece and started to eat it. When Deolinda returned with the tea things he had already eaten three biscuits.

When she had settled down she said, "Well, Mr. Amos get it over with. You have something to talk about, so let's get it out on the table here instead of playing games."

I laughed and said, "It is a serious subject. We want to know about Evangelica and her pregnancy."

That evinced no surprise or reaction from Deolinda and I suspect that she knew the question was coming. She knew most definitely why we were there.

"What is there to say? You know all about it and so I can't see why you are here. Who told you?"

"Amy Macomber told us so that we could get to the bottom of the problem about her husband's death. She also told us that your daughter became pregnant by Jeff Macomber. Is that right?"

"Yes it is. What can I say? He was a pig who lived for his thing. He led his life being led around by his thing. He was a criminal. He was a bad man. You have met Evangelica. You have talked to her. You know he should never have done that to her. It was wrong. But he was no good from the beginning. That poor woman had to live with him all those years knowing he couldn't keep away from women."

"When we first talked to Evangelica, she said he always treated her like a gentleman. That surprises me now," I said.

"Who knows what the girl will say. She could say anything. We know she cannot be taken seriously."

"The next question, of course, is what happened to the baby?" Jack asked.

"That, I will not talk about. That is the big sin on our family name. We cannot keep thinking about it. I confess my sins every week to a priest and he knows, but I do not want to talk about it," she said with a tone of finality.

"Did Evangelica have an abortion?" I asked.

"I told you that I will not talk about it. It is, what do they say, off limits. That's it. Eat the biscuits, lady. Noah likes to dip them in his tea the way the old ladies did when he was a kid. I still do now. That is the best way to eat them."

The subject had changed and I knew there was no way of getting back to it. Yet, I couldn't help but think that there was more to the story than she was willing to talk about.

I couldn't help but comment that my mother had served her tea and biscuits with little Portuguese napkins that had what she used to call "fancy work" all around the edges. They were delicate little napkins in bright colors of pink and blue and red that were brought out and laundered for special occasions. I remember the care with which she washed them and dried them and then ironed them before folding them and using them at tea time. She took a special pride in having nice things for special occasions.

Deolinda laughed and said those things were only for the rich. In her poor circumstances there was not a chance in the world that she would own such things and she had to resort to paper napkins. I couldn't help but comment that my mother never lived in a palatial house the likes of hers and left it at that as my parting shot. Jack looked at me as if to congratulate me on my barb and we left the house a little wiser than when we came in, I thought.

I said exactly that when we were in the car and driving back to the Point, and Marge questioned how much we had learned. She didn't agree that we were much in front of where we had started.

"I think she was talking more than you think she was. I think she told us in no uncertain terms that Evangelica did not have an abortion," I said.

Jack reacted quickly and surprisingly strongly to what I had said. "Noah, I think that needs an explanation. What Deolinda indeed said was that she would not talk about the abortion. I don't think that told us anything."

Marge joined in by saying, "I feel the same way. I think she refused to talk to us about the abortion. I assume she is a Catholic woman and has deep religious convictions when it comes to abortion."

I thought for a moment because I was convinced I was right and I wanted to phrase what I had to say in just the right way.

"The pregnancy in this case is far more important to Deolinda and her family than the abortion, I think. I can imagine that the news of the pregnancy shattered the family's equilibrium. Think about that aspect of it. Here is a family with a young woman who is a beautiful girl. She is sweet and innocent and the kind of girl who doesn't even go out on dates with boys. I'll guarantee that she was chaperoned wherever she went and never left that house alone. The one place where she was safe was working in the Goetzel house where she did her work every day and was productive. Her brothers worked alongside her and her mother was always there working with her. The shock of her pregnancy had to be devastating. I'm sure when the brothers found out that Jeff Macomber was the father, they would have been in a rage and would have wanted to kill him."

Jack said, "I agree with what you are saying so far. But it is the leap to the abortion that bothers me."

"Hear me out. I was brought up with these women. I can't tell you how many abortions I remember growing up. There was no welfare then. Women who became pregnant by their boyfriends and who were having their babies fathered by getting married to them, would never think about an abortion. But, those who found themselves abandoned had very little choice but to have an abortion."

"But, Noah, they are Catholic and abortions would be frowned upon," Marge said.

"But, Marge, they are not Irish Catholics. They are Portuguese. Portuguese women go to church but draw a line between what the Pope and Church have to say along with what their priests and bishops might have to say about their morals and how that translates into action. The defining line for the Portuguese women I know and was brought up among, was always money. The pregnancy meant hardship not only religiously, but also financially. So when a woman was faced with the hardships of bringing up a child without a man to help her and to support her, she turned to the doctor or the women she knew who could remove the child through an abortion. It was only when the movement against abortion became so strong in later years and welfare was allowed women to support their children without a husband that we saw so many children being born out of wedlock."

Jack said, "So what is the point, Noah? I seem to be missing it."

"The point is that Deolinda would not look upon abortion as a shameful thing. In her time and mine, it was a practical answer to a terrible problem. If her daughter had an abortion, it would be a relief to her, not something to be ashamed of. No, I would bet my last dollar that she doesn't want to talk about it because Evangelica never had an abortion. Her child was born."

"I can see what you are saying, and you may very well be right, but what does that have to do with this case?" Marge asked.

"I'm not sure, but I have a feeling there is more to this than we can see right now. It is the iceberg with only ten percent showing above the water. There is something lurking beneath the surface that will explain a great deal."

We drove the rest of the way to the Point in silence and it was odd that the three of us were suddenly deep in thought. It wasn't in our nature to be so quiet, but we found ourselves when we finally arrived in my driveway wondering what we were about. I invited Jack into the house for lunch although I had no idea what I would serve.

"Well, if you are right and the baby was born, where is the baby? Did they put the baby up for adoption?" Marge asked.

"Now, that would definitely go against the grain as far as I can see. The baby might be given to relatives. It is not unheard of that relatives in the Azores would take the child in for a fee, a monthly or annual subsidy to take care of the baby's needs. That was done more than you can imagine when I was a boy. But I don't know in this case. There seems to be no connection to the Azores in Deolinda's family. There are none of the usual signs in the house. I don't know if you noticed but there are no holy pictures on the walls, or the usual lucky rooster that we had in our house. No, I don't think the Azores come into play here. If anything. I would suspect that this is a typical Portuguese family that stays very close."

Jack said, "What does that mean?"

"I mean they live as a closed circle among themselves. They have a limited number of friends. All of their activities revolve around the family unit and maybe a church group with which they are affiliated. It comes from a tradition here in the States of staying close to each other and not mixing in with the outside community, possibly for fear of contamination. You have to understand that when their forebears came to America, they came to an alien community that was incipiently evil in their eyes. They protected themselves from that community by becoming insular and developing the techniques that would keep them apart. They do not participate in the community. For instance, they eat almost exclusively in Portuguese restaurants. You won't find a group of Portuguese seniors having breakfast at MacDonald's. A mother's greatest fear is what happened to Evangelica that she became pregnant by an American."

"This is all very interesting, Noah, but does it have anything to do with the problem at hand?" Marge asked. "I can understand what you are saying, but I am having a hard time relating it to Jeff's death."

"Well, I don't know what to tell you. My gut instinct is that something is just below the surface here and we are missing it. Let's ask some of the questions that need to be asked. Even if we go over some of them again."

While we talked I prepared some linguica and eggs. I fried about a pound in a bit of oil and butter and then added four beaten eggs to form an omelet. This with some home fries which I had cooked a few days before and frozen worked very well and was sufficient for even Jack. Marge and I had a small portion of the omelet with a salad while Jack had the major portion without a salad.

"It seems to me the first question that has to be asked is why did they have a 50th Anniversary Party? That is the most improbable party I have ever heard of, especially now that we have learned that Amy did everything but divorce her husband. Why in the world celebrate the mess they were in? I cannot come up with one reasonable statement to justify that day," Marge said this with a bemused look on her face that was surprising.

Jack said, "I agree. That was absurd. No one has given us a real explanation of it either. I agree with Marge, it is ridiculous to celebrate a marriage no matter how old it is, when it is such a bad one. There had to be a reason for it that has escaped us."

"The next question," I said, "is what happened to the baby that Evangelica was carrying? I think that is crucial here, but I am afraid I have beaten that subject to death."

"And finally, the biggest question of them all. Did Jeff Macomber commit suicide or was he murdered?" Jack asked. "That is the question we began with and that is the question we need an answer to before we close this down. How are we going to get that answer?"

'There may be something in the journals yet. I admit everything has been pretty dull so far, but who knows. I will keep reading and taking notes and maybe something will come up," Marge said almost apologetically.

"No need to feel sorry," Jack said, "You're doing the best you can. We'll just keep plugging away."

The next morning Jack and I met with Amy again and Jack asked the question again that we had asked the day before. "Amy let's level on this. Why did you have that party? You've told us once that it was at your father's insistence. Is that right?"

"Yes, it is. I didn't want it of course because the last thing I wanted was to celebrate a failed marriage. What was the point I asked him over and over again. But, he insisted."

"How did Jeff feel about it?" I asked.

"At that point, he had no choice. He was in the position of having to do exactly as he was told. That's how bad things had become in the house. Dad knew I didn't want the affair, but it seemed that there was no changing his mind. I had a very hard time even showing up myself. I felt like a fool and a hypocrite. Imagine inviting people to the event. How embarrassing it was for me, I can't even begin to tell you. I wouldn't accept gifts so I asked that any gifts be in the form of a check to the giver's favorite charity. At least that way I didn't have to justify getting gifts from well-meaning people."

"That I do remember come to think of it. I was rather surprised at that. So why did your father insist on having the party?" Jack asked.

"I've told you any number of times that I don't know."

"I think what you are worried about is that we will find out that your father wanted to kill your husband and for some reason set up this party as a cover. Am I right?"

"Of course. That has been my worry from the beginning. That is the question that has haunted me for twenty years. Did my father plan to kill my husband? It even sounds terrible when I say it."

"What I don't understand is, even if he did plan to do harm to your husband, how did he know that Jeff would go to the study and rest in the middle of the party? Isn't it odd to think that he would do just that and plan a murder around it?" Jack asked.

"That part at least is easy," Amy said. "Jeff went to the study every day in the afternoon for his little afternoon nap. No one used it then. I was out in the play pens or in the green houses and daddy had finished his work in the morning. So from around two o'clock to five, no one used it. That explains how he got together with Evangelica. That's when she went in to clean the room. But I can't imagine daddy planning such a thing. You know he was ninety when all this happened and although he wasn't senile, he certainly wasn't capable of planning the details of a murder."

"Did he have all his senses at the end?" I asked. "My mother was in her late eighties when she died. and she had a difficult time grasping reality."

"No, Daddy was having a difficult time at the end too. He sometimes went off in flights of fancy. But I think at the time of Jeff's death, he wasn't bad. Although, as I just said, I would have a difficult time thinking that he could plan a murder."

"The point is, though, that he wanted this celebration to take place and would not back down, right?"

"That is exactly right. Daddy could be extremely stubborn when he made up his mind."

So, we had as much as we could get for that meeting and Jack and I went to the study to join Marge who was hard at work on the journals. The weather had cooled down considerably. I thought I could smell the heat which had been turned on in the room. I thought it was too early for the heat but the room was comfortable, and I realized that if Amy were to come into the room that evening it would have to be reasonably warm.

Marge looked excited as she said, "I may be coming up with something finally. Read this."

SATURDAY

THE WEATHER IS VERY HOT FOR THIS TIME OF YEAR. I HAVE DIFFICULTY WORKING IN THE STUDY NOW BECAUSE I NEED A FAN AND THE NOISE BOTHERS ME. I DON'T LIKE THE TERRACE DOORS OPEN EVEN THOUGH WE GET A GOOD

BREEZE OFF THE WATER BECAUSE IT BLOWS MY PAPERS AROUND. SO I HAVE TO SUFFER THE HEAT.

ELEANOR AND I HAVE BEEN MARRIED FOR MANY YEARS NOW AND HAVE HAD A GOOD MARRIAGE. SHE WENT AWAY FOR A WHILE AND IS BACK NOW. I DON'T KNOW WHERE SHE WENT TO. MAYBE SHE WENT TO ITALY TO VISIT OUR DAUGHTER. I DON'T KNOW BUT I AM GLAD SHE IS HOME NOW. I MISSED HER.

SUNDAY

THE HEAT CONTINUES AND IT UPSETS ME. I HAVE TO LEARN HOW TO WORK IN THE MIDDLE OF IT. I GET CONFUSED NOW. THE WORDS ON THE PAGE SWIM. AND MY EYES GROW HEAVY. I CANNOT CONTINUE MUCH LONGER.

WE SHOULD DO SOMETHING TO CELEBRATE OUR YEARS OF MARRIAGE. FOR SOME REASON, AMY DOES NOT WANT TO BOTHER, BUT I AM GOING TO INSIST. I WILL HAVE INVITATIONS SENT OUT TO ALL OUR FRIENDS AND ACQUAINTANCES AND MAKE A BIG PARTY OUT OF IT. WE HAVE HAD A GOOD MARRIAGE AND WE SHOULD CELEBRATE IT.

Marge laughed at the expressions on our faces. I had to laugh at Jack myself.

"Well, I'll be damned. The party was for him. He was celebrating his fiftieth wedding anniversary and he had no idea that his wife had died. Isn't that remarkable?" Jack said.

"Definitely remarkable. The poor man was living in a world of his own making at that point, I suspect. So, what you think from reading this is that he thought the party was for his marriage and not for Amy?" Jack asked.

"Yes, there is no question in my mind now. The only question I have is how Amy did not see what was really happening. Was she so blind to her father that she did not see it?" Marge said.

"It could be that he was going in and out of his delusions. That does happen. He may even have been on medication of some sort that made him swing in and out. The point is that he somehow hid the real reason for the party from Amy and he husband."

Jack laughed and said, "Of all the improbable explanations this is the strangest imaginable."

Marge added, "The man was held in such admiration and respect by his daughter that he may have been able to insist on the celebration without saying much about his reasons for having it. Obviously, he never did explain his reasons. And then there is the matter of his poor speaking habits that Jason mentions. He didn't speak in long sentences and it could have been that they were not used to hearing him give his positions on things, certainly not long explanations."

"Whatever it was, he certainly must have hidden the fact that he wanted an anniversary party for him and his wife. Who would have guessed that? I know who would have known, of course. Deolinda would have known. Would it have been Deolinda coming to him that he thought was his wife? Didn't we hear that she was his mistress after his wife died. Maybe there was a period of time when he was without a woman and then when he began doing whatever he did with Deolinda, he later thought his wife had come back. Is it so hard to speculate that at the age of ninety he would have lost touch with reality and thought that the woman he had taken as a mistress some time before had been his wife returning to him?" I said.

Jack laughed now and said, "I must be some sort of hard realist. You two make such huge leaps of the imagination that I begin to think that I am without any imagination at all. You are stretching the little you have into a major scenario that is going to take some facts to fill in."

"The problem is that we have been working on this for quite some time without getting any closer to how Jeff Macomber was killed. So let's take a few leaps of the imagination and see where they take us. I don't think this is as much a leap as it sounds, but we can leave it here and see what else we can come up with."

Chapter XXVII

Patrick called us later in the day to let us know that he had pretty much decided to call Attorney Desrosiers' death an accident, and he asked us to meet with him. We drove to his office in New Bedford where we wondered if we were going to be questioned again if we parked in the reserved spaces for the District Attorney's Office. I think Jack was hoping to be questioned, but we parked with no difficulty and made our way into Patrick's office.

He began by saying that he had the tapes of the conversations that had been held in the attorney's office, and they clearly indicated that he had contracted with a hit man to kill his wife and her son. There were hours of taped conversations, and the important information had been culled out by a stenographer who then edited her work to give the District Attorney a relevant but limited copy of the phone calls.

"What it comes down to is that they knew that he had a contract out on them, and his wife and stepson immediately contacted the hit man and paid more for the job than the attorney had offered. They turned the contract around on him. You are on the tapes too, you know, but not in the relevant transcripts. It does seem though, that he knew they had turned the tables on him and he was frightened to death.

"Did a second coroner support the findings of the doctor in Woods Hole?" I asked

"Yes. He maintains that he died as a result of a mix of an overdose of sleeping pills and a system full of alcohol. The question for me was to decide whether he committed suicide or whether his death was accidental. I have decided with the latter because I have no basis for saying that his death was a result of his own decision to take his life. I have no basis for assuming that it was accidental either, but since there is an onus associated with suicide and because it effects the insurance claims of his wife, I had no choice in my decision."

"The insurance company might not like that," Jack said. "but I do think you are right. Without proof that he did commit suicide, it is too much of a leap to decide that that was the reason for death and deprive his widow of the insurance money, whatever it might be."

"As it turns out, it is a half million dollar claim. She insisted on it when they married, even though you can imagine what it cost him at his age to take out such a big policy. But the amount doesn't play a part in our decision. There is no other conclusion that I can come to."

"And both coroners agreed that he was dead before he was shot?" I asked.

"There seems to be complete agreement on that. Both have no doubt, whatsoever, that he was dead before he was shot. I can't go into details because I don't know the reasons for the decision, but they have to do with the physiology of the body at death and the effects of wounds after the body stops functioning. At any rate, they can support their conclusion with scientific facts. I have no reason or enough knowledge to question those. So as far as I am concerned this is pretty much closed."

"Is there any criminal offense in shooting a body after it is dead? In attempting to murder someone who is dead, is that a criminal offense?" I asked just to clear my mind of any questions.

"Obviously a rhetorical question," Patrick said. "but, you know the truth of the matter is that no matter how much we feel that the shooter in this case should be punished, Desrosiers is dead and gone and wasn't murdered. Then, I also feel that both Mrs. Desrosiers and her son should be prosecuted for conspiring to kill him, but that doesn't matter either. So, all three of them walk. The shooter is free to pursue his chosen career. That dreadful son walks away with his stepfather's money, and Mrs. Desrosiers finds herself free of her terrible husband at very little cost, both mentally and monetarily. I have neither the staff nor the resources to pursue this matter even though there may be a legal basis for it. I will defer to the Attorney General. If he desires that it be pursued, I will. If not, it is forgotten."

"So you won't pursue this case," I said.

"Oh. No, I won't unless as I said, the Attorney General insists on it," he said.

Patrick obviously wasn't happy having to admit that, but we took his word that considering the other cases he had to pursue that it just wasn't worth it. We left it at that and, after inquiring about Nelly and Peggy and the baby, we headed back to the Point.

I couldn't remember the last time I had seen Nelly or Peggy or the baby, so when we got back, Jack and I decided that it was about time we paid them a visit. Peggy lived in the city but was spending quite a few of her days helping Nelly with her young baby. We went around the back of the house to the kitchen door where we knocked gently so as not wake the baby if she were napping.

The door opened and Peggy gave us each a hug before we could even step into the house. She took both our hands and led us into the kitchen where she asked us to sit for one minute while she told Nelly that they had visitors. It was only a minute or so before Nelly came out of the room leading off the kitchen and she too gave us a big hug and hello.

"The baby just went to sleep so let's have a nice visit. I can't tell you how much I have missed you two. I wish you would come by more often, don't you mother?" she said with a big smile on her face. "I miss running around working on the cases like we did, and I miss you two surprising everyone with your amazing results."

Peggy said, "And, the mornings you met at my house and kept me company. I never see Rico. I understand he is very ill and rarely leaves the house. Noah, do you think you could take me to visit him one of these days?"

I told Peggy that I would be happy to, and that I would like to see Rico myself. Rico was our political expert who had been involved with us in one important case ending in Patrick's election as District Attorney.

Nelly had the good sense to get some food out for Jack, and we all settled down to a half hour or so of pleasant conversation. Peggy was always a delight and was obviously very happy to have her grandchild and her daughter close at hand. Nelly was still becoming accustomed to her new life as a housewife. She had been a successful lawyer prior to getting married a second time after getting an annulment from her first marriage to a cocaine addict. She was a bright, beautiful and delightful young lady in her thirties and we enjoyed her very much.

Before I met Marge, Peggy had been my closest woman friend. She and Jack and I had spent most of our free time together and had taken a trip to Ireland and another to England together. Clarissa had joined us for the trip to England. But, since the birth of the baby, we hadn't been able to get together because she was spending so much time with Nelly and the baby.

Now we sat talking around the kitchen table while the baby slept in the next room. The kitchen had been modernized almost beyond recognition. It had been the kitchen used by the Jackson sisters from whom Jack and I had bought the house as a wedding gift for Nelly and Patrick. The couple had redone the kitchen first because it was in such poor condition that it hardly met the needs of modern life. The old slate sink was our introduction to the house, when Jack was called to unblock it for Elizabeth Jackson who stood helplessly by while Jack and I attempted to loosen the mass of acquired material that had been accumulating for many years. There had been a single bulb hanging from a wire from the ceiling and if it hadn't been for the sunlight neither Jack nor I would have been able to see anything at all.

In a little more than a year Nelly and Patrick with the advice and aid of Peggy had transformed part of the house into something quite special while keeping within their budget. It had the mark of their youth and at the same time was a practical renovation without losing the flavor of the original structure. The back of the house where we were now sitting looked down over the west branch of the Westport River below which flowed into the outlet to the Atlantic Ocean. There was a long sloping green lawn that fell to the water's edge and which was shaded by two large maples that gave it a different look from mine on the other side of the road, which sloped to the east. The partially shaded lawn stippled sunlight and shadow was very inviting and one somehow felt that it should be put on canvas. The view was possible because they had taken out the single window looking out over the back porch and replaced a large part of the shingled wall with a picture window which allowed the light to enter and the inhabitants of the old house to look over the scene with an almost undisturbed view.

We sat and chatted in the kitchen as the sun began sinking in the western sky and its rays peeked through the window. I thought how little we knew about each other's thoughts. Here we were four good friends and yet I couldn't help but think that I knew very little about the other three people sitting with me. What was Jack thinking? Did Peggy dislike her son-in-law? Did Nelly resent the fact that her child had taken her away from her career? None of these questions had any basis in fact but I use them to illustrate that I had no real idea of what was going on in the heads of my friends. Suppose Amy had been harboring strong resentments against her husband, or Jason wanted to get even with his father for what he had done to him, or if Sam Goetzel had had such resentment of his son-in-law that he wanted to end his life. Or had Jeff Macomber become so depressed that he wanted to end his life? All of this led me to believe that we would never solve what I began to see as a crime by looking into the persons involved. I was convinced at this point that Jeff Macomber had not committed suicide, that, he had in fact been murdered.

But my group of friends also convinced me that taking the approach of trying to look into everyone's head, was the wrong approach to take in this case. We needed substantial facts and information, not conjecture here. I sat back and enjoyed the half hour we had together. Peggy had some leftover scones that she had brought her daughter and Patrick for breakfast, and Jack and I both feasted on them. The woman had an absolute gift with scones as well as with Irish soda bread. I had had to teach her how to make a cup of coffee when we had first met, but I could never have approached her ability with flour and her old Irish recipes. Needless to say, Jack was delighted with the scones and with his time with Peggy. He had more than once said that if he had had the opportunity to marry Peggy when she was young, he would have lived his life in marital bliss. He also felt that she had had a very happy marriage, and he did not feel right in wanting to intrude on her memories of a wonderful life with her husband. I thought that was a rather foolish approach to take, but I could not reproach him for his convictions.

I decided that I needed to find some way to come up with facts if we were to get anywhere with this case. But how were we to come up with a smoking gun twenty years after the fact? That was the problem we were dealing with and now I knew I had to come up with some answers or give up the project. One thing we knew for sure was that it would have been almost impossible for Sam Goetzel to have planned and executed a murder. So, in a real sense, he was eliminated as a suspect. Amy would hardly have asked us to investigate the case if she were the guilty party, so I felt she could be eliminated from suspicion. That left Jason as a suspect and I had no reason to feel that he had done the crime, nor did I have any reason to believe he hadn't. I needed some form of motivation on his part to think in his direction and, at the moment, I had none. Money was certainly not a consideration. Then, there was the matter of the pregnancy and the feelings of the family about it. I had no indication one way or the other what we were talking about in that regard. Was the family so angry at Jeff Macomber that they would seek revenge? Was Deolinda the culprit behind the killing or one of her family? There had to be some clue somewhere to help, but as of that moment all we knew was that Sam Goetzel in his declining years planned the celebration for himself and his long dead wife.

Chapter XXVIII

It seemed to me that the place to get our answers was with Deolinda Arruda. I was about ready to give up when Jack said, "Get back to her, Noah. Go visit her by yourself. You know you have something deep down in common. She trusts you because she understands you and you speak the same language. She is the one person who seems to hold the key to this whole mystery."

I wasn't absolutely sure about visiting her by myself, but Marge agreed with Jack that it was one approach we hadn't tried. I think we were all a bit frustrated, and we had to break the case at some point, and the way to do that was to push the envelope just a little harder.

So, on a cool, crisp morning, I rode over the bridge, first into Portsmouth and then into Middletown where I hoped to get Deolinda at home without announcing my arrival. It didn't make any difference to her I am sure, but I wanted to get our visit over with, rather than delay it for several days. I drove into the front drive of the Arruda home and saw Deolinda at the side of the house talking to one of her sons, who seemed to be doing some work on the garden next to the house. She was surprised to see me, but she walked over to greet me.

"So, I get a visit from the great detective, all by himself. I hope you have good intentions. I don't know if your sweetheart would like this. Does she know you are here alone? I think you are very handsome so you had better watch out."

"Oh, come on, Deolinda, for God's sake, let's stop the foolishness. I've got a few things to clear up before we call this whole thing off. So can we talk like reasonable people without playing sexual games?"

"Okay, I apologize. Come into the house. At least we can act like human beings, right?"

She brought me mid-way into the parlor and then went into her kitchen to prepare her tea and bring the biscuits out of their tin to be placed before me as a peace offering. I grew more and more accustomed to her idea of hospitality, and I remembered my mother doing much the same thing when we had visitors at any time of the day.

Much like my mother, Deolinda was culturally illiterate. If you were to ask her who Fra Angelico was or Titian or Ernest Hemingway or F. Scott Fitzgerald, she would have had no idea what you were talking about. My mother had never read a book in her life, and I am sure the same could be said for Deolinda Arruda. Schubert and Mendelssohn or La Boheme were so far distant from them that they would have had to forfeit their lives if identification meant saving them from the hangman. What was true for the arts and literature and music was as true for the popular culture. When I was a child, swing music had no place in our home, neither did any of the music fads that followed, nor any of the songs of earlier periods. Popular music was not part of her culture. And what was true of my mother was also true I am sure for Deolinda. Their lives began and ended with their immediate families and homes and then spread out to their environs in diminishing interest. It never extended beyond the church and the activities within its walls. In an odd kind of way, it did sometimes reach back to the Azores where they had their roots, but only if they had relatives remaining behind on the islands. The Azores was always an unspoken part of their consciousness. Like the fourth generation Irish who had never been to their great-great-great grandparents place of birth and yet acted like they had vivid memories of the Emerald Isle. Like the Portuguese and the Azores those memories were garnered sitting around the kitchen table as children listening to stories.

My mother had what we like to call "street smarts." When she sent me to the butcher to buy chourico or linguica she knew that he would cut a piece that was a quarter of a pound too large to make some extra money on every sale he made to an innocent child. She would say, "Tell the man you want one pound, not an ounce over; one pound do you hear? Tell him more than a pound and you won't pay." She knew every cheat on the street and which beggars were thieves and which were so desperate that they would truly bless the few pennies they were given in charity. Her world was small. She had no idea of the major currents going through the world. When I was just a little boy, the Great Depression was in full force, and from my mother's point of view, it encompassed the few blocks on which we lived. She knew nothing of the great movement to California or the Dust Bowl or Hitler or the horror of poverty being felt all over the western world. Her poverty was limited to five or six city blocks with their tenements and all the people living in them. I'm sure television had broadened Deolinda's view of the world, but I am equally sure that the world was only an adjunct to her more important sphere of knowledge and influence.

My mother managed her finances in such a way that no matter how many times my father was laid off or his hours were cut back, we always had the necessities of life. We had food on the table and when it came time to buy a house of her own at the low prices prevailing during the bad times in the thirties, she somehow had the down payment and enough to do the basic repairs necessary to make our first floor livable. I knew that Deolinda had done exactly that. She would have been careful to take care of her family no matter what the circumstance. Whatever had happened to her daughter, I was sure that the Macombers had paid and paid well for the damage Jeff Macomber had done. Deolinda would make the most of a bad situation.

She joined me in the parlor with her pot of tea on a tray and a plate filled to overflowing with the round biscuits that were shaped like a doughnut but tied in a bow. My mother would roll the raw dough between her fingers until it made a long slim cigar shaped tube and then make a circle with the dough and form a bow as they overlapped. We talked while I ate my biscuits dipping them in my tea to please Deolinda. Then my eyes traveled to the mantle of the fireplace where a row of pictures had been arranged in frames, one next to the other. I couldn't make out the faces too well from where I was sitting, but I determined to take a good look before I left the room.

"I am going to level with you, Deolinda, and then I think we can just about wrap this up," I began. "There is a lot going on here and I don't have answers."

She sat in front of me with her legs crossed at the knee and as she leaned forward just a bit, I could see that she was not the least bit tense. She was completely relaxed, in fact. There was a calmness about her that suggested that she was not the least bit interested in what I was about to ask her. If I was concerned about the case we were working on, she seemed distracted by whatever she was dealing with and that had nothing to do with me.

"The first thing that bothers me is that I know that Evangelica did not have an abortion. I think we both know that that was a lie. If she had had an abortion you would have come right out and said it instead of pretending that you didn't want to talk about it. I know that an abortion in our way of living is no big deal and you know it too."

She didn't answer me, but sat absolutely still. That surprised me because she wasn't the type to sit still under any circumstances and certainly not when she was confronted with a lie.

"So, what do you want from me?"

"Well, for starters, did Evangelica have the baby?" I asked.

"What difference does it make to you? Does it tell you how Mr. Jeff died? Does it change anything at all? If she had an abortion, it suddenly means that whatever happened to Mr. Macomber did not happen right? That is being pretty stupid if you ask me, Mr. Amos. And suppose I tell you that she had the baby, where does that take you? I thought you were smarter than that."

"Deolinda you are doing a good job of skirting the issue and I have to give you credit, you are good. But that doesn't change anything. Did your daughter have an abortion or did she give birth to a baby? You obviously are going to play games with me, but if you think I will give up, you are wrong. All you are doing is making me angry."

"You must be crazy. Let it go. What is the point of chasing something that happened twenty years ago? It's over. Don't be stupid, Noah, it's over."

She said this with a note of finality that made me realize that I would get nothing from her. She didn't stand with her hands on her hips in a final gesture of refusal, but her tone had an edge to it that told me all I needed to know. I rose to leave and walked toward the fireplace to look at the pictures on the mantle. Deolinda suddenly stepped in my way and bumped into me and I knew it had been intentional. I moved aside and managed to step toward the fireplace and then I saw it. And I had the answer I had come for.

There on the mantle were at least ten framed pictures of the family including one of Evangelica as a young girl. It was a photographer's portrait in an old-fashioned style of many years ago. Evangelica was sitting in a high backed stuffed chair, turned slightly to the side with her head turned to face the camera. Her brown hair was in ringlets and she had only the slightest smile on her face. And there was no question in my mind looking at the portrait of the young Evangelica that she was Jen's mother. The woman I was looking at could very well have been Jen. Deolinda saw it and knew that I knew then.

I turned to her and said, "Come on now. Let's have the truth. I want to hear the whole thing."

She was a statuesque woman quite unlike the Portuguese women I had known. The fado singers who sang the almost Moorish like songs of the Portuguese fisherwomen, had a look about them of haughtiness and pride. But, these were not the women I knew. My neighbors among the immigrants of the tenements were downcast, sad women who looked like they had been beaten down in life. There was no sparkle or humor or vivaciousness in these women, only a sense of the fatality of life. My mother, as sweet as she was, expected the worst every day of her life. For her, the glass was always half empty. She was afraid to be happy because she felt that God would take away her happiness as a punishment if He were to look down and see her smiling.

"Okay. But I still say, what is the point?"

"From this portrait I have no doubt that Jen is Evangelica's daughter. Is that right?"

"Of course. Just look at the two of them and you can see it. I'm surprised you didn't see it before even though my daughter is much older than she was. To me she still looks the same as she did in that picture. Yes, that girl is her daughter. Now are you happy that I said it?"

"Happiness is not the issue, Deolinda. If Jen is Evangelica's daughter, then who is the father?"

"The father is Mr. Jeff."

"Then why does Jason say that Jen is his daughter?"

"One question leads to another, so I might as well tell you the whole story right now and get it over with. Mr. Jeff fathered the girl. He got my poor daughter pregnant. He was a no good bastard."

She said that and then seemed to wish she could take the statement back. I had the distinct impression that she was feeling very uncomfortable at this point and I noticed that she kept looking at the kitchen as if she hoped that one of the boys would come in and give her a chance to break away.

"Evangelica was young. She was single and as pretty as she was, she didn't have a man. Then that happened and that was the end of it. Word gets around out here in the country and when they found out that she was going to have a baby, they went running. All the boys wanted no part of her. The poor thing didn't have a chance. So what could we do?"

She looked at me now with such a sad look on her face that I thought for the first time since meeting her, I was dealing with the real Deolinda Arruda. She was no longer playing a role, and what happened twenty years before was as real for her now as it had been then. Her face, so attractive normally, seemed heavy and the wrinkles suddenly emerged as her jaws sagged and her eyes grew heavy with just a hint of tears.

She didn't wait for an answer to her largely rhetorical question, but said, "Let me get something to wipe my eyes with. Give me a minute please."

She rose then and walked toward what I assumed was the bathroom. She was gone for a few minutes and then returned looking refreshed and with her poise restored.

"So you can understand better than anyone else. I decided that if she was pregnant, that the family would take care of her. I decided more than that. I made up my mind that they would provide for her very well."

"So, they did right?"

"Yes they did. They settled a lot of money on her and on her daughter. The one thing she had to agree to was to let the baby be brought up by them. That was the hard part for Evangelica. She can be a foolish girl. We made sure that she had a job working in the house for as long as she could work, so that she could see the baby growing up. For the first ten years she was the girl's nurse and saw her every day, so it wasn't like she was separated from her."

"So, why does Jason say that Jen is his daughter?"

"Why not? Better than a dead old man. The idea was that the girl would be brought up by her father if she stayed with the Goetzels and Macombers. It was my idea. Remember they did it in the Azores all the time. In the Old Country poor people used to sell their babies to people who wanted children and couldn't have them. That way the baby would be brought up in a good house with good people. Look what happened to Mr. Jason. He was a bastard child and now he is a millionaire. Now Jen will have millions too. What better way for the child? She has everything to gain. She has people who love her all around her and we can still keep an eye on her. If anything went wrong we would be over there very quickly. Her mother sees her mostly every day and what is wrong with that? By making Jason her father she is in line to inherit the whole family fortune, right? We made it legal by having him adopt Jen. So it is the best of everything."

"Does Jen know all this?"

"Of course. She is a grown lady now. We had to tell her and since she never knew the bum who was her father, it doesn't make any difference. She is happy living with Miss Amy and Mr. Jason and he is more like her father than her real father who never even knew her and wouldn't have cared for her anyway. Mr. Jason is wonderful to her. She has had a much better life than she ever would have had in our house and she will have a much better future than she would have had with us," she said this with a smile on her face as if to erase the tension she seemed to be feeling earlier.

"So there must have been a financial arrangement between your daughter and the family, is that right?" I asked.

"You know there was. Don't treat me like a fool. We were given a large sum of money by Mr. Goetzel and a trust fund for Jen, so that no matter what happened she would always have money. The way it turns out is that Miss Amy and Mr. Jason love her so much there is no need to protect her, but we didn't know that at the time we made the arrangement. She is a beautiful girl. The funny thing is that she has her mother's loving nature and her father's brains. Who would have guessed?"

"Let's hope that she never decides to go on a ship for a sail," I said laughing.

"This has made me very tired so I am going to stop now. I have told you a lot more than I wanted to, but now that you know I would like you to use some, what do you fancy people say, some discretion. I don't want my daughter hurt or Jen. What is the point? I don't think it has anything to do with Mr. Jeff's death, but now you know what you wanted from me, so leave us alone. I really ask you to leave us alone. Now, I am very tired and I think you should go so I can get some rest."

I said, "Deolinda, is there any chance you can do me a favor? Jack loves your biscuits, do you think you could give me a few to take to him?"

She laughed and I accompanied her to the kitchen where she took an old cookie tin down off the shelf. She opened a drawer and took out a plastic bag and put a dozen or so of the biscuits into it and handed it to me with a shaking hand. She was upset and it was showing.

I thanked her and leaned forward and kissed her on the cheek. It was not something I normally do but I suddenly felt it was my way of showing her that I understood how upset she had become and that I wanted to show her that I supported her and felt for her pain.

Chapter XXIX

I was eager to share my news with Marge and Jack and as soon as I arrived at the Point, I called Jack and asked him to cross the road to my house so that we could talk. The weather was cooler on the Point than it had been in Middletown, so we met in the kitchen rather than on the back lawn overlooking the water.

Jack was at the back door in a few minutes. He looked like he had been napping. His eyes looked heavy and his hair was its usually tousled self. His hair still had traces of his natural blondness but now it was more gray than blond as would be expected in a man a few years past seventy. He was a handsome man and had been all his life. Now, he joined us and as he had done so many times, went to the freezer first to see if there was any Ben and Jerry's ice cream. He found a pint, and after giving me a look as if to say do you mind if I finish the box, took a spoon out of the silverware drawer and sat down to eat and to listen. I gave him the Portuguese biscuits and he smiled, and opened the bag and began to eat his ice cream and biscuits while I told him and Marge the story.

I gave them every particular. They sat silently and listened. When I was finished Jack took a break from his eating and said, "In whose name is the money that was given to Evangelica?"

"That I don't know. Do you think it is important?" I asked. I knew Jack well enough to wonder what he was getting at.

"Not particularly," he said. "I was just wondering. I just think Deolinda Arruda is just shrewd enough not to trust money in her daughter's hands."

Marge was sitting still with her hands crossed in her lap. I loved to look at her when she was deep in thought. There was a serenity that took over her spirit that made her almost angelic in my eyes. When I looked at her, I wished that I could paint. She rose from her seat and went to the stove to put the kettle on for tea. The weather was turning and without the heat on, I could see that Marge was a bit chilled. As she walked she said, "Does it come as a surprise that Evangelica did have the baby? I think not. I think we all expected to hear that. Certainly, you so much as said that, Noah. But it does come as a surprise to me that Jen is the baby and it is more of a surprise that Jeff is the father rather than Jason. In fact, it comes as a shock to me."

Jack said, "I am surprised too, but not shocked. For a family with so few members it seems to me that they have more than their share of duplicity."

"What really strikes me is that we realize that Jeff is the father of both illegitimate children. Jen and Jason are brother and sister, some thirty years apart in age, both living under the same roof but not as siblings but as father and daughter. It is almost laughable except that it is so sad. Think about it. Here are two people pretending to be father and daughter instead of brother and sister. How silly. And why, Jack, please explain to me why this is necessary."

"I really can't see that it is important. Financially, I don't think it has any relevance. Whether she is an adopted daughter of the family or the daughter of a dead man makes no difference in terms of the finances involved. She will be given whatever the family decides, regardless of whether the pretense is that she is a daughter or not. I just don't understand why they did what they did. But that is neither here nor there as far as I can see. The big question is what effect her birth and her staying in the family had on the death of Jeff Macomber. Do you think it had any, Noah?"

"I can't imagine that it did. I just don't know. Deolinda was quite upset when I left her. I had the feeling that there is sill a great deal under the surface here that still has to be uncovered. I have no idea what, but my instincts tell me that there is definitely something being hidden."

We all realized that we were constantly dealing in conjecture and that it would take us nowhere, but there was nothing really solid to hook onto. The next day on our usual visit to Amy Macomber I decided to chase down Jason for a few questions while Jack let Amy know what we had discovered to see if she would break down and give us something more to work on. I felt like we were peeling an onion, removing one layer after another. Marge went to the study to continue her search into the character of the elusive Mr. Sam Goetzel.

I found Jason in the greenhouses preparing them for the winter seedlings. They were about to spray with a fungicide, so we stepped outside while the Arruda men donned their masks and prepared the power sprayers.

"Over the last few days we have learned that Jen is your sister, Jason," I began, and he gave me no particular reaction. It was as if I were talking about the weather, he was so little concerned. "Why did the family think that ruse was necessary?"

"It was grandfather who insisted. He refused to believe that Jen was my father's daughter. He made up his mind that she was my daughter and that was the end of it. He was a very stubborn man once he made up his mind to anything, very much like Aunt Amy and me, I guess."

"The one thing we seem to be getting out of the journals is that as time went on he suffered some lapse of memory and he seems to have suffered from some delusion. Did you find that?"

"Well, he was in his nineties when he died. Wouldn't you expect some form of delusion to occur?"

"For instance, he actually believed that his wife had returned to him. We are pretty sure that his insistence on the 50th Wedding Anniversary Party was based on his belief that the party was a celebration on behalf of his marriage, not Amy's. How did that work? Could you explain it to me?"

Jason actually showed surprise when I asked that. I think it was the first time I had actually elicited an emotional response from him in all the time I had talked to him.

"No, I didn't know that. That explains an awful lot doesn't it? Does Aunt Amy know that?"

"I don't know. I haven't talked to your aunt about this yet. But, let's get back to your grandfather's state of mind as he approached old age. Did you feel he was senile at the time of your father's death?"

"I don't remember him as senile. No, I can't say that. Remember I told you that he did not always talk in full sentences so that habit and the habit we had of filling in for him would hide senility if he were senile, I think."

Jason thought for moment and then he smiled and said, "He would say something like, 'How did...?" and I would say, 'They won 3 to 2." He laughed and said, "Then he would ask, 'And how did...?' and I would say, 'He was 2 for 3 with no home runs.' I knew he was talking about the Red Sox and Carl Yastremski, but any person listening to us would have thought we were crazy."

He smiled at the thought of it and I could see he was carried back to the time when he was with his grandfather. Obviously he had had something very special going with his grandfather and from what we had learned from reading the journals, the feeling was mutual.

"But, from just this much you can understand if he was slipping mentally it would have been hard for me to detect. In many ways he was like a stutterer who couldn't finish a sentence, so I would fill in his sentences for him. I often wondered if I was doing him a disservice, but I got into the habit early and never stopped it."

"How did he conduct his business? He certainly couldn't have been a successful man if he couldn't communicate."

"Oddly enough, he didn't do it in every situation. He spoke that way only when he was comfortable and at ease. He was like a child with what they call a lazy tongue. He spoke in full sentences when he had to, but otherwise everything came out in partial sentences. I was always amazed to hear him talk to my father. He spoke in complete sentences every time."

"So, you feel that had he started slipping mentally, his incapacity would have been masked as far as you are concerned, but your father would have been able to see it?"

"Probably, but to be honest with you, it wasn't that they had very many conversations."

"Do you think he could have killed your father?"

"Mr. Amos, I would be offended if that question were not so absurd. You have to take yourself back twenty years to when this happened. Both my father and Aunt Amy were in their seventies. Grandfather was over ninety years old and could hardly walk. He was incapable, both mentally and physically, of doing anything like this."

'So, I'm sure you have thought about this. What is your best guess as to what happened?"

"To be honest with you, I think he was drinking heavily, he was not in Aunt Amy's best graces, and in a fit of depression, took his own life. That's my only guess. I don't think there was any reason for anyone to want to kill him."

"How about the fact that he had gotten Evangelica pregnant?"

"I know I shouldn't say this, but you are going to know it sooner or later. There weren't many of us boys or men who hadn't slept with her. She was constantly throwing herself at one or the other of us. She was a very sexy woman. It was only a question of time until one of us got her pregnant."

That took me back. I hadn't expected that for one minute. I was shocked. I had a vision of this girl as some sweet innocent thing. I wouldn't have been surprised if he said the same about her mother, but I had difficulty believing it about her and I said so.

"Well, you were wrong about Evangelica but not about the mother. She had become very close to my grandfather after grandmother died and I think she had something going with my father too, to be honest."

He said this in all earnestness and for the first time I thought I was getting somewhere in the case. It had taken this long and now I realized I had tried to make something complicated out of a very simple matter.

I thanked Jason and went directly to the study where I found Marge deeply involved in the journals. She was so engrossed in her reading that she didn't see or hear me arrive.

"Wait until you hear this," I said.

"No, this is more important. Read this."

SUNDAY

THE PARTY WAS YESTERDAY. I SAW ELEANOR HURT JEFF AND I DON'T KNOW WHY. I DON'T UNDERSTAND. IT IS A TERRIBLE THING.

"Well, Marge there it is. Eleanor has to be Deolinda. There it is. And I have just learned from Jason that most likely Deolinda was having an affair with Jeff. How long it had been going on, I don't know, but the fact is that they had been lovers if he is right. Then if we are right and Deolinda is the Eleanor of the journal, we have motive and a witness.

Jack joined us at that moment and when we told him what we had learned he became very thoughtful and sat in one of the leather chairs in the room. Marge and I joined him in the triangle that made up the sitting area. We had all to do some thinking about what all this meant.

He rose from his chair and said, "Amy is the key to all this. I say we confront her immediately and see what she has to offer."

I knew he was right, and so we all three headed for the sunroom hoping that Amy hadn't left it. Fortunately she was still there with Jen just getting her ready to go back to her room.

Jack took no time at all to ask the question about the affair between Deolinda and Jeff Macomber. She was tired and the question was probably unfair under the circumstances. She was quite surprised at the directness of the question and Jack's tone in asking it.

"Well," she said, "I expected this to surface sooner or later. Yes, yes, yes. They had been lovers for quite some time. She was one in a long line of lovers, but she was not his typical affair. She was far more fiery and intense and their affair was not quiet, at best."

"How did she take the fact that he had gotten her daughter pregnant?" I asked.

"You can imagine," she said with a sneer on her lips. "She is very emotional and she made no qualms about how she felt even in front of me which was quite unusual. She even threatened him."

"How did she threaten him?" I asked.

"With his life actually. She warned him to be careful."

Jack said, "He should have listened."

We knew then that we had to confront Deolinda with what we had in the hope that she would confess to the murder of Jeff Macomber. Of course, I had no misgivings in the matter since I did not think that she would. This time we called her to say that we would be visiting her and that we had a few questions for her, so when we arrived I suspect she knew that we had come to some conclusions and that we would be trying to resolve the situation as best we could.

She met us at the door and escorted us into the parlor. Again Marge and Jack and I sat in our usual seats. This time she didn't make tea but seemed to want to get the session over and done with. Both Marge and Jack looked to me to start talking, and I didn't hesitate to do so.

"First of all, I want you to understand that we are here in no official capacity. Jack and I are associated with the District Attorney's Office in Bristol County Massachusetts but have no affiliation with Rhode Island in any way," I said.

"You make this sound very serious," Deolinda said.

"It is. We are here accusing you of murder. The murder of Jeff Macomber."

"I think you are full of shit," she said this emphatically, but I noticed a tightening of her hands in her lap. "How do you prove something that happened twenty years ago, tell me?"

"We're not here to prove anything," Jack said. "That's for the local police to take care of. We will just present the evidence and let them worry about proof."

"And what evidence do you have after twenty years?" she laughed.

"Not a heck of a lot," I said, "but enough to interest the police. We know you were having an affair with him and that you threatened his life when he got your daughter pregnant."

She laughed out loud then and said, "So what? There is a big difference between threatening a man and killing him isn't there? If every woman who threatened a man killed him, there would be a lot fewer bastards around, I can tell you that."

I knew she was extremely nervous when she starting cursing. This was a throwback to when she was younger and hadn't gained the control over her language and herself that she had now. The fact that she was suddenly cursing was certainly an indication that we had gotten to her.

"You were seen. That is the thing that weighs so heavily against you."

"And who was supposed to have seen me? And what did I do?" she asked.

"You were seen shooting Mr. Jeff. You were seen by Mr. Goetzel," Jack said.

She laughed hilariously at that point. "You have to be kidding. Mr. Goetzel. Twenty years ago, he was lucky if he knew who he was. How in the world can he be a witness in a murder? He has been dead for nineteen years himself. How can he be a witness against me? Jesus, you guys are crazy. You too, lady. You're all crazy. You can all go to hell."

"So you deny everything then, right?" I asked.

"Of course. You have nothing and you are fishing. So, now I am going to ask you to leave and I have to say, as much as I hate to say it, please don't come back again." She said this with a haughtiness that made us realize that she felt she had the upper hand. We all knew that she probably did, but at the same time, we knew that she had done it. We also knew that Amy would be relieved to hear that the case had been solved as far as she was concerned. If she had been afraid that her father had committed a crime or worse yet, if Jason had done it, then she need not worry any longer. As much as we knew she would be tired and not need to hear the whole thing immediately, we felt that she should sit down with us along with Jen and Jason and learn what we knew to be the case.

As it turned out I found Jason almost immediately in one of the playpens and I broached the subject to him. He agreed that Amy would want to know immediately and he went into the house to bring her down to the study along with Jen. We went to the study and waited for a few minutes before Jason came in to tell us that Jen was bringing Amy down from upstairs at that moment.

When she entered the room, Amy looked tired and she asked Jason to bring her one of the table chairs to sit in rather than sit on the couch or the soft leather chairs. She looked tired, but, at the same time she looked like she was anticipating an answer to the question she had asked herself so many times. What had happened to Jeff Macomber, her husband?

She signaled to Jen and Jason to be seated and then said, "This must be important or you wouldn't have asked us here. What is it you have found out?"

Jack spoke first, "We are pretty sure we know what happened. Are you ready to hear it?"

"Yes. Let me put all this behind me. I want closure. Let's hear what you have to say."

She looked more frail and defenseless now than at any time since we had known her. Her hands were trembling and the tendons in the back of her hand leading to the muscles in her fingers were taut like the strings of a violin that have been too tightly wound. I felt sorry for her, but I knew we would relieve the tension she felt.

I said, "We believe that Deolinda Arruda killed your husband. In fact we are pretty sure she did."

"Then it wasn't father?" Amy asked.

Jack laughed and said, "He was hardly in a condition to do that or to plan it. Most likely Deolinda went to the study knowing that Jeff would be there and when she found him sleeping, she went to your father's desk, took out the gun, shot him and put it in is hand so that it would seem like suicide. She thought that no one had seen her, but your father had. He looked through the terrace window and saw her, but in his confused state of mind, mistook her for your mother. He couldn't understand why your mother would do such a thing and he never mentioned what he had seen to anyone."

"Then, how do you know he saw anything?" Jason asked.

"He made a note of it in his journal," I said. "He specifically says that he saw his wife hurting Jeff and he doesn't know why. However, we know from his previous entries that he confused Deolinda with Mrs. Goetzal. In this case, he thought the killer was actually his wife rather than Deolinda."

Jason said, "Then, where does this go from here? Can she be punished for killing my father?"

"I don't know," I said. "The evidence is merely a notation in a journal by a man who is long since dead. I think it would inadmissible hearsay. He was also confused while he was alive, so I don't have any idea what law enforcement people will make of the information. The point is, though, as far as you are concerned, you should be satisfied on two counts: first that it was not a suicide, and secondly, that the murder was done by Deolinda Arruda."

"Well, that is a relief to me gentlemen. I can't tell you how long I worried that the murder would have been done by father or arranged by him in some way or even that you might have been guilty of it, Jason. I know that sounds absurd, but it was on my mind and it was a question I needed to have answered to give me peace. Now, for the first time in twenty years I can go to bed and sleep in peace. Thank you, Jack and Noah and Marge. Thank you again and again."

We had found very little, but there was no question in our minds that it was enough. Put together our meeting with Deolinda and the fact that she had had an ongoing affair with Jeff Macomber seemed to give her sufficient motive after finding that he had taken advantage of her young daughter. We were not the police. What we thought had little value in a court room.

It was on the way back to the Point when Marge said, "The odd thing here is that these people made a great deal of heredity. We look at Jason as the hereditary grandson of Sam Goetzel and the nephew of Amy Macomber, and we have all noted that they think alike and act alike. We are told about the work Jason is doing with rhododendrons and how that is related to DNA and the dwarfness associated with his Yaks. Amy is dependent on heredity in the same way working on her azaleas."

In his usual questioning and gruff manner, Jack asked. "What is the connection Marge?"

"Well, consider that Jen is the daughter of a promiscuous mother and a promiscuous father. What could this bode for her future? If all your talk of heredity holds true, then she should inherit those terrible problems from her parents."

"Could that have been what Amy was thinking in having the girl become the daughter of Jason instead of his sister?" Jack asked. "That may be the reason for her deciding that she would not have her share directly with Jason in whatever the estate turned out to be."

"Well, who knows?" I said.

We met with Patrick to discuss what should be done about the information we had in hand and our feeling that Deolinda Arruda had murdered Jeff Macomber in cold blood. He sat and listened politely and when we were finished said that we probably didn't have enough to interest law enforcement officers in Rhode Island. He went on to say that he would have difficulty doing much with the information we had, and he doubted he himself would reopen the case on so little.

I said, "We know she did it. That is enough for us and enough for Amy Macomber. We found out what she needed to know and I think that satisfies her and lets her put the whole thing behind her. She wanted closure and she has it."

"It's a shame," Marge said, "that a killer should get away with murder, but if there isn't enough evidence, there isn't."

And so it ended.

That night over dinner we discussed the case and Jack felt some remorse that Deolinda would walk. He felt that as a murderer she should not go free and that justice would never be served if she continued to live her life as she had done to now.

For my part, I felt that Jeff Macomber had deserved whatever he had gotten. I couldn't imagine a less worthy man. He had betrayed his wife, had a baby by her sister, impregnated a girl who was simple minded after having slept with her mother for years. Why feel remorse that his killer would not be punished? I couldn't see it. Was she justified in killing him? No, no one has the right to take someone else's life.

So, we had done our job. Maybe not as well as a high-powered police department or a private detective agency, but we had our answer. Marge heated up a meatloaf we had made earlier. We baked a frozen French bread and opened a bottle of Italian wine and we were in business. Clarissa was home with Jack and she joined us for a quiet dinner. We were all a bit tired, but relieved to have this case over and done with. It was time to plan another trip. With the cold weather coming, it would have to be to some southern clime where we could relax and enjoy the sun.

The End

CPSIA information can be obtained at www.ICGtesting.com
Printed in the USA
BVOW040654261011

274520BV00003B/3/P